KATE KOMULA

On Ice

A Coments Hockey Romance

First published by Independently published 2023

Copyright © 2023 by Kate Komula

All rights reserved. No part of this publication may be reproduced, stored or transmitted in any form or by any means, electronic, mechanical, photocopying, recording, scanning, or otherwise without written permission from the publisher. It is illegal to copy this book, post it to a website, or distribute it by any other means without permission.

This novel is entirely a work of fiction. The names, characters and incidents portrayed in it are the work of the author's imagination. Any resemblance to actual persons, living or dead, events or localities is entirely coincidental.

Kate Komula asserts the moral right to be identified as the author of this work.

Kate Komula has no responsibility for the persistence or accuracy of URLs for external or third-party Internet Websites referred to in this publication and does not guarantee that any content on such Websites is, or will remain, accurate or appropriate.

Designations used by companies to distinguish their products are often claimed as trademarks. All brand names and product names used in this book and on its cover are trade names, service marks, trademarks and registered trademarks of their respective owners. The publishers and the book are not associated with any product or vendor mentioned in this book. None of the companies referenced within the book have endorsed the book.

First edition

ISBN: 9798376448694

Cover art by Talula Burns
Editing by Reanna Guthrie

This book was professionally typeset on Reedsy.
Find out more at reedsy.com

*To my friends and family that have always supported my dreams.
Thank you from the bottom of my heart.*

Contents

Chapter 1	1
Chapter 2	13
Chapter 3	24
Chapter 4	38
Chapter 5	52
Chapter 6	67
Chapter 7	76
Chapter 8	99
Chapter 9	114
Chapter 10	122
Chapter 11	131
Chapter 12	142
Chapter 13	150
Chapter 14	158
Chapter 15	167
Chapter 16	176
Chapter 17	182
Chapter 18	190
Chapter 19	198
Chapter 20	204
Chapter 21	215
Chapter 22	224
Chapter 23	234
Chapter 24	240

Chapter 25	245
Chapter 26	252
Chapter 27	260
Epilogue	271
Acknowledgments	276

Chapter 1

ELISE

Looking around my now empty apartment, I can't help but think about how much has changed over the past year. Graduating with my Master's degree, being one, and now I'm starting from scratch, so to speak. I place my keys into the drop box, hearing them thud as they hit with a tone of finality. Everything is going to be different now. In a matter of hours, I will be in a new city where no one knows me, and I know absolutely no one. It's kind of nerve-wracking in a way, but then there is little to no pressure and no expectations either. I can be myself and not worry about letting anyone down.

My car is full of my belongings. Everything that wouldn't fit was sold and added to my savings so that I can find a nice home and furnish it the way that I want. Well, almost everything. There are a few small things that I put into a portable storage unit, a fancy way of saying a box with wheels if you ask me but hey, who am I to judge, that I couldn't part with- the desk that my father had since his youth and my mother's antique cedar chest. Until I can find a house or condo, I will be staying in a hotel. One that is, conveniently, right across the street from my new job. I take one last look at where I came from before setting out on my new adventure, excited for what is ahead of me.

The drive goes faster than I expected and yet it felt like I had been sitting in the car for hours. When I was younger, my dad and I would go on trips together, and the drive seemed to fly by, but I wasn't the one driving. I was the one asking to stop every hour to go to the bathroom, or the one wanting snacks. Now my back is tight and my butt is numb from sitting for so long, and I can't wait to stretch. Pulling up to the hotel, I'm greeted by the doorman who, decked out in the full Hollywood-type uniform that you would only expect on the big screen, greets me with a smile and truly welcomes me to my new home. *Well, sort of home.*

"Welcome, Miss, I can take your things inside if you would like to proceed to check-in," he says, opening the door for me.

I smile and thank him before making my way to the young woman at the front desk. She looks exhausted but pulls out a bit of enthusiasm as she looks up my reservation and get my key. I sleepily make my way to the room, praying that room service is still an option because the thought of having to go out again for food makes me want to throw a fit. Tomorrow is my first day on the job, maybe I should pray that it goes well–along with there

CHAPTER 1

being food.

***

I woke up earlier than I intended, both anxious and nervous for what is about to happen. The uncertainty of what I'm walking into made it hard to sleep deeply, even though I was exhausted from the drive. After taking a long hot bath to try and relax my tight muscles and calm the nervous butterflies swarming my stomach, I take my time doing my hair and makeup, wanting to make a good impression on my first day. Not that it really matters. I doubt that anyone will be worried about how I styled my hair today or what shade of blush I went with. It's a brisk morning, and I'm glad I grabbed my light jacket to wear as I walk across the street to where my office will be for the foreseeable future. I take a deep breath for one last wish of courage and confidence, straighten my simple wrap dress, and make my way through the entrance, where I am greeted by a guard. He escorts me to my office, and on the far wall, I see a large window that overlooks the practice ice.

There is something about hockey that I can't seem to shake. The thrill of it all makes me feel like a kid again, watching my first game with my dad. The pure joy of it makes my heart swell with happiness. My dad would be thrilled if he could see me right now. Who am I kidding? He would be more thrilled to see this view! He always wanted a boy, but instead, he got me– a super girly, hair and makeup always done kind of girl. Luckily for him, though, I also happen to love sports–especially hockey.

Now, here I am in the arena of the Comets, which just so

happened to be the one and only team we could ever agree on. I'm nervous but excited to be here- mostly nervous. I mean, who moves so far from their childhood home alone and starts from scratch? I swallow the emotions bubbling up as I think of him not seeing this with me. I take a calming breath, pushing what I'm feeling down far enough to ignore for the time being.

"Elise?" I hear my name called from across the room and turn to face the man that I've had several video meetings with prior to accepting my position with the team.

"Hi, Ben. It's great to finally meet you in person."

"Likewise." He smiles confidently, extending a hand towards me. I shake it firmly, not wanting to seem weak in what is traditionally a boy's club. "I see that you were checking out the team."

"It's hard not to with that view," I exclaim, unable to contain myself.

"I know that we weren't your first choice of teams...."

"Well, that might not be entirely true. I love this team. I just thought that I may get distracted because I tend to get really into the games, and this being my favorite team in the NHL... You know what, now that I think about it more, this is probably the only team I was meant to work for."

"We felt the same way. Welcome to the Comet family officially. You're not required to come to the games for your work, but I can tell that we won't have to twist your arm to attend a couple here and there. We typically encourage our staff to come to as many games as possible. You're here to help with our outreach and public relations in general. Some of our players can be troublemakers."

"Ben, you and I both know that is an understatement" I chuckle and he joins in as I turn to follow him as he shows me

CHAPTER 1

around the arena. "Especially lately with the ever-so-popular captain and whatever is going on with him. You all have kept things pretty hush hush, but with how he's been handling things, it's only a matter of time before the press starts asking questions.". They did some remodeling over the summer, and I can still smell the fresh construction scent that takes me back to my youth when I would go to work with my dad and uncle. I smile at the memory as we continue on

"That," he looks over pointing his finger at me smiling, "is exactly why we needed you here, no bullshit. You've got it, Elise. You know the sport, and you know how to make people look good. You did wonders with that kid in your hometown." He stops outside of the offices and I make a mental note of where the people are that I will be working with once things get into full swing.

"That was easy, these are adults that don't have their shit together. He was a kid who was just at the wrong place at the wrong time, truly. He was hanging out with the wrong crowd. Sorry to be so frank, but I find that sugarcoating things only makes it worse in this business. Especially since everything that I've worked on has been more clean-up rather than being proactive."

"Not an issue here. That was a big selling factor when it came to hiring you. You're not afraid to get right in there and set people straight," he says, clapping his hands together as though pleased with himself. "It's easy to get turned around here so don't be afraid to ask anyone for help. I know that I mentioned the main issue, but other than that, we try to be a big part of the community. Just the minor fires that need putting out here and there."

"I'm sure that isn't completely unheard of. It's not like ESPN covers hockey unless it's the playoffs. It isn't like people really follow the personal lives of the players." I throw my hands in the air dismissively, thinking about all the things they choose to focus on rather than the games most times.

"We have been trying to keep certain things from the public... ." He wrings his hands together nervously, and I'm instantly worried by his tone. How bad can it possibly be?

"What exactly am I hiding this time, Ben? You didn't give me much to go on, and don't think I didn't notice and look over the non-disclosure agreement in my HR packet." I stop instantly, placing my hand on my hips, bracing myself.

"Well, not hiding. Wilkes, as you seem to already know—He's a private person. There was a lot of debate about his private life. Even his sexuality was a mystery until he proposed to his longtime girlfriend. Then when she was six months pregnant, she died in an accident. That was this past winter... Drunk driver." His tone shifts from matter of fact to a hint of sorrow. "He had a rough time right after and isn't handling it well."

I take a deep breath and can only imagine how he is feeling losing the people that he loved. He was about to have a baby, too. Then to have lost all that suddenly. My heart instantly hurts for him. Unfortunately, this is something that I know all too well. Even though I have never had that kind of love.

"I know that this is probably not what you wanted or expected to walk into your first day, but you are exactly what we need here, and we are hopeful that you can help us." He shifts on his feet nervously avoiding eye contact with me. "And him," he adds.

"I'm not a psychologist," I say with a sigh, finally making eye contact with Ben again. "I can't make any promises, but I will try." Knowing a fraction of that loss may help me reach him,

CHAPTER 1

but that all depends on him.

"That's all I can ask for." He smiles as we walk through a tunnel and onto the ice.

"Holy shit..." I gasp, feeling my jaw drop to the floor. Being level with the ice at a professional arena is something that I never tire of. The crisp cool feel in the air, the fresh scent of the ice, and the sound of skates slicing along the frozen surface all illuminated in front of me is every hockey fan's dream. Seeing the players practicing I can feel a hum of energy that waits in anticipation of a roaring crowd. "This view is my new favorite."

"It's pretty amazing, right?" He eyes me as I take it all in. I can't help but think how much my dad would love this.

* * *

LIAM

I stop mid-ice when she walks in. I can't help it. She is gorgeous in this effortless, low maintenance kind of way. She isn't trying to impress any of us. I'm not sure that she even cares about us out here, but she is visibly in awe of the sights from where she is standing. She isn't Kaylee, damn it. No one will ever be her either, so why am I thinking about this random woman whom I've never met?.

This girl, whoever she is, makes me feel like maybe I can breathe again, or at least feel a bit of attraction towards someone—which has been a rare occurrence. Losing Kaylee has been unbearable—the hardest thing that I have ever had to go through. I lost my best friend and our child. Random girl or not, nothing can make me feel that loss less than I already do.

"Wow, they brought in a hottie in to replace Brett," Will Spencer, my teammate, comments as he stops beside me on the ice, removing his gloves and helmet.

"Replace?" I ask, taking a drink of water as I watch them walk closer.

"Yea, don't you read your emails? He wanted to spend more time with his family. Apparently, keeping up with you was too much work for the old man." He hits my arm in a joking way as if he can make it less awkward.

"Yes, blame me...." I glare at him as I feel a bit of guilt creep in now that I know I'm a major factor in why someone left their job.

"You've had a lot going on lately, and we all know you will get to a better place eventually, but until then, they need PR that can keep up."

"Have I been that bad?" I question my friend, my brow furrowed as a sour feeling spreads in my gut.

"Yea, but we still love you, bro. Just get over your funk before the season starts, ok? We deserve a playoff run." He puts his gloves back on and picks up his stick again.

"Get over it? Trust me, Spencer, I'm trying." He nods and skates away. I keep looking over at her, trying to figure out what it is that makes her so different. Aside from the obvious. She has a curvy, almost full figure and auburn hair. I huff, shaking off whatever trance she has me in. There isn't anything special about her. My eyes flick in her direction again as I take a drink from my water bottle trying, and failing, to ignore her presence.

CHAPTER 1

Shit, who am I kidding? She's gorgeous. I hope she has a terrible personality or a horrible voice. Maybe a snaggle tooth. Yeah. That would make her less attractive. I see her talking with the coach, laughing at what I can only guess is one of his many dad jokes. Well, shit, her smile is adorable. Coach calls me over, and I pray that her voice is annoying as I skate slowly over to where they are chatting.

"Wilkes! This is Elise Connors, our new public relations expert. You're probably going to be working together a lot." He gives me a pointed look.

She extends a hand. "Hi, it's nice to meet you, Mr. Wilkes." Damn it, her voice is adorable–yet strong and confident. A freaking beautiful contradiction. I glance awkwardly at her extended hand, then back to my gloves. The sprinkling of freckles across her face scrunches up when she smiles, lowering her hand back to her side. Who knew the freckles could be so hot?

"It's Liam. Mr. Wilkes makes me feel ridiculously old - like Coach." I try to joke, and it's super lame. I know it is by her reaction alone. She lets out a small laugh, but it is so short I almost miss it. Her smile widens, though, and I'm more frustrated that it's perfect. I scan her body now that she's closer. Her perfectly rounded ass and hips would normally make me want to hold on for dear life. Normally. If I were available, but I'm not. Someone that had a body like hers would have drawn me in–made me want to try everything I could to get her home. I can feel my jaw tick as I clench my teeth together.

"Hopefully by the end of the week," she comments in response to a question I missed. "Does that sound ok with you, Wilkes?"

"Uh, yea. I suppose that will work." I blink, trying to clear my head.

"Great, we can go over some things then. I look forward to any input that you may have." What the hell am I supposed to have input on? I need to pay attention when she speaks from now on, or better yet, I need to not be this distracted by her looks. Shit personality, that's got to be the flaw. "Ok, well, I will let you all get back to practice. I need to get settled into my office. I will see you all later."

Watching her walk away might be worse than staring at her like an idiot when she was talking.

The rest of practice goes off without a hitch, and I escape before anyone can invite me out for food or ask how I am coping with everything. I'm sure that someone will make a comment about Connors– probably about her appearance– and then I would defend her. That would lead to questions about if I wanted to call dibs on the new PR girl. I do. Even if it's just to keep the others away from her. Although she seemed unphased being around professional athletes, which honestly makes me want to keep her away from the team even more.

* * *

ELISE

Holy man he is huge. Big, bulky, and so hot. I'm sure his bicep is as big as my thigh!

Ok, so probably not–but still. Just keep your cool, Elise. You're here to do your job, not fawn over a man that is lashing out because he just lost his girlfriend and their unborn baby a couple months ago. Besides, I doubt that I am his type. Not that

CHAPTER 1

anything can or will ever happen. I take a seat at my desk with a huff, taking a look at my agenda and adding my meeting with Wilkes to this week. I email him a quick reminder as well.

Mr. Wilkes,

As per our earlier conversation, I look forward to our meeting on Wednesday the 21st at 10 am, prior to your morning practice.

-Elise Connors

After spending the day getting settled into my new office and acclimating to my surroundings, I feel prepared for the normal day-to-day of the job, but I'm honestly worried about how things will go with Wilkes. He could be receptive to what I need to do to help him, or he could make things very difficult. I'm hoping for the former. But preparing for the latter. Always prepare for the worst; that's something that I, unfortunately, have had to do most of my life.

It's late afternoon when I head back to my temporary home and I've just made it into my room as my alarm goes off for my standing appointment I have had since I was a teen. "Hi Dr. J," I greet after starting the virtual therapy session. Kicking off my shoes, I settle in for what could be an emotional hour. It's always one extreme or another when we talk, I'm either bawling or feel ready to take on the world by the end.

"Hi Elise, how are you settling into your new surroundings?"

"Straight to the point, I see." She smiles at me, and I am so happy we've been able to continue my sessions even though I'm no longer in her city. "It was ok. Settled in as much as I can, considering I'm in a hotel for the time being."

"And the job? Today was your first day, right?"

"Yeah, it was. Being in the arena was amazing, and it was so hard not to totally freak, but it was good. Spent most of the day getting acquainted with my surroundings, setting up the office, those kinds of things. There's a lot of events planned that I have to weigh in on and oversee but nothing too crazy until a few months from now."

"Sounds like you'll be busy."

"I'm sure of it."

By the end of the session, I'm emotionally drained but in a good way. It needed out. I needed it, and Dr. J knows me better than anyone else. She's not quite old enough to be considered a mother figure, more like that older cousin that you can turn to when you're having a difficult time. She's seen me through it all, the highs and the lows. I'm not sure I could handle this monumental change if I had to stop seeing her.

"Ok, that's all our time for the day. You know, though, that if anything comes up, I can make time for you. This is a lot of change happening all at once, so it's perfectly normal to feel overwhelmed or even scared at times."

"Thanks, Dr. J. Have a great rest of your week." We say our goodbyes, and I walk to the bed, flopping right into the middle. I know I should be doing anything other than laying on the bed, but right now, I'm just too mentally exhausted to move.

Chapter 2

ELISE

Wednesday morning came, and he didn't show. So, I rescheduled, and again – no show. Which led me to this – about to lose my cool because he is, once again, about to bail on me. However, Liam Wilkes has no idea how resilient I am. I don't take no for an answer. I brace myself, take a deep breath, and walk into the locker room, not caring that the players were filing in for the day. "Wilkes!" I shout as he walks from the other room, "Three times I've scheduled a meeting with you, and yet each time *you* are nowhere to be found. You really had to make me track you down."

"What the hell are you doing here?" he asks, looking at me like I am crazy. Just a week ago, this man wasn't able to focus on a simple conversation, and today he's an insufferable ass. Seems about right. What the hell is his problem? Actually, I know his problem—the reason they were so desperate to have someone here to reign him in.

"As I already said," I reiterate with as much calm as I can muster, "we have had several meetings scheduled, and you have failed to show up. So, here I am."

I wait, staring him down for a moment. I want to see if he will make things any more difficult for me. For the first time since our initial meeting, he looks me in the eyes, and I can almost see the wheels turning, trying to figure out how he is going to react and suddenly feeling like I made a mistake when I chose my dress this morning. My simple wrap dress is great for running around the office but not so great when you need to command authority. I have to avoid fidgeting in attempts to make sure there isn't too much cleavage showing. News flash, there is always too much cleavage in a wrap dress when you're a thick woman.

"You are messing with a bull, honey," he finally says, leaning against his locker as if he is completely unbothered. The smirk on his face catches me off guard for just a moment, but I quickly recover and steal my gaze. The locker room is filling up now, rather than the few players here and there, and they're watching us now. I don't break eye contact with him, though. Regardless of how this may look, I am in charge here.

"I'm not scared of you, Wilkes," I state bluntly, even though it may be a little bit of a lie. He is intimidating, his sheer mass, alone, is enough to make me feel inferior, but I will not let him think that.

CHAPTER 2

Finally, he's walking towards me, and I won. I can let out the breath that I had been holding in, waiting for him to finally comply. I spoke too soon, "What the hell are you doing?" He bends and in one quick motion, picks me up and throws me over his shoulder. *Fuck*. His hands are strong and rough–a lethal combination that I didn't prepare for. He holds my waist with one arm, keeping me tight against him. With any other man, I would be turned on by how effortlessly he lifted me. It isn't something that I have ever really experienced–being someone who is bigger than what fashion deems average. But this isn't a normal situation. He's not just any man, and I try my best to maintain what level of professionalism I can while thrown over his broad shoulder.

"You wanted this meeting, sugar," he states, and I can hear the smirk. He is very proud of himself.

"I can walk, Wilkes!" I shout, trying not to slide off and bust my head open on the concrete floor of the arena, but that just makes him tighten his hold.

"Too late now." I can see the doors of the locker room close behind me. Faces of his teammates laughing, disappearing as I bounce against his shoulder with each step. This must be a regular occurrence because nobody seems alarmed by his sheer lack of professionalism and infuriating—what is this even? The exact reason they needed to hire someone to handle PR.

"You made your point, showed your team that I am not in charge, now put me down." He lets me slip a little further down his back, and I let out a yelp as I reflexively wrap my arms around his waist to keep from falling. The deep breath I take to settle my nerves fills my lungs with a fresh minty scent that almost makes my mind wander. Almost. He smells amazing, yes, but instead, I'm filled with thoughts of what he's seeing. My ass is probably right in his face at this point. *Great. M*y fat rump in this solid muscle body of a Greek god's face. Thank goodness his personality is shit at this point because if I even thought for a moment that I could like this man... *ugh*. "How about you try not to drop me on my head? You need me, Wilkes. I'm not sure anyone else will be willing to help if they find out you injured me."

* * *

LIAM

Why did I decide picking her up and carrying her out of the locker room to her office was a good idea? I was pissed that she barged in scolding me like a child. I thought I made it clear I wasn't interested in her help. You would think that bailing on the meetings and avoiding her as much as possible, apparently I need to spell it out to her. I'm not interested in her or anyone else's help..

I need to distance myself from her, and yet, I have her thrown over my shoulder, and her arms are wrapped around my waist. Her voice was so damn soothing even though she was pissed at me. I could feel the tension slowly leave my shoulders, and by the time I make it to her office, I feel calmer than I have in a long time. I set her down rougher than I mean to, but that might be a good thing. She steadies herself by grabbing a hold of her desk, then squares her shoulders. She looks furious, and honestly, the flush on her face is sexy.

CHAPTER 2

"Next time you touch me, you better hope I'm feeling generous. Because I will not hesitate to take us both to the ground."

"Next time don't barge into my locker room," I say with as much malice dripping from every word. her. She straightens her clothing and hair. I can't deny that her curves are gorgeous. She's so damn hot, but I need her to hate me—not want me.

"Next time don't force me to take action," she scoffs, crossing her arms across her chest. I lose the battle and glance down briefly at where her arms are folded, quickly shaking my head to stop myself thinking too much about it.

"What the hell did we need to talk about anyway?" I stay standing, not letting her think she won by getting me here.

"Other than you being a huge asshole to your teammates? Or maybe we should look at how you went from crowd favorite to the team's biggest nightmare. We could also discuss how you became someone who just might blow up on a child who asks for an autograph. Quite frankly, Wilkes, I don't understand what's wrong with you."

"Like you would understand," I mutter.

"Try me," she says, looking at me like she is waiting for a big epiphany. She takes a deep exasperated breath before adding, "Look, I know the basics. And it's terrible. I don't expect you to just get over it. I know that isn't possible. However, you need to figure something out so that you don't let it control you so much."

I can feel my blood pressure rise at her comment, my face and ears growing hot. "Oh, I'm so sorry that the death of my fiancée and our unborn baby is causing such a problem!" I shout towering over her. "When everyone that you loved is ripped out of your hands, that changes a person." How fucking dare she? Am I just supposed to forget them, and everything that I planned for us?

"Not always, that's not good enough," her hands rest on her hips, silently telling me that my reasoning is bullshit. "People lose the people they love every day and they don't act like assholes!"

"Yeah, well, what would you know? I'm sure you've had this perfect life, it sure seems that way. Worst thing that's probably happened to you was not making the cheer team in middle school or whatever. You have no idea what I am going through." My shoulders are tense, and my frustration just grows with every second that passes.

"What I know is that you are not a defender. You don't need to get into fights left and right on or off the ice this season. We hire others to do that. You need to find an outlet for your anger? Go out for drinks with the guys, take up a class. Hell, maybe you should talk to a psychologist."

I scoff. "No, therapy was a joke."

"Ok, then don't do the therapy thing. Heaven forbid a man talk about his feelings with a licensed professional to maybe better himself. Damn it, Wilkes! Figure your shit out. I highly doubt that they would have wanted you to behave like this because of what happened. Let me help you. It's my damn job." Something shifts in her eyes as she talks. She goes from angry to indifferent, maybe even sad in a short moment. I'd rather she be pissed at me. She should yell–throw things even. Anything besides showing pity. I hate the pity.

"Fine, can I go now?" I rub the back of my neck trying to ease the growing tension there. I can't take this a moment longer. I want nothing more than to get to work and take out some of my frustration on the ice.

"You know that this isn't over, right? We have to work

CHAPTER 2

together on this, Wilkes. I can't help you if you don't let me." Her tone softens as she looks me directly in the eyes. I don't say anything. I wait for her to continue. "Just go..."

I turn quickly to get away from her. There is something about her that makes me want to let my guard down, but I can't afford to do that. Not now. And probably not ever.

* * *

ELISE

"Ugh!" I groan. "This man is infuriating." I sink into my desk chair, running my fingers through my hair. "Daddy, why is this so difficult? How did you survive without Mom? I can't get through to him, I just wish that you were here to give him advice, and I could really use a papa bear hug right about now."

I look at the picture of us from my graduation. We were both excited for my future and sad to not have Mom there with us. I know that Wilkes is hurting, but grief isn't a good enough reason to be an ass to the people trying to help you. There must be a better way to channel his shit-tastic mood into something less d-bag like. Am I terrible for being so mean to him? Well, not to him, but in my mind about him? What kind of person am I that I get pissed at myself for not actually being mean but just thinking what everyone else is thinking?

Focus, Elise, you have a charity event to finish planning. There's no time to beat myself up about Wilkes. I just wish I could get through to him–help him work through this. I close my eyes and try to stretch my neck to relieve some of the stress I have been feeling while trying to figure out what to do with Wilkes. I could let my mind wander and think about what I would want to do with Wilkes if he wasn't a heartbroken, selfish jerk. Sure, he has every right to be upset about what happened, but there are a lot of people trying to help him, and we are getting nowhere!

Resting my head in my hand, I look at my desk calendar. I know that it's archaic, but I have always been more of a pen and paper kind of person, physical books, sketch pads with pencil, and other tactile mediums. That's when I see it. I'm supposed to be in a meeting right now–in the locker room. *Son of a bitch.*

I grab my notes and coffee and kick off my heels, choosing to carry them to get down there a little faster. If that jerk Wilkes would have just shown up at our meeting, I wouldn't have to practically run through the arena to make this.

I stop to catch my breath, slide back into my heels, and fix my hair. I will not let him see me frazzled. I will appear calm and confident in front of him, regardless of how I actually feel. And yeah, I kind of felt hot and bothered for a moment, a very brief moment, as I was hanging on for my life a little bit ago. But he will never know. I refuse to let him see me as anything but professional. Squaring my shoulders, I push the door open and walk confidently across the room.

* * *

LIAM

CHAPTER 2

What the hell is she doing here? I thought I was done having to deal with her today. But no. She strides in as though we didn't just fight. She looks all business, with her binder in her arm and a coffee in her small hands. I shake my head and, with a sigh, go back to lacing up my skates. I can't look at her and keep my cool.

"Alright, guys. Listen up," Coach says, his voice booming in a way that demands attention. "Elise is here to let you know about what's coming up with our outreach."

"Thanks, Jim," she starts. "Alright . . ." I go back to my usual routine, neglecting to listen to whatever she says. She drones on, and I hear her but I am not listening until she suddenly stops. "Hi pumpkin, I'm so sorry to interrupt you," her voice can only be described as a teacher trying to get the attention of a kindergartener. I let out a slow breath, stopping the laugh I want to let out but the audacity of it. Instead, I look up slowly, starting with her black heels that lead to her strong calves, thick thighs, and curvy hips. She is gorgeous; her waist tapers in and accentuates her large... "Eyes up here, Wilkes."

"Sorry, sugar, I'm trying to get ready," I say with a smug smirk. I can tell she hates the pet names I keep using, and it honestly keeps pushing me to use them. To put that distance between us a bit more, of course. Not because I'm positive she would taste so incredibly sweet.

She sets her glare on me, crosses her arms, and in an almost scarily calm voice says, "And I'm trying to work too. Should I mention that the contract you signed when you started playing also makes you contractually obligated to attend and participate in events that the team holds? Like the one I'm trying to tell you about right now. So, do everyone a favor and focus real hard. I know that you have the attention span of a toddler."

"You're drooling, Wilkes," Will Spencer whispers with a nudge to my arm. "You're calling dibs, aren't you?"

"What? No!" I deny forcibly, but quietly so she can continue to talk about the back-to-school shop with the team event, and season ticket holder events coming up.

"Oh so, you won't mind...," he trails off glancing at Elise then back to me.

"Why would I?" I scoff. I almost don't believe myself as I say it. I steal a quick look at her myself before adding, "she's not Kaylee."

"You've got to start working through some of that," he says, letting me wallow for a moment. "I'm not saying to forget her. I know that's not possible."

I sigh, not wanting to say it again for the millionth time. Will knows more than everyone else how difficult these past months have been for me.

"It's fine, man, but seriously." He eyes me, trying to get a read on what I'm actually feeling. "Are you ok with me asking out the PR goddess? I mean, she isn't your usual type."

"Do what you want, Spencer."

Why does it bother me so much that he wants to ask her out? It's not like he doesn't have a point. She isn't my type- typically. Lately, though, she's physically everything I need. Shit, she is so pissed at me too, which is another thing that makes me want her more. I guess I should play it up to keep some distance between us.

I catch her eye as she finishes up whatever part of the events she is talking about, and without her saying a thing, I can tell she wants to throw her perfectly organized binder at me. Instead, she just shakes her head at me as she walks out. At least making her think I am a total jerk looks like it will work. She already

CHAPTER 2

hates me.

Lights flash, red, blue, red, blue. I'm running, trying to find her, trying to get to her in time. My feet pound against the linoleum floor. My footsteps are all I can hear, along with the sirens and shouting of doctors. The halls stretch, and no matter how fast I run, I can't get any closer. I can't get to her. I can't do anything to help her—to save her. I need to be with her. My heart is racing, and the hall starts to disappear. Everything is turning black, and I know I can't save her.

I sit up fast, trying to catch my breath as sweat drips down my neck. My blood runs cold, and I have a sick feeling in the pit of my stomach. It's as if I'm there all over again. I can even smell the sterile air of the hospital. The dream is too real. It's always the same, and I never get to her in time. Just like it was. That day haunts me in my sleep as much as it does when I am awake. The day I lost everything. I have that dream—no—nightmare, at least once a week.

Maybe Elise was right. I need to do something about this. The sleepless nights are messing with my rationale. I can't believe that I'm agreeing with her after all I've been trying to do to keep her away from me.

Chapter 3

LIAM

This is complete and utter bullshit. I can hear the sound of the team's families gathering in the players lounge and I turn the other way. I know that I have to be here for the annual 'Family fun day', but do they seriously expect me to be around all these families and not hate every part of it? Fun day my ass. I wish I had a drink right now. I can't though. Otherwise, I'll be in even bigger trouble with the club, I can't have another chat with my manager about the team's 'concerns for my future'. It's bad enough that I've been given a glorified babysitter. I walk through the halls of the stadium, turning into the visiting locker room where I know I can be alone for a bit.

I can't fight the building rage as I pace–rage for the crap hand I was dealt. Being around everyone that reminds me of what I lost is ridiculous. It's like I can't go anywhere without being reminded of what could have been. I grab the nearest thing, throwing it as hard as I can against the far wall. It does nothing to make me feel better, but I take more things off the shelves that were ready for the visiting team and throw them in a blind rage. I should have been here with my family. With Kaylee and our child. I should have had that to look forward to. I shouldn't be spending nights alone in my living room, waiting for an acceptable time to go to bed or checking to see if it's late enough to have a drink.

"What the hell?" I hear as my fist goes into the wooden locker divider. I punch again, not wanting to see her face. This isn't about her, and every second she's around feels like she's putting herself into my mess—a barricade between what I have with Kaylee—what I should have had with her. "WILKES!"

"Leave, Connors."

"No." She slowly steps closer. "Your hand is bleeding."

"Fuck. Just leave me alone!"

"What the hell is your problem?" She steps directly in front of me. "Not only are you literally hurting yourself to the point that you're bleeding, you're destroying property and making a shit ton more work for the staff. How big of an ass are you?"

"Seriously, leave me alone." I need something to release this rage, and she needs to not be here when I do that. I fight back the urge to yell at her, to force her out of the room.

"I'm not leaving. Not when you're acting like a child." She walks over to the mess of things I have made, grabbing a towel and wetting it in the sink just outside of the main locker room.

She makes her way back over to me and softly pushes me towards the empty chair. "Sit down."

"I don't want you here." My jaw is clenched to the point that it almost hurts as the guilt trickles in, but I'm not ready to admit it yet. She hasn't looked me in the eyes—not that I've noticed anyway. For some reason, that makes me angrier. Am I so pathetic she can't even look me in the eyes?

"Tough shit," she says calmly, taking my bloodied hand in hers. She silently cleans the blood from my knuckles, it feels like she is pressing harder than she needs to. "I'm not a doctor, but it looks like you just broke the skin." She wraps my hand in gauze before standing up and heading to the door. "Take all the time you need, but you're cleaning this up. If you want to act like a child, you can get a child's punishment."

I nod once, refusing to look at her. Scanning the room, shame washes over me. I'm right back to day one, throwing and punching things out of anger. I'm not proud of myself, and I know that Kaylee would be furious with me and probably make me clean up the mess just like Elise is. Nothing that I do numbs the pain. Even drinking after that first month out at the cabin didn't stop the nightmares from creeping in every night, reminding me of the day the life I was so sure of was lost.

Things have to change. I'm just not really sure how yet.

* * *

ELISE

CHAPTER 3

As the pre-season events started wrapping up, I could tell that Wilkes tried hard to prevent something like the locker room incident from happening again. We didn't discuss it. In fact, we barely talked beyond what was necessary. For the most part, the events have gone smoothly, and I'm surprised how well Wilkes behaved. He showed up and participated without needing me to push him along. He's been great with the kids that have come up to him, and honestly, it would be sweet if I didn't know what he's still going through. To be fair, he is still cold towards me, but if he's staying out of trouble, I guess it doesn't matter. I can handle the cold, as long as he behaves.

The season will be starting soon, and the upcoming events should be simple enough to put together. A few simple meet-and-greets with season ticket holders, and a drawing for a locker room seat for opening day. I take a break from sitting in my office and end up in the lower bowl seating of the arena–half asleep and half trying to figure out what to do with Wilkes. He's doing better with the fans, but he's obviously still working through everything.

"Elise, hey!" I hear from behind me. "Connors!"

"Shit!" I jump. "Sorry, no one calls me by my first name here. I almost forgot who Elise was!" I turn to see a smiling Will Spencer and an indifferent Liam Wilkes. My eyes lock on Wilkes for a moment longer than I wanted, and I'm surprised to not see pure disdain there, but something else. Something I can't quite grasp.

"The perils of working with a lot of men. We tend to go right for the last name for some reason," Will chides. He's handsome–in a real boy-next-door kind of way. He isn't as rugged as his friend and teammate but has a leading man in Hollywood look. He'd definitely be the kind of guy I would have gravitated towards during school. He was incredible to work with over the pre-season, and I find myself talking to him more and more each time we crossed paths.

"True. What are you two doing up in this neck of the woods? It's not the typical player hangout after all," I comment, looking at Will but unable to not steal an occasional glance at his brooding friend. He hates me. That much is obvious, but he is still very tall and very handsome.

"Well, honestly, I was looking for you." He nods in Liam's direction. "And I'm his ride for today"

"Oh..." I whisper, looking at Wilkes again.

"I should have taken a cab," Wilkes mutters under his breath, and I flinch at the tone. It pains me more than it should.

"So, why were you looking for me?" I ask, shaking the uneasy feeling that Wilkes gives me.

"I thought maybe you would like to get some food," he offers with an easy smile. It's a little awkward honestly. Is he asking me out in front of his friend? "I know you just moved here and probably don't know anyone yet."

"That's really thoughtful, Will, thank you. I kind of have plans though. There hasn't been much time with all the charity events and the season starting up." I stand from my seat and make my way towards them, planning on going to my office to work a bit more.

"It's fine, no need to try to ice my bruised ego..."

"No, it's not that. I've been living across the street at a hotel for like 2 months now and I need to find a place to live.. Hotels are pretty depressing after a while." I take a moment to catch my breath, and Will lets out a laugh. Wilkes, on the other hand, is engrossed in his phone. "So, I actually have a date to meet some realtors. Hopefully one of them won't be a total asshat."

CHAPTER 3

"Oh yikes, I don't envy you at all."

"Thank you," I say, oozing sarcasm. I giggle- not entirely sure where it came from.

"Here," Wilkes practically shoves a card into my hand. I look at him in shock for a moment before taking it from him. "My realtor. Let him know I sent you."

"Thank you. I appreciate this," I say, grateful for the little bit of kindness he just showed. This is the first time he hasn't actively avoided speaking to me, and if I'm not mistaken, he may have cracked a smile. A small one but still. I honestly don't know exactly how to take this sudden helpful side of him—other than to just enjoy it while it lasts.

"Don't mention it." He turns away from me toward Will, adding, "Spencer, can we go now? I'm starving."

"Yeah. Are you sure you don't want to join us, Elise? A girl has got to eat..."

"I don't want to impose on guy time," I comment, looking between them. As much as I would love to get something to eat and not be on my own, yet again, I also don't want to come between friends. It's obvious that Wilkes doesn't like me, even professionally. I doubt he wants me to actually go with them.

"Oh, shut it, Connors. Like Spencer said, you have to eat at some point." The scowl on his face almost makes me laugh. "Ok, I just have to grab my bag." I climb the few steps from the lower bowl to the mezzanine where they are waiting, and my stomach growls slightly at the thought of a full meal. "Just give me a minute and I'll be right back."

"Awesome!" Will says with a triumphant clap. "I'll bring the car around." He smiles wide before turning towards the exit.

I'm about to have lunch with two of the city's most eligible bachelors, albeit, one lost his fiancée and their child only a few months ago, but the other one isn't grieving. Yes, it can be written off for my job but at least I have that going for me. I have to admit that if Wilkes wasn't so mean all the time, he would be the kind of guy that I would fall hard and fast for. I can't say that I know much about him—not that he has given me a chance. Every time we speak, it's all business; team photos, meet and greets with the tiny comets (the youth league that practices here), and random social media posts that feel incredibly scripted in the moment. That's all really. He hasn't given me much beyond that. It's difficult when the client doesn't speak to you about things other than business. I never know if what I'm doing is helping them at all that way. Not that I should ever intertwine my personal life with him, that would be a big misstep.

When I make it to my office, I grab my things and get ready to head back out, but an alert draws my attention to my email.

Miss Connors,

I received your information from Mr. Wilkes, and I would love to help you in your search for a home. Mr. Wilkes gave me a few guidelines that you were looking at, but I would love to sit down with you and go over what you are looking for in more detail. Let me know what works for you, and I will arrange it all.

Sincerely,
Robert Bates
Metics Realty.

"What guidelines?" I ask myself, hurrying out of my office. I have questions to ask Wilkes, and I don't want to make them wait longer for me. I reread the email as I all but run to where I left Wilkes. I suddenly slam into something hard, and I can only describe it as a brick or cinder block wall. It knocks me off balance, and the force sends a cold feeling in the pit of my stomach.

"Shit, Connors," I hear as I feel something grab my waist, stopping me from falling over. I let out a groan as the dizziness hits me from the abrupt movement. I lean my head against the brick wall, and take a deep breath, trying to let the dizzy feeling pass. "Are you ok?" The voice is gentle and calm as someone cradles my face with their other hand. It's warm and calming. I feel grounded by that touch and the dizziness subsides little by little.

"Why is the wall talking?"

"Connors, I'm not a wall Are you ok?"

"What?" I look up finally. "Sorry."

"It's fine. Are you ok?" Wilkes asks with actual concern in his voice. He really is handsome– when he isn't a jerk. I don't think I've ever seen him look so caring. He surely has never looked at me with anything other than indifference. Why do I feel so comfortable with his hands on me? I shouldn't. But the bulk of his arms around me feels better than I thought was possible.

"Distracted, I'm fine. I ran into a wall," I almost shout in disbelief, confused and disoriented.

"You ran into me," he laughs. And what a laugh! It sends a shiver down my spine, and I can't help but smile.

"Oh... shit. Wait, how did the realtor get my email? And what are these guidelines that you gave him?" I ask, remembering the questions I had for him.

"Can you stand on your own?" He ignores my question, and I realize I was still leaning against him to support myself. I have my hands resting on his arms. They're thick and solid like branches.

"Yeah," I gasp. "I mean of course I can". I push slightly away from him, feeling his hands on my waist still steadying me. I feel dizzy again almost instantly, "Yeah, no."

"Alright. You're not ok. We're going to go down to the locker room to have the team doctor take a look."

"He's a physical therapist, not an actual doctor." I feel him pick me up as I argue. "What are you doing?"

"You can't stand on your own," he states firmly. His concern is almost cute. I can see why his fiancée fell for him.

"I'm fine, really. I probably just need to eat. I was running late and didn't have breakfast."

"You haven't eaten...since when? Did you eat yesterday? Damn it, Elise, how stupid are you?"

I roll my eyes at his anger. Never mind, it's not cute.

"Geesh, thanks for being an ass! I had a late lunch yesterday, ok!" Why does he care anyway? He's been so cold towards me since our first meeting, and now he's almost human. Maybe he isn't as bad as I had thought.

"Earth to Connors." I shake the fog from my head and look him in the eyes. They're impossibly blue. I didn't know they could be that blue. He gently brushes a lock of hair from my face. I swallow and am taken aback by the gesture. "I thought you were going to pass out on me there."

"Where did Will go? I'm kind of starving now that we've been talking about food." I flash him a smile hoping that he forgets about taking me to the 'team doc' who wouldn't be able to do anything for me anyway.

"He's getting his car. Should be here soon," he answers in a gentle way that I didn't think he was capable of. "Can you stand on your own?"

"I don't know," I say incredulously. "But please put me down."

CHAPTER 3

"I don't know if I can then," he replies with a smirk tugging at the corner of his mouth. Is he actually teasing me? This is a new side to him that I'm not sure I'm prepared for.

"Are you going to be a jerk again when I'm no longer dizzy?" There is a full on smile on his face now as he gently sets me down. "Thank you," I whisper.

"Will's pulling up," he states as we walk the remaining few yards to the door. He stays close by as if waiting for me to pass out. His voice is calm but quieter than I was expecting when he speaks again. "I just told the realtor to avoid certain unsafe areas, especially for someone on their own. Since you are new here, you wouldn't know where the safest places would be and whatnot."

"Oh. Thank you, Liam."

"You called me Liam." He looks shocked.

"You called me Elise- you were calling me stupid though, too. So, there's that." He laughs. I don't think I've heard him laugh before—not this laugh anyway. He's pretty handsome when he's not being a jerk.

"You didn't drive, did you? I normally see you walking in the mornings." I'm a bit shocked that he has noticed me walking.

"I didn't. It seems kind of silly when I'm staying across the street."

"We'll drop you off after you finally eat something," he says, opening the door for me.

"You say that as if I haven't eaten in days," I reply, stopping a few feet from the door.

"You haven't eaten in a day," he comments, eyeing me in a concerned way rather than judging. I would have expected him to be anything but concerned, honestly. "You're here alone, as far as I know, so you need to take care of yourself."

"Now you're concerned? Ok. You're like the big brother that I never wanted," I say with as much sass as I can muster. He looks confused and a bit upset but opens the car door for me to sit up front.

"What do you want to eat, Elise?" Will asks as we both climb into the car.

"I'm honestly not sure what there is around here. I've been eating a lot of room service and things at the office restaurant thing."

"Seriously?" I hear Liam scoff from the backseat.

"Yes, seriously. You're not the easiest person to reign in, Wilkes. It has taken a lot of my time and energy trying to make you look good again," I say calmly, eyeing him from the mirror. "I get that you're going through something terrible, and I'm grateful that you're no longer getting trashed and punching people. You're still messing with my food." I smile after seeing him let out a silent laugh. Our eyes meet through the mirror, and we can't seem to look away. His piercing blue eyes draw me in. He is handsome when he lets go a bit.

"Seriously, though. What are you hungry for?" Will asks again, trying to hold back a laugh. I almost forgot he was here aside from someone having to drive the car.

"Um . . . Oh! A burger sounds amazing right now," I answer, finally breaking eye contact with Wilkes.

"We should go to Frank's place," he suggests from the back.

"You think she can handle it? Do we want someone else knowing our secret?" Will asks jokingly.

"She can handle it."

***

CHAPTER 3

LIAM

She is different than I thought she was. The first weeks here, she was all business and no fun at all, but the first charity event we did was where I saw a different side of her. I still need to keep my distance, but maybe she wouldn't be so bad as a friend. Even if she is gorgeous, and when she ran into me, I enjoyed feeling every one of her soft curves against me. Her personality is pretty fucking amazing. But Will—he wants to ask her out, and I can't cock block my friend because I may or may not have a thing for a girl for the first time since Kaylee died..

We sit in the corner booth, Elise between the two of us. We joke and learn a little about the new girl.. She's an only child, but she doesn't seem as spoiled as others that grew up alone. She's a lot more than the privileged girl that I thought, which isn't making it easy to stop feeling something for her. Not that I know what that something is—beyond lust.

The waiter comes up and takes both of our orders as Elise finalizes what she wants. "I'll have a double cheeseburger, medium, with cheddar cheese and bacon. Don't bother with the bun. That would just be a waste. Fries are good- can I get pickles too? Oh! A chocolate milkshake, please," she says with a smile and thanks him before he walks away.

"Damn, you're not shy, are you?" I muse.

"What?" Her face falls a little, and I'm not sure why. "I'm hungry," she mutters, looking away from me and I scramble to fix what I said.

"I think that it's more that I'm impressed you don't pretend to eat, like a lot of women." I'm disappointed in myself that I didn't realize sooner that she probably has had people commenting on her eating habits before.

"Seriously, Wilkes? I tend to get hyper focused on what I'm doing and before I know it it's hours later and I haven't had anything besides a granola bar with my coffee. If someone wasn't such a huge pain in my ass I probably would remember to eat., but no. Instead I'm handling your mess on top of the regular events and charity things that have to happen." Her voice is so easily teasing- I've picked up on this a few times now. She'll say something, and the other person will be unsure if she is joking or serious. A punch line delivered with a straight face and her soft, sweet tone. Kaylee would have loved her. I can feel the melancholy smile on my face. Thinking of her still makes my heart ache, but it's getting easier, and maybe someday, I can find someone as great as Kay or Elise. I'm not saying I would date Elise... no. I mean, she's pretty, and I'm sure she would make a great girlfriend, but she's too close already. I can't be a jerk to her forever. It's best to keep her as a sort of friend. A friend held at a distance.

"What do you mean you didn't want to work here?" Will asks her. I zoned out again- not listening to her speak, lost in my thoughts again.

"I didn't want to be distracted. This has been my all-time favorite team, and I get really into the games."

"How into it are we talking?" I ask, genuinely curious. "Jersey? Sign holding? Face Paint?" I pictured her completely decked out, banging on the glass, and honestly, it would be ridiculously distracting.

"No face paint, I have sensitive skin. But, when I was younger–the signs." She laughs. "Oh, and profanity. So much profanity."

"I don't know if I believe her. Do you?" Will asks.

"No. We're going to have to see this."

CHAPTER 3

"That's the problem." She laughs. "Now that I work for the team, I'm going to have to behave myself!" Our food arrives, and we dig in, our conversation slowing but still making me smile more than I thought possible.

The rest of the afternoon goes by quickly, and I can honestly say I wasn't expecting to have this much fun. I almost forgot that everything is different now. As much guilt as I have for that day, for not getting there in time to be there for Kaylee and our child, I know that she would want me to move forward in life. I can't let the guilt eat away at me forever. I need to have fun and start living life again. I just wish it wasn't a life without Kaylee.

Chapter 4

I feel insanely better after finally settling into a routine. A routine with regular meals- in fact. The guys may have forced me to eat a couple of times. One of them would walk in and leave a bag of something on my desk when I wasn't in the room. This is why I am so happy to have found a boxing class nearby. They have been making sure I am fed, but they also contributed to the extra ten pounds I have gained in the past couple of weeks. I make my way into the building and towards the classroom that I have been to a few times already since my move and stop in my tracks when I see him.

"What are you doing here?" I ask, dropping my bag next to him. He looks up at me, taking a break from trying and failing

CHAPTER 4

to wrap his hands for class.

"Someone," he starts, with a pointed look my way, "suggested I take up boxing to help with my anger issues and grief or whatever." He goes back to his task, winding the hand wrap haphazardly around his large hands.

"I didn't mean this class," I say, unable to concentrate on anything other than how much he is struggling with his wraps. Well, that and how the muscles in his hands flex, wondering how they would feel against my skin. Ew, gross, Elise. He's not into you that way, and you sure as hell shouldn't think of him like that either.

"It's the closest to the arena," he says, matter of fact.

"Oh dear Lord. Let me." I sigh, unable to watch him fail yet again at the task. I take one of his hands and undo what he attempted, starting over correctly. I don't say anything while I take my time to make sure it's done the right way, but I do notice how big his hands are. They make mine look small. All of him makes me look small, and I am by no means a straight size girl. I've always been thicker and curvier. I get one of his hands wrapped, and he offers me the other. This is when I realize I should not have removed my extra shirt from my gym bag. It will get far too warm for the sweatshirt I currently have on, and I don't know how I feel about wearing just my sports bra and leggings in front of him. "There you go," I say, releasing his hand quickly, missing their warmth almost immediately.

"Thanks," he says, flexing his fingers. There is something about him flexing his hands that is undeniably sexy. I shouldn't be thinking this about his hands though. "I guess I will have to learn how to do that."

"It gets easier the more you do it," I say, wrapping my hands quickly. I've done this countless times, so it comes naturally.. I can't look at him. I can't fall for one of my clients. After lunch the other day, finding random snacks or meals left on my desk, cordial run ins here and there as we pass each other in the halls, and now today with him here, it's proving difficult. I feel drawn to him in a way that I can't quite put my finger on. Luckily, I don't have much longer to overthink it all because the instructor is calling for our attention. I pull off my sweatshirt, deciding to ignore his stare as much as possible. Soon, the class will be in full swing, and I will be able to block out the world- the world and Liam Andrew Wilkes.

I started boxing classes after all the crap back home. It helped keep the demons at bay. That was the goal I had in mind when I suggested it to him. I guess I should have been clearer on the class not being the one I was in. As we get warmed up I can feel his eyes on me, I'm not sure if it is because he's trying to figure out what he's supposed to be doing or because I'm practically half-naked. I didn't expect to see people that I work with at this class, I really didn't expect him to be here. This sports bra doesn't leave much to the imagination, it does it's job but still. I tug at the fabric trying to cover myself a bit more any way possible. The hour seems to fly by, for the most part- I catch him looking at me several times and I try to shake the exposed feeling I have when I catch him. He seems a bit winded though. Sweat is dripping down his face. His shirt clinging to his chest a bit.

"How in the hell?" he says, chugging water once the class wraps up. I can see the heavy rise and fall of his chest as he catches his breath.

"You didn't pay attention to the class levels when you signed up did you? Or was that a macho man kind of thing?" I laugh taking my towel to wipe my forehead off.

CHAPTER 4

"How do you keep up with that?"

"What exactly is that supposed to mean?" I tease with a smile as I throw the towel in his face. He catches it and swipes it across his face as if I hadn't just used it myself. "I'm full of surprises. Obviously."

"Obviously." He smiles. He is undeniably handsome when he smiles, and it's genuine. But damn him! Just when I stop thinking about him in a primal way he does something cute and ruins everything. I'm not sure how long I can resist. And I must resist. I mean it's just a physical attraction, after all. It's not that I like him as a person.

"I am surprised that you handled this as well as you did though. It's different from hockey," I say. I turn away from those sapphire eyes to pull my sweatshirt over my head, feeling too warm really for it but wanting to not have my torso so exposed around him.

"Uh, seriously? Have you tried hockey? You might be singing a different tune after that," he says as we walk out of the studio. "I mean we all have our strong suits. You might be the one out of breath after a little bit of that."

"Meh. I've played a time or two." I shrug knowing that he is just trying to egg me on.

"Meh?! Seriously? Give it a real chance, Connors, and tell me it's not harder than you thought. There isn't anyone there right now, and I just happen to have special access being Captain and all..."

"Yeah, you're not special. I also have access. You know this. You're not going to impress me because you have a key to your job," I say with sass.

"I wasn't trying to." His voice is quieter.. His eyes are locked with mine for a moment longer than I would have expected.

Then it's over sooner than it happened.

"Nope, now I have to prove myself to you. Prove that I can handle a little skating."

"A little skating," he gasps.

"Meet me there in about thirty minutes. I'm going to put on some warmer clothes, and you can show me how it's done, oh great one," I say with a smile, looking up at him.

"Thirty minutes it is." He smiles.

* * *

"You showed up." He sounds surprised as I walked into the arena.

"You sound surprised?"

"I'm not sure that I expected you to come honestly," he says, rubbing the back of his neck. He thought that I wouldn't come—that I would go back on what I said. I guess that's not too far off for someone who lost so much. "I grabbed you some gear."

"Well, sorry to say you wasted your time," I smirk, setting my very large bag down on the ground between us.

"How the hell do you have hockey gear?"

"Again, I'm just full of surprises, Wilkes," I laugh at his confusion.

He shakes his head, and I swear I see a smile. "Do you want to lace up in the locker room?"

"Wait, seriously?" I jump a little in my excitement. "Yes. Holy hell! Yes! It's like a teenage me's dream to go through the tunnel onto the ice in a professional arena. Honestly, if things had gone

CHAPTER 4

a bit differently, I would have been at the last winter Olympics."

"What?" He looks shocked and genuinely confused. "What happened?" he asks as we take a seat to lace up our skates.

"That's a story for another day, but for now..." I stand and hold out a hand to him, shaking his hand once before letting it fall. "Elise Connors, left wing. I earned this gear along with a full ride to play for my division one college. Played all four years of my undergrad. That's the basics..." I trail off, noticing how he is looking at me. Almost like he is realizing I am more than the girl that has been, and will continue to bust his balls every chance I get.

"Wow. Not what I expected," is all that he says. We make our way through the locker room and down the tunnel before he adds, "You're kind of surprising."

"So are you." I take a deep breath seeing the ice from this perspective and take the first step onto the freshly smoothed ice letting myself glide to center ice. "I forgot how amazing this is!" I move around the ice enjoying the feel of it beneath my skates for the first time in forever. "So, Wilkes, are you ready to be shown up by a girl?" I ask with a teasing smile.

"Shown up?" He skates in smooth circles around me. "You do realize that I am a pro right? And you haven't played in how long?"

"Yes, I realize that. I also know that you're a cocky son of a bitch too, but here we are. You're about to get your ass kicked by a girl, and I'm about to make a professional hockey player feel fantastic about himself." I can't help but laugh at the terrified and amused look on his face. "I mean, scientifically speaking, I am smaller and more compact. Therefore, I am faster and more aerodynamic."

"Scientifically speaking," he chuckles, his eyes tracking me as I come to a stop in front of him.

"Yes, exactly! See they were wrong about you. You are smart" I wink before skating off again.

"Hey, I went to college."

"I know. That's what I keep telling them," I say, doing one of the spins I learned in my early skating days.

"Ok, what the hell was that?"

"Oh that?. Well, I'm not entirely proud of it, but before I became obsessed with hockey as a kid, my mom had me in figure skating. Then one thing led to another, and Dad's love of hockey rubbed off, and we changed gears a bit. So yeah... that was a one-foot spin."

We stay for hours: shooting, skating, I even did a few more tricks that I remember from my figure skating days. When we've worn ourselves out, he even walks with me back to my hotel room, and I can't shake the familiar feeling of a first date. Not that this is a first date. I would have to be crazy to think that, but there is a slightly awkward feeling now that we aren't going to see each other for the rest of the day. I also don't want or need to get involved with a still grieving man. So maybe it was just nice to have a friend for the day. I haven't spent time with anyone since moving here- let alone just let go and had fun. It was easy and I wasn't overthinking any of it. Yeah, Liam Wilkes will be a great friend to have. Even if he is ridiculously handsome.

"Thank you for today. I needed this more than I thought," he says his brow furrowing slightly, obviously deep in his thoughts.

"I did too, so we are even. Friends?" I smile up at him, "Even if I'm going to be so sore tomorrow."

"Hey, I know we just spent the majority of the day together

CHAPTER 4

but, do you want to get something to eat?" He sounds nervous- it's kind of cute, and a part of me wants to say yes.

"I can't..." His face drops, but he regains his composure almost as fast.

"Right, it's not very professional. Sorry, I...."

"It's not that," I, without thinking, want to correct him before he thinks I'm shooting him down or something. "It's just... well, I kind of have a date. I think."

"You think?" he chuckles. "You either do, or you don't."

"Well, Will asked me out, but I don't know. He's a nice guy, don't get me wrong, but he reminds me more of a brother. I'm not sure there is chemistry there... but we will see I suppose."

"Does he know that?" He asked, his shoulder relaxing slightly.

"I guess I'll find out." I shrug and smile. "I did have fun today, super surprising actually. I mean it's you, after all."

"Gee, thanks, Connors." There it is. A real smile from him that is so rare it makes my heart flutter a bit. Probably because I want to see him happy, not because he's so much hotter when he smiles, right?

"You're welcome- see you tomorrow, Wilkes."

"See you tomorrow, Elise." I feel a flutter in my stomach at the sound of my name from his lips. It's not often that he uses my first name and it hit me more than I expected. He walks away and I catch myself watching him, wishing I could have spent more time with him. I know I spent all day with him, I get that, but I don't really want that to end. I shake the thought from my head and close my door.

A short while later, I am in the middle of my biweekly therapy session, hair air drying for my date. We discuss how I'm settling in and I find myself talking about the team, specifically Liam. "You talk about this coworker a lot." Dr. J comments.

"Well, yeah" I blink, not sure how to explain myself. Do I really talk about Liam that much? "I work with him a lot. I see him every day."

"It sounds like more than just working. They way to describe how you are with each other. " I'm a bit thrown by this comment. Everything I've done has been to help him. Sure, it was fun but it was to help him deal with his grief, so it was work related.

"HA! What? You're delusional, Doc."

"If you insist that's all it is then forgive me but..."

"I mean, we are friendly now. Nothing more," I reply. My mind trailing back to him leaving today and how disappointed he looked when I told him about the date. A date I was looking forward to, if only for the company until I saw that look.

* * *

LIAM

I know I told Will to go ahead and ask her out, that I was completely ok with it, but I can't shake the weird feeling in my stomach when she mentioned going on a date. I return to my new condo, the one I bought after Kaylee, after my summer-long bender in the middle of nowhere, and try to distract myself from wondering how it's going. I know I told Will I was completely ok with him asking her out but I can't shake the weird feeling that's settled in my stomach since she mentioned going on a date. I tried watching Sports Center, reading a book, even cleaning but nothing keeps my mind off of them out together for long. I don't want her, It's not like I want to date her, so why am I so concerned? She's just too... too, perfect. Shit. How weird is it going to be to lust after a friend's girlfriend? It's just lust.

She isn't Kaylee. She never will be.

Thankfully, Will shows up letting himself in as usual and breaking my train of thought. I try to ignore how deep in thought he looks and the questions that have been running through my mind.

"Hey man, what's up?" I ask calmly, glancing his way from my place on the couch.

"Not much."

"Why are you all dressed up?" I have to know something. Anything.

"Hung out with Elise," he says heading to the kitchen to help himself to whatever I have in there.

"Oh? You finally asked her out?" I turn a bit his direction on the couch, and try to smile at him. I feel like a stereotypical sorority girl waiting for my friend to dish on how their date went. I hope that it both went well and terrible at the same time.

"Yeah, it was fun." Will returns from grabbing a drink and slows as he looks at the built-in shelves my mom and interior designer set up. I can tell he isn't going to give me much more than this, and it's infuriating, especially since I had been sitting here for well over an hour thinking about their date. I'm beginning to understand why women hate us.

"Nice. Going out again?"

"Maybe," he says, stopping. I know that he is looking at the one picture I have displayed of Kaylee and me. The only one that I can bear the sight of. "She reminds me of Kay."

"How so?" I ask as I watch him stare at his sister's picture.

"Like I feel like I need to take care of her, in a brotherly way, she's been through shit too." He smirks then walks over falling onto the other end of the couch.

"I'm sorry. I forget, sometimes, that you lost her too." I keep it at that, not wanting to drag up all the emotions again, knowing that it's not what he needs or wants right now.

"It's fine, I appreciate how much you loved her." We sit in silence watching but not paying attention to the TV. "You like her, I can tell. Don't be a complete ass and pretend you don't. You did that with Kay. You made my sister happy, now I know it hasn't been that long, but you deserve to be happy again."

"So, the date was horrible and you're pawning her off?" I joke trying to lighten the mood.

"No, she's great. We had fun but both realized it was platonic, no chemistry. Not like you and Kay had. Not even close. I saw you trying not to look at Elise at lunch the other day, and at the arena...You like her."

I'm in shock at his words. "It's only been a few months...and"

"I know how long it's been," he cuts me off. "She was my sister, after all. And it's closer to a year... Kaylee wouldn't want you to not move on. It's been hard watching you struggle through this. I know how much you loved my sister and I'm happy that she had that love in her life." I swallow the lump that has formed in my throat, and nod willing myself to keep it together.

"Do we have to hug now or something?" I joke in attempts to lighten the mood.

"Don't you dare." He takes a long sip of his drink, most likely his standard whiskey neat, and that's the end of our conversation, but not the end of my train of thoughts.

. It's not often that we speak about Kaylee, when we do it's short and overdue. Like when he showed up at the cabin I spent this past off-season to be away from everything and everyone who reminded me of her. He came unannounced and started shouting at me about how Kaylee would hate what I had let myself become. How I had turned into a completely different person. He was right of course. I was completely different. I went from working out every morning, eating well, and making time for my family and friends to sleeping most of the day away, eating whatever I could find, and drinking myself into a stupor. Ugh.

"I've been thinking," I say, breaking the silence after a good 20 minutes.

"Don't hurt yourself."

"Funny... but really. I've been an ass to everyone." Will shoots me a look that was undeniably saying 'no shit'. "Maybe we are overdue for a team dinner or night out. I should invite Elise too, as an apology."

"An apology... ok. Let's do it." There is something about his tone that makes it known that he doesn't feel like it's just an apology. I pull out my phone and send a group message to the team and a single text to Connors. Will takes his glass to the kitchen and places it in the dishwasher, ready to head back to his place.

To EC: Hey the team is planning a dinner. Saturday at 7 pm. You should join us.

From EC: That sounds great :) Thank you for the invite.

To EC: Of course. I owe you.

From EC: You don't owe me anything. I mean it.

"Later man," Will says as he leaves my place. I wave him off and continue texting her.

To EC: Well thank you nonetheless. How was your date?

From EC: Oh that... it was ok. But like I said we're not anything more than friends- he's like the big brother I never had.

To EC: That's a shame. The date. Not the friends part.

From EC: Who knows what better guy is out there for me although with friends like you and Will that might be scary.... I can always use new friends though. I don't know many people here yet outside of work.

To EC: Very true.

Well shit, friend-zoned. Probably because I've been so much fun to be around. Making her job more difficult. I guess being friends is better than ignoring each other aside from when we have to work together. It's going to be difficult, though. If not impossible. What am I concerned about being friend-zoned anyways? It's not like we would date each other; I'm her job. She is responsible for my image and the teams. She's not here to date me.

From EC: Goodnight Liam.
To EC: Goodnight Elise.

Lights flash, red, blue, red, blue. I'm running trying to find her, trying to get to her in time. My feet pound against the linoleum floor; they are all I can hear, along with the sirens and shouting of doctors. The halls stretch, and no matter how fast I run I can't get any closer. I can't get to her. I can't do anything to help her, to save her. I need to be with her. My heart is racing, and the hall starts to disappear. Everything is turning black, and I know I can't save her.

Another night, another nightmare, same as always. Another night of reliving the worst night of my life. A reminder of everything I lost. Everything I will never have again. I take a deep breath sitting up in my empty bed, and I can't think of

CHAPTER 4

a way to get past this. Will knows me more than just about everyone else, and knows that I'm not one to show my feelings right away, which might be why he compared Kay and Elise. The beginning of things with Kaylee I didn't want him to know that I was falling for his sister. Now though when it comes to Elise, I don't want to know what my feelings are either.

I need to keep my distance, that's the only way, better to let myself be friend-zoned and fast.

Chapter 5

[1] ELISE

Getting back to the office on Monday was rough— I was still very sore from skating after boxing but remembering how much fun it was put a smile on my face. There were several things I needed to get through in preparation for the team's annual PR opportunities. Luckily there was a rough outline of these events already in place. It's just a matter of making sure the social media department would be ready for them, as well as making sure that the funding is in line. Liam would have to be

---

[1]

at all of these if we wanted to make sure the fans believed he was back to his 'old self.' I hate that the media is using that to describe how he has been since New Year. Of course the man is going to be different- he was happy and planning the rest of his life with someone, only to have it be torn away in an instant. I wish I could tell people to just leave him the hell alone, but that's not my job. My job is to make him appear 'normal' again, whatever that is.

There wasn't practice today, but I had seen several of the players walking through the halls to get to the workout room. Most of them came in on off days to get in some sort of practice, in an attempt to get ready for the upcoming games. Soon enough, things would be very busy with the season underway. I need to get things going on my home search before things get too hectic. My phone dings and I glance down, seeing a new email from "realtor." I type out a quick reply just as my body slams into something.

"Shit," I gasp, nearly falling on my ass.

"Watch where you're going Connors," I hear him snap. "How many times do you have to run into people before you stop walking around with your nose in your damn phone." I pull away as if I was burned. I wasn't expecting him to talk in that icy tone, not after we had spent some time together and finally started to feel like friends, if not just polite acquaintances.

"Sorry, I didn't..." I stammer, trying to reconcile the difference in how he is towards me today and how he was just two days ago.

"Obviously not." His demeanor was so different from the man I had talked to the other day. "What is so important that you can't watch where you're going?"

"Not that you care, but I'm setting up house viewings," I say, confused by how rude he was acting towards me. What could have changed in such a short amount of time?

"Finally moving out of the hotel. How the hell did you afford to live there for this long anyway? There's no way you make enough for that." I can't form words to respond. I just blink up at him. Trying to hold in the anger and hurt that is brewing inside me. He looks me up and down, shaking his head as if putting together some invisible puzzle. "Oh, so that's how. I'm surprised you have time to do any actual work then."

"Dude, what the hell," I hear Will's voice from behind me, "that was uncalled for."

"For the record, Wilkes, I have enough money on my own that I don't need to sell myself to afford things. But let's break this down for your tiny jock brain, shall we? My mom died when I was in middle school, and my dad invested the life insurance money so I could go to college without being in major debt afterward. However, as you damn well know, I had a full ride. So guess where that money sat for another seven years growing interest." I forced my voice to stay steady, though I could feel my blood starting to boil over. I want to give him a piece of my mind but I can't let my emotions get the best of me right now. I refuse to cry in front of him. Taking a deep breath I added, "Kindly keep your damn mouth shut next time you have an opinion on my ability to pay my bills, and how I do it."

"Wilkes, that was uncalled for." I could see Will standing next to me, but I was too enraged to register his presence.

"I have work to do," I say, turning away from them. I hate him. I hate that when I'm mad, I cry. I can't look at him. I can't let him see the tears pooling in my eyes. What the hell just happened? I hear Will practically yelling at him as I flee. I thought that we were cool, friends at least, but now. Why did

CHAPTER 5

his words hurt as much as they did?

I walk as fast as I can to my office and pack my things for the day. I need to get out of the building before I regret everything and try to make things better- even though he was the one in the wrong. I pop my head into Ben's office beside mine and let him know I was going to work off-site for the rest of the day to 'get a fresh perspective'. Despite the fact that the perspective I got a few moments ago was exactly what I was here to set right again. I make my way out of the arena, avoiding as many people as possible; especially Liam Wilkes.

* * *

To think I was almost giddy a few short days when I got those texts from him, now I have been avoiding him like the plague. Aside from work-related things, he hasn't said much at all. He has, however, acknowledged my existence, which is a bit better than before we spent the afternoon skating. But I was hoping it would continue on that level at least. Now I realize what they truly mean when they say one step forward, two steps back. I'm not entirely sure if I could be his friend after his not-so-subtle accusation that I can be bought.

At least I have Will to help make things less weird. I'm glad I have his friendship, but it's too bad we have no romantic chemistry- it would be so easy. We get a long way better than Wilkes and I ever could, and we have a surprising amount of things in common. Honestly, if it wasn't for my new friend, I don't know if I could stay here after this season- not with Wilkes' crazy mood swings.

I am honestly taken aback when I see the man I've been trying to avoid, Liam Wilkes, standing in my office doorway next to Will on Friday afternoon. I hadn't expected to see him at all outside of required events after Monday's fiasco.

"Hey, Connors," Will says with an easy smile. "Are you still going to join us tomorrow night for dinner?"

"Wouldn't miss it," I reply, giving Wilkes a quick glance to see if he has any objections after this past week. "Where and what time? I will meet you all there."

"I'll pick you up around 6:30," Wilkes says before Will can process the question. Why the hell was he offering to drive me after what he said?

"I am perfectly capable of driving myself," I reply, honestly confused and slightly scared of what might come next. The wounds from his words were still fresh.

"It's probably a good idea to get a ride," Will said matter-of-factly after a moment of me staring Liam down. "This is kind of a last hurrah before games start, and knowing the guys and the wives/girlfriends, it's going to be a bit crazy."

"Thanks for the warning," I say, a bit worried now. I tend to say what I'm meaning after a few drinks. I let out a breath and give in, "Ok fine. When should I be ready? And is this casual, or do I need to dress up? Also, please say casual because I would like to not have to dress up outside of work. No more heels, please."

"Casual, jeans and a button-up typically for where we're going," Will answers.

"I'll be there to get you at 6:30."

"I could just get a rideshare," I say sharper than I intended.

"Nope," Will says semi-offended. "What kind of people would we be to let you ride in a stranger's car at night? You could be murdered."

CHAPTER 5

"You've been watching too many crime dramas, Will Spencer." I smile. "Besides, I can hold my own. You don't even know, my friend."

"She has a mean right hook," Wilkes says with a smirk. I smile, my mind flashing back to the fun day we had last week. "Just call her Rocky."

"I'm missing something," Will says, looking between us.

"I will be there, and I promise not to be murdered nor murder anyone. How's that?"

"Probably a good plan," Will says with a smile. "Let's get out of the lady's way, Wilkes!" I can't help but laugh. I noticed at the last preseason event, that, aside from hockey, Will had a talent for making people laugh. We had invited season ticket holders to watch the team practice and meet some of the players. Pretty much every person who spoke to Will had a smile on their face. People were happy to see Liam too, but it was different; something felt forced with him that day. I'm not vain enough to think it was because of our conversation the day before. He was probably having a hard time with all the families that were there. We have one more event before the regular season, and then hopefully, it's smooth sailing from there. Hopefully. After they leave, I get out my phone and text him.

To LW: I don't have to go tomorrow if you don't want me there.

From LW: Why do you say that?

To LW: Oh idk the fact that we've barely spoken this week. Oh and you basically calling me a whore.

From LW: I'm sorry. It's weird right now.

What the hell is that supposed to mean? Weird right now? I don't bother responding, what's there to say after all? I thought we were going to be friends but, apparently, that's too difficult for the both of us. Maybe I should just tell Will that I don't feel well and stay 'home.' I could say that my meeting with the realtor took longer than expected... but what realtor would be doing home tours that late? I lean back in my desk chair and groan. Why is this so complicated? The ping of a text coming in sounds, and I sigh, picking up my phone again.

From LW: I want you there.

I let out the breath I didn't realize I was holding in and remind myself that he is going through something terrible, probably still navigating this new life without someone, well, two someones, that he had been planning on forever with. He's going to be a bit messed up. I still am.

* * *

LIAM

Man am I nervous. I mean she most likely hates me. Rightfully so after Monday. At least she is still coming tonight— probably because it's the entire team, not just Will and me. If it were, she would have said no, that's for sure. As I walk to her room door, I take a deep breath and steady my nerves before knocking. A moment passes with no answer, so I knock again. The door swings open quickly, and she looks completely stunned to see me, "Uh...Hi?" she says, obviously confused. "I thought that we decided I was just meeting you all there?"

"Well, I... shit, this isn't easy for me," I sigh. "I'm sorry. I was an ass, and I know it."

CHAPTER 5

"Ok." She walks back into the room, grabbing her jacket, she turns back to me as if waiting for me to continue, but I'm at a loss for words, not just because I know I was wrong but because she is stunning. "If you are expecting me to just forgive you for calling me a whore, in my place of work no less, you are sadly mistaken."

"I deserve that," I say, wincing at her words.

"Are we going or what?" Her face is so stoic I can't look her in the eyes without feeling worse for how I acted. She pushes me gently out of the way as she closes the door, before turning down the hall towards the exit.

"Yeah." I frown, not knowing how to make things better. She remains silent as we walk to the car and for most of the drive. I turn the radio on to pretend there isn't an uncomfortable silence. Not that it really helps. She just sits in the passenger seat quietly. It's unnerving, especially since she is usually very chatty and bubbly.

"I really am sorry," I say when I can no longer stand the silence.

"That's great for you, showing remorse. It doesn't change what you said," her tone was cool and collected; it terrified me. "You have no right to say that to any woman, ever. You're lucky that it was me and that I was in shock by the harshness of it because I would have decked you. If you had said that to me in a bar or anywhere other than my work–I wouldn't have hesitated." She was still so furious with me, and for good reason.

"I wish you had punched me, slapped me, something," I admit, glancing her way as my grip tightens on the steering wheel to stop myself from doing something stupid like taking her hand and begging for her forgiveness.

"Yeah, because that would have gone over real well," she

said, flailing her arms around. "'Member of PR Staff Punches Widowed Captain.' I can see the headline now, and the mess that I would have to clean up all on my own. While you would go around playing the victim."

"Valid point." I stop talking then, letting the moment simmer there. I need her to know that I recognize how terrible I was towards her. The plan to keep my distance worked too well. I pushed too far.

"I just need time to be mad for a bit, ok? Can I have that?" she asks, her tone softening. I nod, not daring to look at her or ask any questions.

I don't say anything else. I went too far, all because I couldn't control my emotions. The worst part is that I'm not even a widow, not really. Everyone treats me as if I am. It's not like Kaylee and I were married and had already built a life together. We hadn't had a chance. And the only person outside of family that has tried to treat me like I'm not some fragile piece of porcelain that needs to be handled delicately, I've been treating like crap.

* * *

ELISE

He is smart enough to stay silent, I'll give him that. It wasn't the first time I had been called something along those lines. All through high school, I was a tease or a prude, and while in college, every time I went out on campus, regardless of how I dressed, someone was bound to make some sort of comment.

CHAPTER 5

But from him, especially after the weekend and the time we spent together, it hurt so much more than I ever thought possible. Honestly, it shouldn't have hurt so much. We haven't known each other that long. I sigh before breaking the silence again. "Where are we going anyway?"

"Mitchell's. It's a nice place, we go there a lot as a team. They always have space for us; the owners are big fans," he says with a faint smile. "It's not much further."

"Oh." I take a look around. "Where... Who is all going to be there?"

"Most of the team was able to make it work, and the WAGs."

"Oh." He pulls into the parking lot, and I'm instantly nervous. "Being thrown to the wolves."

"The wolves?" He parks the car before letting out a laugh, "That's a good way of describing them."

"That's not comforting," I say, turning towards him and really look at him for the first time since the incident.

"Will and I won't let them get too crazy," he offers. We get out of the car and walk towards the door. He stops, looks me in the eyes, and says, "I am sorry."

"I know. And I'm not scared of the team, obviously, I've never been great with women. Probably because I've always played sports." I state matter-of-factly. The downside of choosing a male-dominated pass time was the only teams available were mostly filled with men.

"I'm not great with women either," he says with a chuckle.

"Obviously." I can't help but smile at this.

"They're going to love you. Everyone seems to." I smirk at him, apparently buttering me up is his new strategy to make me forgive him. "Just be a little wary of Jenna and Brooke. They're kind of... well... bitches."

"Wow," I laugh and can't help but swat at him. "Seriously?" I catch his eye, and it makes me happy to see a real smile on his face again. They're so rare that if you blink, you might miss them. "Well, since I know who to avoid if possible. I still would feel awful if I stopped you or Will from meeting a nice girl, but I also don't want to be left alone with strangers... so."

"You can't do any more damage. I seem to be doing that on my own. Something about being a grieving d-bag does that well enough."

"Yeah, you know? You're right, you can be a huge tool," I say straight-faced.

"Wow," he says looking genuinely shocked. "I wasn't expecting that."

"You're allowed to grieve, but you're not allowed to be an ass. Especially to those who are just trying to help you." He watches me intently as I speak. "It may be my actual job to help but I thought that we were becoming friends too. So yeah..."

"We are," he whispers, his head dropping slightly. "I hope that we are." I place a hand on his arm as a comforting gesture, feeling the heat radiate through his jacket, warming my always slightly cold hands. He lifts his face enough to look me in the eye, and his piercing gaze holds me there in that moment for longer than I had planned. I note the slight stubble on his face, the richness of his cologne, and then the bob of his Adam's apple as he swallows. My whole body is warm now, all from being near him. I smile and step back, letting my hand drop from him.

Clearing my throat, I say softly, "We should head inside." All he does is nod before stepping to open the door to the restaurant for me. We walk back to the table where most of the team is seated chatting away. A few stop to say hello to me and Liam, and I notice a handful of the women sitting there giving us disapproving looks

"Those two, stay away from them," he leans in and whispers as he pulls out my chair before shrugging out of his jacket. Seated between him and Will I feel less nervous, but I can feel the anxiety of meeting new people in a social setting creeping up on me. In a professional setting it's completely different; I am in charge, it's my situation to control— but this, this has never been my strong suit. "Are you ok?" He asks, his voice low so only I can hear him.

"Yeah, I just don't feel comfortable with meeting lots of new people." I know people think that with what I do for work I'd be used to it, but meeting new people for the sake of socializing is completely different.

"You?" he asks, visibly confused. "You, the person who barged into the locker room..."

"That was different. I didn't care what you thought of me." I smile, watching his face.

"To be honest, I thought you had bigger balls than half the guys here." I can't help but laugh at his words. I think back to that and remember being terrified of him for a moment, between me yelling at him and being thrown over his shoulder.

We continue chatting, with Will joining in when Liam's attention was elsewhere. Bottles of wine are brought to the table like pitchers of water and we order our entrees. As I'm finishing my first glass of wine one of the other women I recognize as Tom's wife Sarah, decides to talk to me.

"So, Elise, how are you liking it here, now that things are gearing up?" she asks from across the table. She seems friendly and Wilkes didn't warn me about her at all.

"Oh, well. It's never a dull moment with these guys," I smile. "Exhausting getting everything ready but now, it's mostly making sure certain people don't get into trouble. Like this one," I point towards Wilkes, "and him," Will, "and him... him too..." I continue to point at the other men at the table. "I'm ready to enjoy the season a bit between working." We continue in easy chatter, I promise to help keep her husband in line, and she smiles, thanking me for any help she can get.

Soon the food arrives, and if I didn't say that this was the best steak I have ever had I would be lying. I can't help the moan that escapes my lips with that first bite, and if I didn't know any better, I would have sworn that Wilkes let out a frustrated groan after. We eat and drink until I know that I have had too much wine. I glance around the table, taking it all in, noting the comradery that is apparent between the team and the friend groups of the significant others. This night with everyone is what I had hoped for when I moved, maybe not with the team, but still. This city is starting to feel like home.

"You're new here right? Where are you staying?" Sarah asks leaning over to touch my arm as the table starts to clear.

"I just put an offer in on a condo just on the other side of the river. But right now, I'm in the hotel across the street from the arena."

"Let me know if you need help with furnishing- I'm a buyer, so I can get you a good deal." I take the card she offers me, and tuck it into my purse.

"Deal." I smile. Liam stands up from the table, and I watch as he walks out of the room, then I turn towards Will. I smile at my friend, glad to have him around to help me navigate not just the team stuff but with the new city as well.

"I'm glad that you two seemed to have patched things up a bit," he says quietly enough that the others can't hear him over all the talking. "Monday wasn't a good day."

CHAPTER 5

"I feel like that is an understatement."

"No, more than that. It's not an excuse for his actions at all, but Monday was Kaylee's birthday," he explains, his voice turning sad and slightly distant.

"Oh, I'm sorry, Will." I take his hand and squeeze it. He'd explained to me previously that Kaylee was his sister and they were close, and despite that it would never happen for real, Liam was his family.. I had confided in him too. Letting someone know the darker sides of my life was cathartic, something we both had needed.

"It's ok... I just wanted to let you know why... he wasn't taking the day well and I dragged him there to work out."

"Thank you for telling me," I reply. My eyes snap to Liam as he walks back into the room, watching him stop to talk with his teammates at the far end of the . I can't help but notice the smile on his face, as if this night was a catalyst for him to mend bridges and repair the friendships that his grief had torn apart.

He makes eye contact with me as I sip on the rest of my wine, finishing the last bit in my glass. "We're heading out- got a section at Park Patio. Some of the guys are coming with us, but old men like Tom are headed home," he jokes.

"Hey!" Tom shouts, helping his wife get her coat on. "You try staying out all night in a couple of years, you won't be able to hang out either." They're pretty adorable together, and you can tell that they are in it for the long haul.

"I'm sure you're right, gramps," Sarah says, condescendingly patting his arm, and I giggle at them both, probably because of the many glasses of wine.

"Not you too, Connors." He places his hand over his heart in mock hurt. He turns towards the door, placing a hand on Sarah's back to guide her past us, making their way out of the restaurant.

"Sorry, Tom," I say, standing as Liam pulls my chair out for me. "Thank you," I smile at him, and our eyes lock on one another. Liam doesn't say anything else, just follows behind Will and I to the parking lot before we head out to the bar.

Chapter 6

LIAM

The evening was more fun than I have had in a while. Elise may have been a big factor in that though. She stayed close the whole night. Will and Elise had more to drink than I think either of them had planned, and Will is currently lying in the back seat of my car, snoring loudly, as I drive him home before dropping Elise off. She's singing along with the radio, slightly dancing in the front seat. I smile, hoping that tonight wasn't a one-off, that she has or is in the process of forgiving my stupidity. The ten minute drive to Will's place was too long for her, though, when I pulled into the driveway and parked, she flung her door open.

"I need water," she slurs slightly when I get over to her side of the car. I wrap an arm around her waist to keep her from stumbling. I can't deny that I enjoy the feel of her leaning against me. "You're like the new superman hot, you know that? Henry, what's his name."

"Oh, is that so?" I smile down at her, walking her into Will's house - deciding to deal with the awake one before the passed-out one. "Thank you."

"You're welcome" she smiles, as one of her hands lightly slides across my waist, as I get the door open and lead her into the living room.

"I'll get water for you once I get Will in, ok?" I clear my throat trying to avoid thinking about what that touch does to me. It's been so long since I've been with someone that the slightest brush of her fingers messes with me for a moment.

She takes a seat on the sectional, waiting as patiently as someone who has been drinking can, and gives me a thumbs up. I jog out to the car and see Will trying to open the door to get out and I get there just in time to stop him from injuring himself. Slinging his arm around my neck I help him into his house and toss him on his bed then walk to the kitchen and get the water for Elise. When I get back to the living room, she's curled up on the couch. Her shoes are on the floor and her feet are tucked beneath her with her jacket thrown onto the ottoman. "I have your water," I say, kneeling in front of her.

"Thank you." She sounds sleepy, but takes the glass and sips it watching me. "I'm really tired," she whispers.

"My place isn't far. I have a guest room if you'd be ok with staying on this side of town." I shouldn't have her so close, not when she makes me feel things I've been avoiding. Not when I

CHAPTER 6

want her to touch me again, and not in the mostly innocent way she did moments ago. But she's drunk, and it's late.

"That means sleep sooner, so yeah, let's do that."

She finishes off the water and puts her shoes back on as I take the glass to the kitchen. She seems to walk just fine this time around, but I stay close just in case, my hand resting on the small of her back. I drive the short five minutes down the road to my place and park in the garage. I show her the guest room and hand her sweats and a shirt that she can wear to bed. "My mom left some stuff here after her last visit, face wash at least."

"Liam," she says quietly from the door.

"Yeah?" I swallow the dread that I have, unsure of where this is going, especially after how I treated her a few days ago.

"I forgive you." She closes the door before I have a chance to react, and I stand there for a moment feeling relief wash over me. I change into a pair of basketball shorts, brush my teeth, and climb into bed tossing and turning. My mind drifts to the woman in the bedroom down the hall and I imagine her wearing nothing but my oversized t-shirt..

* * *

It feels like only a few seconds later when I hear a knock on my door, and I am genuinely shocked when I see her standing there in my clothes. Not because she's here but because she is stunning. I take her in; she's gorgeous standing there in sweats too big that she had to roll the waistband for them to stay on her hips. Her usually perfectly styled hair lay in a messy bun atop her head, and she's more beautiful now than when she's put together. I'm staring, and I can't stop. She steps back about to turn around, and my hands reach for her of their own accord. One hand wraps around her hip and the other slides behind her neck, stopping her from leaving. My hands at her hip and neck holding her there. Her breath hitches and she rests a hand on my chest, looking up at me through her lashes as if searching my face for something. I see the resolve settle on her face moments before she pushes up onto her tiptoes and presses her lips to mine. She's soft yet eager and I let her take the lead, holding back until her hands slide around my neck, and she's pressed against my body. Feeling her soft curves against me is enough to push my restraint, and I lift her so her legs wrap around my waist, kissing her deeply as I walk to the bed with her in my arms.

"Wilkes," she moans in my ear when I trail down her neck, kissing and nibbling on her skin. Her hands leave my body for a moment to pull the shirt over her head. Exposing her lace-covered chest, I take a good look before pulling her close, kissing her, our tongues dancing together. My hands slide to her full breasts, and I can feel her hardened nipples through the lace. She grinds against me when I rub my thumb over them.

I groan against her lips, pressing my hips against her showing her what she has done to me. I want her naked beneath me. As much as I'm enjoying the view as is, I know it can only get better. "These," I kiss her the lace of her bra, "are magnificent." I take her nipple in my mouth and give it a little tug, "but this needs to go." I slide a hand behind her and unhook the offending material. Her nails graze my scalp and I continue to lavish my attention there, switching sides to remove the barrier of her bra. She is grinding against me more and more with each movement I make.

CHAPTER 6

"Liam," she says, pulling my face towards hers, our mouths joining once again.

"Are you going to come from this?" I ask tweaking her nipple with my fingers.

"Yes," she gasps. "But I need more." her hands slide down to the waistband of my shorts and...

I snap awake, drenched in sweat and hard as a rock. It was a dream, a very vivid dream, and I can almost feel her still. Well, not her. "Fuck" I say aloud before getting out of bed and heading to the bathroom for a shower... a cold one.

* * *

When I wake up again, it's early morning. I lay in bed for a moment, thinking about last night's dream and how I was glad it wasn't the usual one I have had most nights since the accident. Shaking both thoughts from my head, I make my way downstairs, stopping on the bottom step when I see Elise wrapped up in a blanket on the couch. The dream comes flooding back, and I know I have to do whatever I can to keep from thinking about it too much. "Good morning," she says sleepily from where she sits.

"Morning. Did you sleep down here?" I ask, not wanting to sound interested. I shouldn't be thinking about how much better I probably would have slept if she had been in my bed.

"No, well, kinda. I woke up and was thirsty, so I got some water and took a seat here. I planned to head back to the bed, but then this blanket. Have you felt this blanket? It's like touching a puppy. It's so soft. And well, I fell asleep here instead, in a bundle of puppies." She snuggles deeper into the blanket and I chuckle.

"I can see where my mom got it... coffee?"

"I saw some cocoa when I searched for a glass for my water..." She smiles hopefully.

"Cocoa." I stare at her for a moment, unsure where it could have come from before I make my way into the kitchen. My mom must have bought it and marshmallows the last time she was here, shortly after my two month long cabin 'retreat' as she called it. I called it the grief-themed drunken bender once the season was over. I packed a bag, left the city for a cabin in the middle of nowhere for two months, and wallowed. When I got back, I decided I couldn't live where we had planned to raise our child anymore and moved into the first place I found that wasn't too huge, and close enough to the arena. I take a sip of my coffee before making my way back to the living room where she waits.

When I hand the mug of hot chocolate piled with marshmallows to her, she gives me a huge smile and takes a tentative sip. She sits there silent for a moment, deep in thought, before asking, "Is hot cocoa considered soup? I mean, you eat marshmallows out of it."

I'm not sure this is what I thought she would be saying. "I don't think it's soup." I take a seat on the opposite end of the couch, and sip my coffee, not sure how she is able to drink the super sweet hot chocolate so early in the morning.

"Yeah, but cocoa comes from a plant/bean, so technically, isn't it a fruit of sorts?"

"Well, yeah, but—" I pause thinking how she might not be entirely wrong.

"So, I mean, how would it not be soup?" Her hands are flailing about as she talks, something I've noticed she does a lot.

CHAPTER 6

"You make a valid point." An unexpected laugh escapes my lips. She had been thinking about that for a bit longer than I had, and I can't say that her logic wasn't sound. She's chatty in the mornings- I make a note to have coffee ready early the next time she stays here. Wait, the next time. There isn't going to be a next time. She may have forgiven me last night for being a jerk to her, but that doesn't mean she'll want to stay here again. One drunken touch and a dream later and I'm planning on her spending nights with me and needing coffee ready, so I'm prepared for the chatter. What's wrong with me?

"Thank you for my soup, Wilkes" she adds, closing her eyes as she takes another sip of her drink.

I clear my throat and give a simple, if not curt, "You're welcome."

We sit in comfortable silence for a while, both just sipping on our drinks. She's nice to have around, I almost always laugh at some point during our time together, and she calls me out on my shit which is surprisingly rare. I glance her way, and she smiles at me almost timidly. I don't know if I've ever seen her timid!

"Ok, I'm sure I said something embarrassing last night; I tend to be too honest while drinking... So, spill. What did I say?"

"Nothing I would consider embarrassing." I smirk, thinking back on the night. "Want to watch a movie? I'm sure Will will be over soon and want to order some food in…"

"Sure… nothing super loud though, please?"

"Of course," I smile, finding just the right movie to watch. I watch as the realization hits her, "I mean, unless you telling me that I look like Superman is embarrassing?" The opening credits roll on the 2013 Superman.

"Oh no," she pulls the blanket over her head, "I didn't!"

"You did, but it was the nicest thing anyone has said about me in a while, so..." Which isn't a lie at all. Aside from complimenting my skills on the ice, there hasn't been much positivity surrounding me.

"I'm mortified," she gasps, burying herself further into the blanket.

"'The new Superman hot. Henry, what's his name?' I believe that's what you said." I hear her groan from under the pile of fluff and I laugh; her reaction isn't what I expected, not that I know what I expected. She always does the unexpected. As the movie plays she gradually comes out from under the blanket, watching my apparent doppelgänger.

About halfway through the movie, she sits up abruptly, "I'll be right back," she says, answering her phone with a quick hello.

I pick up my phone and order breakfast through a delivery app from one of my favorite places. Unsure of what she likes, I make sure there is a variety of choices. I hit complete on the order just as Will walks in the front door and asks, "What are we eating?" He stops walking when he sees Elise's cup sitting there on the coffee table. "You've got company?"

"Yeah, Elise is here. It was late by the time we got you inside." I explain as if I have something to hide. I know after they went on their date he said they're just friends, but I still feel guilty.

"Gotcha..." he starts, giving me a look as if to ask if he should leave.

"Food is on the way, I figured that you'd be coming over."

"HOLY HELL!" We hear her shout, and I am about to go to her when she all but runs back into the living room, "I got it!" She breaks out in what most would describe as a happy dance, I would describe it as adorable.

"Got what?" Will asks, finally taking a seat on the couch as far from Elise as possible, as if to not sit between us.

"Hi, Will!" she says sweetly, clearly happy to see her friend. "I put an offer in on a place, and they accepted, and since it's a new build, everything is good to go!" She does another dance that makes me feel happier than I should for someone else. When she stops, I know that I want to see it again. I need to see it again. "They're going to let me know when the paperwork is ready!"

"That's great," I smile. "I ordered some brunch, I guess we are celebrating." She takes her seat on the couch smiling from ear to ear.

"What are you two watching?" Will asks, sitting between us. Elise and I exchange looks, and she smiles at our private joke.

"Superman," I say simply before pressing play again.

Chapter 7

I have a house! I signed the papers this morning and will be able to get moved in and settled while the team is out on a two-week-long road trip of games. Luckily I have an awesome intern that is able to go on this trip so I can settle in while getting a bit of work done at home. It will suck to miss out on the trip, but having a place to come home to after a long day at work will make it worth it. I see the team off and make my way back to my office, getting my things together and heading to my new home before the furniture is delivered. I finally checked out of the hotel this morning and loaded my car back up with everything. I will sleep in my house tonight even if I have to get an air mattress.

I made Will promise that he would keep an eye on Wilkes so I

CHAPTER 7

could take some time getting settled and finishing up my part of the gala that will be taking place in a little over a month. The gala is a fundraiser for the youth teams. Players donate time to the teams, but this event funds their equipment and gear. It's one of my favorite things that the team does and is great press, making my job a little easier. The last thing I need is to have to deal with a random blow-up from Liam while they're in another state, especially when that state is on the other side of the country.

I pull into the garage of my newly built condo and begin unloading the bags filling the back seat and trunk. A few hours later, the delivery men arrive with the furniture and get everything unloaded and set up where I want it. The things I had in storage are being delivered in a week, but at least now I feel like I have a home. The kitchen and dining area are sparse except for a fairly large dining table that I had to buy because it reminded me of a time when I had a large family to spend holidays and birthdays with. The two empty rooms upstairs will eventually be turned into a home office and guest room and the couch I bought is oversized to fit the large living space. It will be perfect to have friends over, even if right now, my only friends seem to be the two hockey players.

I sigh. After so long in a hotel, the space suddenly feels too big, and I feel very much alone. I grab a container of sesame chicken from the counter, my laptop, and a drink then head to my room. Settling on my bed, I pull up my emails and get to work— hoping to drown out the emptiness. Just as I start working, my phone alerts me to a new message, and I can't help but smile at his name.

From LW: Hey, everything going ok?
To LW: Yep! All set!

From LW: That's great :)
From LW: I'm glad you're settled in, but honestly, a little bummed you're not on the trip with us.
To LW: I know I am too. You better behave!
From LW: Behave? Me?
To LW: Please? For me?
From LW: Ok ok. Just this once.
To LW: Thank you, friend!

I set my phone down and get back to work planning the gala, stopping every so often to eat my dinner. The final details were still needed, but the event was shaping up. I was looking forward to seeing it come to fruition and enjoying the evening as a guest too. I realize that I need a dress for the event, and I send a message to Sarah, who I have gotten to know a bit since the dinner, and we plan to meet tomorrow to go searching for gowns. Yawning, I adjust in the bed so I am laying on my side and fall asleep after a busy but exciting day.

When I wake the next morning, I have drool crusted to the side of my face— I must have been more exhausted than I thought. I stretch and take my empty take-out container to the kitchen. I'm just about to pour a glass of water when there is a knock on my door. 'It's 8 am on a weekend', I think, 'who would be here this early?' Opening the door, I see a package addressed to me, and I rack my brain, trying to remember if I had ordered anything that hadn't yet arrived. Taking it into the kitchen, I grab a knife and open the box to find a note that reads:

Congrats on your new home. Enjoy your soup.
-Liam

CHAPTER 7

I laugh and pull out a container of hot chocolate, a bag of marshmallows, and the same blanket that I loved at his house. I get out my kettle, heating water for a cup of cocoa, and send him a quick thank you.

I can see why he was engaged, from what I hear, to a very sweet and kind woman. He puts up an exterior that makes him seem unapproachable or like he doesn't care about anything other than his job, but he is very kind and giving. When he interacts with children at the events we hold, he's a completely different person. Instead of the steady focus that is plastered on his face while on the ice and the calm, if not cold vibe he gives off every other time, he is playful and engaging. I'm intrigued by him more and more lately.

It's about mid-afternoon when I get dressed and head out to meet Sarah at a local boutique to find our dresses. I'm hoping to find something today since the next few weeks are going to be insanely busy leading up to the annual fundraising gala. It's nice to have a woman to talk to after spending so much time with guys, and I've really enjoyed getting to know her. When I get there Sarah is already there looking through the racks. She stops when she sees me, bringing me into a tight hug. "Elise, how are you?"

"I'm good! How are you?"

"You know, I'm just so happy to get out of the house. Thank goodness my mom is here visiting and could watch the kids. I needed to get out."

"I'm so happy to help."

We start browsing together, chatting along the way. She asks about my new place and offers her help again with helping me finish furnishing it. We decide on a date after the gala to check out a few of the clients she works with for the rest of what I will need to make my place feel like a home. It feels both amazing and weird to have a friend that isn't a hockey player again, but mostly good.

Luckily we were both able to find dresses, I can't wait to hear what Tom thinks of the gorgeous burgundy dress Sarah picked out. It's obvious she doesn't get to go out as much as she would like to with the kids and busy hockey schedule, and I'm glad she's chosen me to hang out with.

"Did I tell you that I have basically been assigned to be Liam's babysitter for the gala?" I ask on our way out of the store.

"I can see why. You're a good influence on him," she says, matter of fact. "He seems to be coping a bit better with everything. It's nice to see him not as miserable, finally. Like he's moving forward with his life."

"I didn't know him before everything happened, obviously, but I was hoping that others were noticing a difference."

"Yeah, Tom said he picked up boxing."

"I only saw him at a class. I didn't know he's been keeping it up," I comment, taken back a bit. "It was something that helped me through some tough things, so I mentioned it in passing."

"Well, it's working." I hope she is right, that Liam has found an outlet that is helping him. He deserves to be happy and to not let the grief continue to build up under the surface.

The two weeks fly by, and I honestly miss the company of Will and Liam. I realize I need more friends though, rather than relying on my job to give me companionship, platonic or otherwise. Thank goodness for Sarah and what will hopefully be a good friendship there.

The two weeks fly by, and I realize I need more friends. Rather than relying on my job to give me companionship, I need to get out and meet some people. Thank goodness for Sarah and what is already turning into an amazing friendship.

The team won seven out of the ten games they played, and it's looking to be a great start to the season. Will and Liam stop by when they land and I can honestly say I missed them. While Sarah has become a good friend, there's just something about spending time with my first friends here that I was lacking while they were gone

"CONNORS!" they shout, walking into my house as if they live here too. Seeing Liam with a smile on his face, as if he's happy to see me, makes my heart flutter slightly; he's so handsome when he smiles.

"Put on something pretty; you're coming out with us," Will states as if it was already decided. They make their way into the living room and stare at me expectantly. "Maybe lose the ponytail and glasses. Just a suggestion."

"Hello. How are you? Nice to see you. Those are normal greetings." Sarcasm drips from the words as I stare at them fighting the urge to smile.

"Hi, Connors," Will smiles, then claps his hands, "now chop chop. We're going out."

"But, I'm all cozy," I say, pulling the blanket that Wilkes bought closer to me.

"You're never going to meet anyone hiding in your house."

"And you think going out with two large hockey players will do anything?" Thinking it was an obvious answer, I don't bother moving. I just look back at my laptop and try to figure out where I was in my work.

"You're going," Wilkes says, taking the laptop from me and closing it sharply.

"You better hope that saved," I snap at him. I had worked all day on the prep for two weeks from now, and I think auto-save was turned on but the thought that it might be lost...

"Come on, we'll be wingmen."

"Wingmen, yeah ok," the snarky tone seems to make them hesitate. I stand and walk towards my stairs. "Look, we can go out, whatever, but the wingmen thing... that's not happening. The men I am attracted to aren't attracted to me."

"That seems hard to believe," Liam mutters and I spin around quickly to look at him intently. He has no idea the struggles that women athletes go through.

"I'm 5'8", so a smaller guy isn't going to cut it. I'd prefer not to feel like I could beat the shit out of the guy I'm dating. I'm not into hookups, which is all that is offered to women of my body type." I sigh and add, "so yeah, we can go, but don't waste your time trying to find me, someone."

"I don't think it's that tricky," Liam comments.

"Yeah, you know you're right because athletes totally go for thick girls and not thin waifs of women. And then when I tell them that I'm a collegiate athlete; that goes over so well. Better at sports and not tiny!? The men just flock to me," I say sarcastically, not bothering to look at either of the men standing before me. "I mean look at your dating histories! None of them have thighs like these or childbearing hips!" I throw my hands up in exhaustion, this is the life of a mid-size thick girl. Always the friend, never the romantic interest. I finally look at them, Will is smirking at my outburst in amusement, but Liam... his slow-rolling gaze over my body has me a bit shocked and my breath hitches.

"No offense Elise, but I don't think that's entirely accurate. I mean, we did go on a date," Will says with a bit of a chuckle draw-

CHAPTER 7

ing my attention back to him and away from the appreciative eyes of the hottest hockey player I have ever met.

"Give me thirty minutes," I say quietly before I trudge up the stairs. If they're making me do this, I'm going to look hot as hell. I start in the bathroom, plugging my flatiron in to heat as I put on a full face of makeup. I curl my hair and make sure to add extra hairspray because I will dance, and I will get drunk. I make my way to my closet, picking out the sexiest outfit I have that is still appropriate to go out in. I slip on a little black dress I may have purchased while drunk. The skin-tight black bodysuit and a black mesh dress over it hugged my ample curves. I'm covered, but everything is on display, just to prove a point. I slide on a slinky pair of black heels and grab my clutch before making my way downstairs. "Ok, let's go."

"Fuck," I hear Wilkes breathe out. I'm not sure if it's a good thing or not, but I decide to take it as a compliment and smooth my hands along the dress letting them trail along my curves a bit. I notice Liam's eyes following my movement and smirk knowingly.

"Where is the rest of your dress?" Will asks, his brow furrowed. If I wasn't already irritated about having to go, I would have found his protective brother act endearing, but I wasn't in the mood.

"If you're going to complain about what I'm wearing, I'll gladly stay in," I comment, placing a hand on my hip, lips pursed in defiance as I look between them. They don't say anything but turn and make their way to the car. Wilkes pauses while I lock the door before walking near but not with me. I walk a stride ahead of him with as much confidence as I can muster in a dress I never intended on wearing out.

I'm silent the whole way to the club, partly because I didn't want to go at first, and part because I want to make them regret making me come. When we arrive the bouncer doesn't bother carding any of us— perks of going out with hockey players, I suppose, and we're led to a VIP section and I know how to get back at them. I'm going to get so drunk and make out with someone random. Ok so maybe not make out, but flirt heavily. Yeah, flirt, heavily.

A waitress comes quicker than I've ever seen at a bar, the first round of drinks even faster. My vodka sprite has extra cherries in it, just how I like it, and I wonder which one of them remembered that detail. I perch on the edge of the seat making sure to show off my curves as much as possible as I sip my drink. A bottle of vodka is brought over for the table along with several shots to share. I lean forward to take one in my hand, knocking it back quickly, then another before they have even grabbed one themselves.

"Umm, maybe slow done just a bit there Connors," Will says, eyeing me.

"You forced me to come out, and now I'm drinking too much?" I glare in his direction, daring him to say something else as I take another long sip from my glass.

"I wasn't expecting you to down them so fast." He holds his hands up in surrender.

"And I wasn't expecting to be forced out of my home tonight. Yet here we are" I reply, snarkily. Being an only child, I'm not completely sure, but I can only imagine that this is how a typical sibling relationship would go. Wilkes laughs from between us, and I turn jabbing my finger at him. "You, don't even start."

"I didn't say anything," he holds both hands up in the air as a surrender.

"Good because odds are one of you will have to carry me out

CHAPTER 7

of here," I smirk, throwing back another shot. "Now, are we just going to be perched up here in the ivory tower? Is that what you all do when you go out? Or is dancing permitted?" I stand up, sip my drink, and smile at them both. Even though Will is acting like an overprotective brother, I want us to have some fun before I get too drunk. They stay seated, so I shrug and weave through the crowd until I find a spot close enough that I know they can see me but far enough that they can't ruin my fun.

I start swaying to the music, feeling the bass dictate my movements. I can see them sitting there, Will is scanning the room, but Wilkes is watching me. I give him a quick wink before turning away, trying not to think about how I can still feel his eyes on me. I keep dancing, enjoying myself for the first time since the team dinner.

I feel a hand on the small of my back, thinking it's one of the guys, I smile and turn towards them. Except it isn't. This man is tall but not nearly as bulky as either hockey player I came here with. His eyes are a deep brown and his hair is black and tousled. He is handsome but doesn't compare. He doesn't say anything at first, he just joins me, dancing. I can see Wilkes over his shoulder stiffen slightly and his eyes narrow. I can't help but smile at the reaction.

"Do you want a drink?" the man asks, standing a bit too close for someone I don't even know the name of. I nod and walk with him to the bar, knowing to never let a stranger buy me a drink and not watch the bartender make it. "Shot?"

"Sure," I say just loud enough to be heard over the music. I watched them make the drink and take one in my hand before making eye contact with the man again. I see his face go from flirtatious to shocked in a matter of seconds.

"You really shouldn't take drinks from strangers," Wilkes

whispers in my ear, wrapping an arm around my waist from behind. He holds me closer than I expect and I sink into his hold a bit.

"Holy shit," the now wide-eyed man mutters, "you're..... you're Liam Wilkes, from the Comets!"

"Hi, thanks for dancing with her while I caught up." I can't see his face from this angle, but I can hear the territorial tone in his voice. Liam's hand spreads against my stomach, not letting me move a fraction of an inch away from him, and I don't hate it. In fact, I'm relishing it.

"No problem man..."

"Come on babe," he says, taking my hand and leading me to the dance floor again. "You wanted to dance..." His lips brush my ear, and his breath is warm against my neck and face. My breath stills for a moment, unexpectedly.

"I did," I reply quietly, turning so that I can see him a little better. "I didn't need you to save me."

"Again, you shouldn't accept drinks from strangers," he reiterates, looking down at me through his thick lashes. Even in the dark, his blue eyes are piercing. If I wasn't already a bit tipsy, I might have been after that look. His hand is on my back again, holding me close enough that I know no other guy is going to attempt to flirt tonight. There goes part of my plan for the night. I don't want to admit it, but it feels different dancing with him. Comfortable and safe, but also like my skin is on fire.

"I watched them make the drink- like I have for the entire time I've been able to drink. I've been getting free drinks from men at bars for a while." I throw an arm around his neck; if he's going to ruin my chances with anyone else, I might as well enjoy this as much as possible.

"We have bottle service Elise," he states bluntly.

CHAPTER 7

"Part of it is the game of seeing how many drinks you can get for free, Liam," I tease. "The flirting and coy looks." I give him an example of what I mean, running my fingers through the hair at the nape of his neck. "I know I don't need them to get drunk tonight." I see the bob of his Adam's apple as he swallows then wets his lips.

"Ok, I get it." He smiles. His hand that was on my waist a moment ago is now on my hip, the other still on the small of my back. Being this close to him, even if it is just him keeping others away from me feels good, like we fit together. It would be a bit unnerving if it wasn't so incredibly hot.

"I need to... I'll be back in a bit," I whisper, taking a step back and leaving the warmth of his arms. His hands fall to his sides as I turn to walk away, then he grabs my hand for just a moment. I smile at him before making my way through the crowded club to the ladies' room.

I'm about to leave the stall when I hear it, "Did you see who is here?" I can't help but smile, knowing that they've spotted the very hunky hockey players.

"Liam Wilkes? Did you see who he is with?"

"Ugh, yeah. She's huge." I gasp, deciding to stay in the stall a bit longer. I'm used to this being a bigger girl. It's not the first time someone used my size as an insult not knowing how much my body can do and how strong it is. I typically have no issues with how I look, and I get plenty of male attention, but there is something about when other women say negative things that just hurts more than you want it to.

"We'll see how long that lasts; he's too hot for her, and I plan on getting my hands on him."

I can feel the tears forming in my eyes as they say things I have thought about myself since I was a teenager, and worked hard to get over. But in that moment, I'm a teen again and dislike how I look. I wait until I hear them giggle walking out of the bathroom before I peek out of the stall. Not wanting to chance them still being in the room when I make my exit I take a moment to make sure I don't run directly into the girls. I make my way to the table expecting to see both guys there, except it's only Will Spencer, my actual friend, and he gives me a concerned look. I take a deep breath, trying to calm my nerves.

"What's wrong?" he asks when I take a seat.

"Nothing too far out of the norm." I can't talk about this now, or ever, my hands are shaking in both anger and defeat. I look everywhere but at my friend trying to shove down the body image issues that I have worked so hard to overcome.

"Then why do you look like you're going to cry?" he asks, obviously concerned. The perils of becoming friends with a perceptive and brotherly guy. He knows too much and sees too much.

"I'm fine I. just need a drink," I state, filling my glass to the brim. I start to chug it, searching for Liam, wondering if he is looking for me too. I feel like we've been here for hours, my mood has shifted, and I am more tired than I should be.

"Elise, what's wrong?" Will leans closer, placing a comforting hand on my shoulder.

"Just something I overheard in the ladies' room." I try to just brush it off as if it's nothing, but I can't. I can't ignore it, as much as I wish I could. The high school level drama still digs even now.

"What? I know it has to be something. Kay used to tell me about the shit girls would say when she came out with the team." I look away from him, and he continues, taking my hand and comforting me in a way that I wasn't expecting. "They don't

CHAPTER 7

know shit, Connors." I scan the crowd again, and my eyes land on what I was dreading.

"Oh really?" I stand. "Then what's that? Because what I'm seeing is one of the girls that said I was too ugly for him with her tongue down his throat." I bite the inside of my cheek to keep my emotions in check. How can he flirt like that with me and then make out with some stranger? He can turn away a guy that I was just flirting with for the sport of it, flirt with me, and then turn around and make out with the same girl that was talking shit about me. "I'm leaving."

"Wait just a minute," Will says, standing in front of me. "You're not leaving on your own. I'll get the car— I've been drinking water most of the night. Liam can get a cab."

"Will, I just want to go," I reiterate softly, trying to maintain my composure. Trying but on the edge of failing.

"Ok, let's go." I see him take out his phone, probably telling Wilkes that we are leaving and to find a ride, and also to settle the tab. I walk ahead of him as quickly as I can, holding myself together. I refuse to cry because he chose a stranger over me, but the sting of her words echo in my head. I know that this wasn't a date, I know that he didn't have to stay with me. It doesn't change the fact that what happened tonight hurt. Will opens the door for me, and the cool air of October hits me. I take a deep breath and turn towards where he parked. "He's messed up."

"That might be an understatement." Will wraps me in a tight comforting hug, and I feel a few tears collecting at the brim of my eye, threatening to break free. Tears for the girls' words, tears for Liam, and for me thinking that he might like me enough to not make out with the first pair of size four legs that walked his way.

"For what it's worth," Will says, letting go of me to open the car door. "I think you would be the best thing to happen to him in a long time." I can't say anything, but I hug Will again, knowing he has quickly become my best friend. "Ok, let's get you home. Do you want nuggets?" I nod brushing away a single traitorous tear that runs down my cheek, before letting go of him and sliding into the car.

* * *

LIAM

I try to gently remove the random girl from my face, without being an ass. I know Elise wouldn't like me causing a scene. Especially in public. "Yeah... no thanks," I say, shaking my head before walking back to the bar, where I had been heading to start with. I was getting more cherries for Elise's favorite drink, and hopefully, we could dance a bit more. The girl smelled like cigarettes and a sickeningly sweet perfume. I can still taste it. It was so bad, I want to scrub my mouth with a Brillo pad, but I'll settle for a shot back at the table. With the glass of cherries in my hand, I make my way back to where I left Will, except the table is empty. Pulling out my phone, I see a text from him from fifteen minutes ago.

From WS: Elise is upset about something. Had to leave. Grab a cab.

Shit, did she see? I throw two hundred on the table as a tip and order a rideshare punching in her address instead of my own. Pulling out my phone, I dial her number, "Please answer Connors." It rings and rings until it goes to voicemail. I try again

CHAPTER 7

and this time it goes straight to voicemail. "Damn it." The car pulls up, and my mind is racing as I climb in and the driver heads towards her place.

I was just standing there like a chump, content to wait for Elise when the girl walked right up to me. She flirted, if you can call it that, followed as I tried to get to the bar, and just when I was about to tell her to move on, she threw herself at me. She either saw or something terrible happened. Maybe that guy?

The fifteen minute drive is terrible. I jump out of the car as soon as they stop and jog up to her front door. I turn the handle-locked. At least she isn't leaving her home unlocked. I knock, probably a bit more aggressively than I intended, but when the porch light flickers on, I let out the breath I had been holding in. The door swings open, and I see her standing there in shorts and a t-shirt, wearing the glasses from earlier with her hair piled on top of her head, holding a baseball bat like she knows how to use one. She's angry. I can see it in her red-rimmed eyes, I just don't know why.

"Elise," I start, wanting so desperately to explain what happened and see why they left.

"What in the actual hell, Wilkes!" She pokes me in the chest with the baseball bat she has in her hands. "What are you doing here?"

"You left. Just out of the blue...."

"Out of the blue," she scoffs, and I take that as she saw. Exactly what I had hoped hadn't happened. "You know what I find hilarious? You stopped me from just flirting with a guy. Yet it's totally fine for you to play tonsil hockey with some rando!!"

"That's not what happened," I state firmly.

"Yeah, ok." She shakes her head and turns to go back inside.

"Let me explain!"

"Fine," she says through her teeth. "But be quiet. Will is asleep on the couch."

"Ok." I follow her inside, locking the door behind me. I slip off my shoes and walk into the kitchen, where she goes back to eating a chicken nugget. I smile at the sight. She may have looked like a wet dream at the bar but now? I like this completely dressed-down Elise so much more.

"So," she says, snapping me from my thoughts. "Some grand explanation?"

"Are you going to listen or have an attitude?" She gives me a look that tells me to choose my words carefully. "Look, tonight was fun, and as much as I shouldn't have enjoyed it, I was looking forward to more of the same—"

"I'm glad you enjoyed a stranger's tongue down your throat," she snaps. "How much fun you had tonight doesn't really affect me, now does it? I'm so sorry you felt the need to leave early." She is visibly shaking but her voice is hushed and almost terrifyingly calm, she's holding back right now.. "I know for a fact she would have done very dirty things to you. I heard her describe in detail everything she wanted to do. I also heard your new girlfriend or hookup say terrible things about the huge girl you were with and how you'd be so glad to have someone hotter."

"First things first, you're fucking gorgeous. I don't care what anyone says, I would have spent the whole night with my hands on you." I take her face in my hands and her eyes snap to mine quickly. Now that I have her attention, I explain, "I was waiting for you to come back, I decided to get more for those damn cherries you like in your drink when some random girl came up and started talking to me. I was trying to be polite because some PR woman told me to control my emotions and not let

CHAPTER 7

people get to me. Then I tried walking away and she followed still trying to talk to me, when I turned to tell her to kindly fuck off, she threw herself at me. It was only a few seconds of hell, but I guess that's all it took for you to think the worst."

"But…" Her eyes search mine, as if she was trying to search them for a hint of a lie.

"But nothing, that's what happened. It was awful, and then I went to the table looking for you, only to find out you both had left."

"I thought you…"

"That I what? Didn't like you? Damn it, woman, I've been fighting it since the beginning! I freaking like you!"

"BRO! SHUT UP!" We hear from the living room. Will is not enjoying our argument messing with his sleep schedule.

"Let's go upstairs so we don't bother him," she says softly, wiping her eyes gently with the sleeve of her shirt. I nod, letting her lead the way. As we walk, I notice that her place is still pretty empty, work must be keeping her too busy to get everything furnished. I also notice again how beautiful she is, even in comfy clothes with no makeup on and her glasses. She leads me to her room, shutting the door after I walk in. "You, what did you mean? Since the beginning?" Her brow is furrowed in actual confusion.

"Since I carried you out of the locker room, there was something… I liked your guts. You didn't back down. Then the burgers with Will. You seemed to fit seamlessly. Boxing. Skating. The team dinner. Do I need to go on? I will if you need me to. I can't stop thinking about you. You're gorgeous. Seriously. That dress tonight, Elise, I didn't want anyone else seeing it, but it felt damn good to claim you at the club. There were so many men watching you."

"No, there weren't." She looks down avoiding eye contact with me; it's as if she believes it. She actually believes that no one likes her romantically.

"There were," I say firmly, taking her face in my hand and holding it up so she was making direct eye contact with me as I kept going. "And I hated it. I hated every second of that guy touching you."

"I know how you feel, but at least the guy thought you were a god among men. That girl Liam, that girl and her friends. You didn't hear what they said about me. Then to see her with you... it was terrible." She pulls away, turning her face from me for a moment.

"It was terrible, like licking an ashtray." I shiver just thinking about it.

"I have an extra toothbrush and mouthwash you might want to use then," she smiles.

"That would be fantastic." We stand there for a few moments, her face scrunched up in thought. "I should go... You're probably tired."

"I don't really have anywhere else for you to sleep- but my bed is pretty big. Unless you want to sleep in the oversized chair in the office?" She offers shyly like she isn't sure she should suggest that we share her king-size bed. "It's late and you should get some sleep too."

"There seems to be plenty of room here."

"I still have your shirt and shorts from the last night we went out. I'll let you change while I finish getting ready for bed," she says, handing me my clothes. They smell like her now, fresh linen and something I can't quite place. I change into them while she's in the bathroom. When I am done getting ready to sleep, I find her on her bed covers pulled back and her face in deep

CHAPTER 7

thought. "Just so we are clear. Nothing is happening tonight. Just sleep."

"That's fine," I reply, getting into bed with her. I haven't slept next to someone in a long time. It's strangely comforting having the weight of someone in the bed with you, the warmth radiating off their body. I will have to fight the urge to pull her as close as I possibly can.

"Ok," she sighs. "You have to turn off the light though. You're closer to the switch." I get out of bed and walk to turn out the lights— getting back to bed is trickier than I had hoped, but when I lay back down, I'm surrounded by warm blankets that smell like her. I can't hide the groan that escapes my lips. "I don't get why you let her kiss you— it looked like it had gone on for a minute."

"I was in shock for a moment, and she was like an octopus- I couldn't figure out how to remove myself without just grabbing her face and shoving," I say honestly.

"Yeah, that wouldn't have been good, someone would have sent that out, and I'd have to clean it all up." I hear her soft short laugh, and roll over to face her.

"Are we ok?" My brows pinch together,

"I don't know, but I am too tired right now to figure it out tonight," she yawns.

I can't see her face fully, but I can feel her presence next to me. I want to pull her to my side and have her fall asleep in my arms, but I stay where I am on the other side of the bed. Instead, I whisper a simple "good night" and try to fall asleep.

Lights flash, red, blue, red, blue. I'm running trying to find her, trying to get to her in time. My feet pound against the linoleum floor, they are all I can hear along with the sirens and shouting of doctors. The halls stretch, and no matter how fast I run I can't get any closer.

I can't get to her, I can't do anything to help her, to save her. I need to be with her. My heart is racing, and the hall starts to disappear, everything is turning black, and I know I can't save her.

"Liam," I hear, "Liam, wake up." My eyes snap open, and I see Elise sitting beside me in her bed, and I'm brought back from the dream. The dream I've had on and off for almost a year now. "Are you ok? You were thrashing around like crazy." She scoots close enough to touch as I sit up.

"Just a dream," I mutter, trying to shake the images from my head.

"Ok," she says wearily, placing a hand on my cheek as she searches my face. "I know, kind of anyway, how it feels, you know. Losing the people you love, if you need to talk about it."

"Not something I want to talk about with the woman I've had sex dreams about." I grab her wrist gently, holding her hand there, enjoying the feel of her soft touch.

"Umm, excuse me?" She says with shock written on her face.

"You heard me," I smirk at her before laying back down to try to go back to sleep. Only then noticing how much closer we were now. I take a chance and pull her into my side like I had wanted to earlier. She tenses up but soon relaxes into my hold.

"You know today sucked," she says quietly from her spot against my chest. "It's a historically crap day. Did Will say something?"

"About what?" I ask. "Why was it a crappy day?"

"Oh... I thought that's why you both dragged me out. Never mind." She hides her face from me.

"No, tell me." She doesn't say anything. Just props herself on her elbow to look at me again. It's dark, but I can see the frown on her face. "I'll tell you what the dream was if you tell me what today was."

CHAPTER 7

"You first," she whispers.

"I have a recurring dream of that night, when Kaylee died. Running into the hospital, but I never get there in time to do anything."

"Recurring? As in, how often?"

"It used to be every night," I confess, "now at least weekly."

"Oh," her voice is small. "Today is a bad anniversary... not like ex-boyfriend bad anniversary." She turns her face into my chest, "Today's the day my mom died."

"I'm sorry, I didn't know that was today," I answer, brushing her hair out of her face. "Will didn't mention it. Just that we needed to go out." She nods against me, laying here with her talking about our dark days feels, not sad, but like we have a bond. Sharing the darkest parts of ourselves changes things, for the better. It's a good feeling knowing that she understands in a way.

"So, when I was having fun and enjoying today, I didn't think about her much, but then it crashed back down on me. When the illusion that you... that we...I don't know." She tries to roll over and away from me, but I grab her waist and hold her close.

"Hey, you're not going anywhere right now," I say softly. "I enjoyed our bubble very much. And there was no illusion..."

"Please don't... don't be all Superman sexy right now." I laugh a little. I want to tell her that I want to spend an absurd amount of time proving to her that it was real, that I know she is gorgeous, and that I don't want to leave this bed until she understands what I mean. But I don't, I can't, not right now anyway.

"You know that day that you destroyed the visiting locker..."

"The locker room, yeah." I jump in trying not to think about that day. "It wasn't one of my proudest moments."

"I felt that though, seeing you just lost in the rage and sadness.

I knew what that was. I went to the ladies' room just down the hall and cried. Because I had no clue what to do to help you. I still don't really." She pauses for a moment while I give her a hug that is long overdue, a thank you for letting me break down, but holding me accountable sort of gesture. "We're both kind of screwed up in our own ways, aren't we?" she adds in a whisper, and I can feel the warmth of her breath against my chest.

"Yeah. I'd say so." There is more to her tone, but I let it slide because I can also hear how tired she is. She sighs as if on cue and nestles closer to me. Closer both physically and emotionally.

Chapter 8

ELISE

It's about an hour into our biggest event of the season, a huge fundraiser that supports the youth team. It's the classiest event I've ever been to, also black tie. The team, all in tuxes, don't look as rough as they normally do. I can't help but smile, looking around at them. They've been busy with games and practices these past few weeks, so while this is technically work, they deserve this break from playing and workouts to enjoy an evening. Each donor's table is chosen randomly; they have no idea which player they will be dining with until they get seated. I'm wearing the new formal gown I bought with Sarah. It is floor length and has a low back in a deep shade of emerald green to complement my auburn hair, which I pinned to the side with a simple silver comb. I feel like a million bucks.

At least I do until I see Wilkes' face with his brow furrowed. I walk towards him- taking a deep centering breath. The seating chart they put together has us sitting next to each other, I can only assume because he behaves himself when I'm around, and they want me to babysit, but after our chat that night at the bar, it doesn't feel like babysitting. Honestly, we haven't discussed it at all. Just stolen glances, friendly hangouts with Will and other teammates, and the occasional game- but that was me watching him. We've been in this in-between friendship and flirtation stage for a few weeks now. I take a breath and make my way towards him, readying myself for anything that could happen.

"Wilkes." I nod, setting my clutch down at my seat.

"Connors," he says after clearing his throat.

"I hope you'll be on your best behavior tonight," I tease, glancing around to check the last-minute details just to be sure that everything is perfect for the night.

"I promised others I would be on my worst behavior," he smiles. I laugh, knowing that he will behave; it's my job after all.

"Your bow tie is crooked," I say, straightening it quickly. The guests are starting to come in. They take in the whole event with fresh eyes that I don't have the opportunity to do, having been here most of the day directing vendors and making sure every detail reflects the team in a positive way.

"You and everyone else did a great job. It looks amazing," he comments, glancing around the room, a cool calm expression on his face.

CHAPTER 8

"Thank you." I smile up at him, taking in how the almost romantic lighting is playing off the strong angles of his face.

Cocktails are served, and hors d'oeuvres are passed as the evening gets underway. The team mingles with everyone making sure they don't linger too long with a particular group. I spot Sarah, her arm draped over Tom's, from across the room and she peels herself away from him meeting me at the bar.

"This is the best gala I have ever been to. It's absolutely stunning. I mean it, truly," she says as soon as she is close, giving me a hug.

"I have been an absolute wreck this entire week, so thank you for at least pretending that it turned out a fraction as good as I had hoped for."

"I'm serious, Elise, it has never been this good, and I know that was a big part thanks to you."

"Oh my goodness, you should stop now. I'm just glad it's done. We can enjoy it now." I take her hand and give her a spin, hyping up my friend. "And can we get a little commotion for the dress!!!! The back of the dress!"

"Oh, stop," she waves me off, laughing as she twirls on her own.

"No, seriously, I hope that Tom was completely gobsmacked when he saw you."

"Just a little bit," she laughs. "It's been too long since we've been out. I think he forgot that I can look like this. Dinner with the team was my first time wearing jeans in months."

"I'm a little jealous. Jeans are the worst." I grab each of us a fresh glass of champagne off the passing tray.

"You should wear that dress every day for the rest of time, I mean, seriously!"

"I always wanted to be a princess when I was little. I just need a tiara." I laugh just thinking about wearing this to a meeting with our executives, with a crown.

Sarah and I chat and walk around the room for a while. It's been longer than I expected when Wilkes catches my eye from across the room. There is something off about his eyes, and it's not what I was expecting to see. I excuse myself from the conversation that I was in and walk towards him. He looks on edge, and before I can blink, he is making his way quickly towards me. Taking my hand, he leads me out of the room and around a corner into an empty hall.

"What's wrong?" I ask, trying to keep up with him in my heels.

He doesn't answer me, just pulls me closer, placing his hand on the back of my neck, the other on my hip. One step forward from him, and my back is completely against the wall in the hallway just a few feet from the event where a couple hundred people are expecting to see their captain. He smells amazing per usual- it's intoxicating, really. Being near him has become routine, but this is different. I can feel a heaviness in the air between us, an unspoken and unacknowledged want. Ok, so it was spoken, but nothing happened, and it didn't feel like this. This is different. This feels like unbridled lust. I was not prepared for this.

"Liam, we really should get back in there," I breathe, looking him in the eyes again, noticing the pained look on his face again, "What's wrong?" This is one of the biggest fundraising events we have for the team, and the star player should be the focal point. Instead, he pulled me out here, away from the crowds, away from everyone. However, something is obviously bothering him. I sigh heavily, running a hand along his arm, trying to comfort him the best I can when there is all this

CHAPTER 8

electricity between us.

"I needed a moment, away from them." His thumb caresses my neck where he holds me. I want to ask why I needed to come with him, why he is holding me here, why he is looking at me like we are the only ones in the building. "You ground me, Elise. I don't know how else to explain it right now. Please, just a moment longer," he answers my unspoken question. I place my hand on his chest, feeling the steady beating of his heart.

"Ok, we can take a moment," I whisper, looking up at him. His forehead almost touches mine, and I can feel the warmth of his body radiating around me. "Do you need anything?"

"No, just stay here with me." He takes a deep breath pulling me a little closer. His hand slides to the small of my back. I gasp at the gentle but sudden contact that holds me flush against him, my heart is racing "You look amazing tonight."

I let out a breath I didn't realize I had been holding in, and my eyes flutter shut to savor this moment. Being this close to him, has me feeling drunk almost. I might ground him, but he exhilarates me. "Liam, I..." I stop when I feel him gently coaxing my face to his. His lips press firmly against mine; this is the moment I've dreamt about for a while now. His mouth moves against mine, and I swear his fingertips are on fire as they press against my skin. After this kiss, I don't know if we can be just friends again.

He's pressed against me, hip to chest, I can feel his heart pounding against me as our lips move against each other eagerly. And while I don't want to stop kissing him, I know I have to. I pull back slightly, breaking the contact and regretting it instantly. I want to kiss him again, but a part of me is worried about everything that will change now.

"Wait, not yet," he pleads, his voice soft and deep, his

forehead resting against mine.

"We have to go back, unfortunately," I whisper, dreading that I have ruined the little bubble that we are in, or were in, I suppose.

"I know," he sighs, kissing my forehead lightly before taking a step back, his hands remaining in their places as if he doesn't want to break contact completely just yet. I don't want him to, either.

"You don't have to stay the whole time. Just until all the dinner is over—"

"As long as you're here, I'm here." His tone is far more serious than I expected. I want him here with me, but what will people think? It hasn't even been a year since he lost everything.

"I'll probably be late..." I start to explain, knowing I should be here to make sure the entire event runs smoothly.

"Promise to let me know when you leave, I want to see you after." He lets his hands fall from my body and tucks them in his tux pockets. He looks as if James Bond and Superman had a baby. I would let this man impregnate me just to keep looking at him like this.

"Ok," I smile up at him, "I'm going to the ladies' room to make sure I'm still all put together. I'll see you in there." I place a quick peck on his cheek before walking away. I put a bigger sway into my hips, knowing that he is watching me.

Thank goodness for long-wear lipstick, I think as I check myself in the mirror. Luckily everything seems to be in place; everything seemingly normal. Everything except someone who should just be a work acquaintance pushing me against a wall and kissing me so hard that I can almost feel his lips still there. Yeah, that's not normal, but I wouldn't want to change it. I wouldn't want to never have felt his mouth on mine. Even if it never happens again, I wouldn't regret it, not one bit.

  Making my way into the main room, I notice that people are headed to the tables. I see Liam already chatting with the few people sitting there already. I take a deep breath and head over to take my seat. He pulls out my chair, letting me sit before he takes his place beside me with a smile on his face. I can't tell if he is feeling that much better after the few minutes he took out of the room or if he is masking how he actually feels. Either way it feels good to see him smile.

  Dinner starts arriving, and most of the chatter slows to light conversation at the table. I'm cutting my filet when my hands still in shock as I feel his hand go to my thigh, just where the slit of my dress falls open. I glance towards him and see that he is chatting with the couple to his right, unaffected, or so it seems. I continue with my meal, trying to ignore his hand beneath the table as it runs gently along my upper thigh. He gives it a squeeze before he bringing his hand up to cut his steak; the warmth and weight of it is instantly missed.

  Throughout the meal, he found ways to be closer to me, an arm around the back of my chair, leaning in to talk in hushed tones between us about the event, etc. But when he slides his hand back to my exposed thigh, moving the fabric more out of his way, I feel my pulse quicken, and I suck in a deep breath. I cover it the best I can with a sip of water. He strokes the top of my thigh with his thumb, as if it were a common gesture, and not something incredibly inappropriate to do around strangers.

  I have no clue what the conversation is about, my focus only on his fingers brushing the apes of my thighs every so often. He knows what he is doing, playing as if there was nothing happening, but then he smirks when I squirm slightly beneath the table or have to take another sip of water. His hand feels like it's burning against my flesh, warming me from the inside out, and I have to move away from him. Using the only tool that I have to make a momentary exit, I excuse myself from the table, feigning a catering issue that they need help with in the kitchen. I made my way out of the room, and Sarah gives me a questioning look as I passed her table. Liam Andrew Wilkes will be the death of me.

I take a few minutes to cool off, literally, before heading back in and taking my seat next to Liam. "Crisis averted," I say with a smile. I cross my legs and practically fold my skirt around my legs to avoid him trying more under the table.

The rest of the evening goes smoothly. After a while, Liam leaves, making me promise to let him know when I was on my way home, and now that I was almost there, I'm a ball of nerves to see what I will be walking into. I spot Liam's car parked out front as I pull into my garage. I know that he said he would be here (I mean the man knows where my hide a key is after all) but I'm a bit surprised to see him still in his tux, bow tie undone and hanging loose around his neck, sitting on my couch with a glass of water in his hand. I take my time kicking off the heels and setting them on the stairs for me to carry up later before finding a seat near him but far enough away that he can't touch me just yet.

"I think we need to talk," I say, not looking at him. I didn't want to risk my feelings for him to distract me this time.

"That sounds ominous." I can hear his smile. I take a deep breath as I pull the pins out of my hair, releasing the tension that they created. "I'm sorry, I'm sure you didn't expect anything to happen tonight with us."

"Us... is there an us? After the club, we both didn't seem to make any moves to start anything. So, I assumed that was a one-time drunken thing..."

"It wasn't... I don't want it to be." He reaches for me, and I stand back up, walking around the couch, knowing that if he touches me now, I will lose my nerve to have this conversation.

"What do you want then? Because honestly, I'm terrified. My job will be the one affected if this doesn't work out. If the owners find out! Shit, what if they find out," I throw my hands in the air in frustration, and let them fall to my sides. "This could go way worse for me than it ever could for you!"

"Ok, so we keep it quiet. Nothing at work... I don't know how I will manage, but if you're concerned," he's right next to me now, his hands holding mine. "If that's what you want."

"I don't know what I want. I'm so confused," I admit, finally looking him in the eyes. I take a deep breath and search for an answer. "You would keep this between us for now?"

"I'm pretty sure Will knows something is going on."

"True, can't hide it from him, considering you came out of my room, plus he was at the bar. Ok, say we try this... What if it doesn't work out? What then? You and Will are the closest thing I have to family Liam..."

"What if it does work?" He tenderly brushes his fingers over my cheek.

"Since when are you an optimist? This is terrifying." I see him deflate slightly as if he is sure I'm about to say that it will never work, that we can't be more than friends. "Liam, I...ok."

"Yeah?" His smile is wide and bright.

"But, we have to be professional. I have a job to do and so do you." His hand is cupping my face holding me there, eyes roaming over me as I speak. "I want to be clear Liam, I can't lose you and Will if this doesn't work."

"You won't," he whispers. I sigh and lean into his touch.

"You know you can't promise that," I add, wishing I was wrong. I bury my face into his chest, hiding from my want and my fear.

"I just did."

He gently lifts my face to his, and when his lips are a breath away, I state flatly, "You're a cocky bastard you know that."

"Damn it, Elise," he laughs.

"Are you staying?" I ask timidly, not sure if that is too much too soon.

"Of course I am." He stands up, pulling me along with him. "Now I've been dying to ask... why did you leave the table earlier with the fake need to check on something?"

"Shut up," I gasp. "Ugh, you just had to keep touching me, and all I could think about was your damn hand! It was very distracting. I needed to refocus. It was still work." We make our way upstairs, Liam grabbing my heels on the way. "It wasn't very nice of you to do that, by the way."

"I'm so sorry." I know he isn't sorry, just from the mischievous smirk on his face.

"Bull..." I can't help but smile, mostly because I'm not very sorry about it either. In my room, I take my heels from him and place them in the closet where they belong. Then I turn my back to him, asking for help unzipping my dress. Yes, it's a lower-backed dress and I don't need help, but I don't want to do the twisty struggle of reaching the zipper when he is standing right there. "I'm going to get ready for bed... I don't have anything for you to wear this time, though."

"I'll manage," he says in a husky tone I haven't heard from him before, not even when he kissed me earlier. His hand lingers at the small of my back, where my skin is now exposed. It sends a shiver up my spine as he lets his fingers graze my skin. I can

CHAPTER 8

feel his warmth on my back, and my eyes flutter shut. I have never felt this comfortable with a man in my home before, in a non-platonic way, that is.

"Liam, I really would like to wash my face and put on comfy clothes," I say, turning my head slightly to see his face. He places a soft kiss on my shoulder before stepping back, allowing me to grab my shorts and shirt. I go into my bathroom and, after closing the door behind me, take a deep, grounding breath. I take my dress off and hang it on the back of the door, pulling on my pajamas. I wonder what, if anything, he is expecting tonight. If what happened in the hall or his hand under the table was any indication, he might be thinking about more than I am willing to do right now. I take my time brushing out my hair and washing my makeup off- maybe this way he will have cooled off a bit? Who am I kidding? Maybe I'll be cooled off a bit by the time I'm done.

I go through my whole routine, full skincare, and nighttime dental routine, stalling yes, but also a bit of prep. When I can't stall anymore, I walk back into my room. I watch Liam fold his tux and place it in a small duffle. "You have an overnight bag?"

"I had it in my car... not that I was expecting this. I just grabbed it in case you didn't kick me out." I don't say anything. My eyes are just locked on the bag. "Elise, I don't want you to think I expected anything."

"Ok," I say flatly.

"Don't... Do you remember what I said in the hall earlier?" He takes hold of my hands, snapping me from my thoughts.

"I was a little distracted."

"You ground me, Elise. I needed to step away because someone asked about Kaylee... and I wanted you there to help me. I didn't plan past getting out of the room." He is calm and quiet, not what I am used to from him. "I enjoyed what happened after, but I don't expect anything else to happen. I grabbed the bag on my way here because I was hoping to at least stay."

"I wasn't expecting it at all. Any of this, really," I admit. His eyes are locked on mine, the icy blue somehow brighter than I ever thought possible. I place my hand gently on his face, trying to think for a moment. "This is a little terrifying," I add.

"Terrifying, yikes," he laughs.

"It's just a big gamble. Maybe not for you, but for me."

"You don't have to worry about that. I'm pretty sure Will would choose you over me anyway." It's my turn to laugh now. "I'm going to brush my teeth and get ready for bed. Tonight is up to you. Everything is."

"Not going to lie, Liam. I never would have thought of you as a sweet type of guy. You sure know how to put up a front."

"I'm going to get ready for bed before you figure out all my secrets too soon." With Liam in the other room, I crawl into my bed and wait, feeling really stupid for being all in my head about this. But he won't lose anything if this doesn't work out. I will. It doesn't stop me from thinking about tonight and how much I want to kiss him again and how good his hands feel when they're on me.

When he finally comes out of the bathroom, I am lying comfortably on my bed, eyes closed. I hear the flick of the light switch and then feel the dip of the bed as he slides in with me. He is close but not touching me. I hate that he's not touching me. I take a deep breath and place a hand on his cheek. It's shy, I know this, but I'm not sure what to expect after tonight. He must take it as a sign that I'm ok with this because he scoots closer and wraps an arm around my waist, letting his hand rest on my back beneath my shirt. The warmth that settles there is comforting; it feels right. He smells like spearmint and ice, cool and refreshing, and I take it all in.

I lean in closer, our lips centimeters apart. I want him to kiss me. I want so much more than that too. He brushes his lips against mine- slow and tentatively. He is holding back, it's both endearing and annoying, but not enough. I slide my hand to the nape of his neck and run my fingers through his hair like I did at the club, and it earns me the groan that I was hoping for. His lips part and become more eager.

He has me as close as I can possibly get, his hands glide seductively over my body. I gasp, not expecting the fire that trails where his hands roamed. He smiles against my cheek before trailing kisses down my neck. "Liam," I whisper, holding him there, not wanting him to leave. I feel his questioning hum against my neck. I tighten my grip on his hair slightly and guide him back to my mouth, kissing him hard. Our mouths clash in a sort of dance that has me on fire. The kiss in the hall was hot, partly because of the chance someone would catch us, but this is so much more.

He rolls onto his back, pulling me, so I'm partially laying on top of him. His hands are in my hair and cupping my ass. I feel his heart pounding against my chest, my own racing right along with his. "You're so damn beautiful, Elise. I've wanted to kiss you for so long."

"You were an ass, though," I joke, smiling against his mouth. "Never would have happened three months ago." He squeezes my ass before rolling, so that he is hovering over me. My breath is heavy as he traces my face with his fingertips, slowly making his way down my neck, across my chest, and to my side before pulling me so my back arches towards him. "Fuck."

His lips find mine again, but this time our hips are aligned with one of his legs between mine. I remove his shirt hastily, and as soon as it's gone, I run my hands over his sculpted chest, honed in years of training. He is solid, and actually makes me feel small, like he could protect me from whatever happens. I want every inch of his body pressed against me.

"I couldn't keep my hands off of you tonight. I tried to behave, though..." he starts between the open-mouth deep kisses that he has resumed. "That slit in your dress drove me crazy." His fingers trail up my thigh where the slit had been. "I wanted to slide my hand between these thick thighs." He rubs his thigh against my core. I can't fight the moan that escapes my lip, even though it's muffled by his mouth on mine. "You're a bombshell, Elise. And I want to make you feel so insanely good."

I push him impatiently, hard enough that he rolls onto his back, and I straddle him. He rests his hands on my thighs, eyes locking with mine. For a moment anyway. When I reach for the hem of my shirt, his eyes follow. I take my time lifting it slowly over my torso, teasing him slightly before he raises a brow as a question. I remove it completely, and he sits up, instantly trailing his mouth across my chest. His rough, calloused hands feel like heaven on my skin.

"Damn," he groans. "I knew these would be amazing ever since that boxing class."

"I knew you were looking," I state as I grind my hips against him. He smiles mischievously, and I know I'm in trouble. He takes control. I bring my mouth to his, and before I know it, he's over me once more, pinning my hands to the bed. His body rolls over mine, and I arch against him involuntarily. I can feel how hard he's gotten now, and a moan escapes again.

CHAPTER 8

* * *

LIAM

I'm vaguely aware of where I am when I wake up, but I'm more aware of her curled up into my side. Last night was more than I expected, and way better than I dreamed- literally. Now that I think about it, I didn't dream last night. At all. Not the usual reliving nightmare or the Elise sex dream either. She breathes steadily next to me. I brush a strand of hair out of her face and watch her sleep. She's gorgeous. I mean, it helps that she's still completely naked under the blankets.

She stretches next to me before sliding her hand across my abdomen. I see her smile, keeping her eyes closed as if willing herself to go back to sleep. I lean close and whisper, "It wasn't a dream," before placing a kiss on her forehead.

"Good," she replies, "but I'm also cold and want to sleep more. Where are my clothes?"

"Nope!"

"Nope?" She laughs, sitting up on her side to look me in the eyes.

"No clothes," I grin, pulling her close. "I will keep you warm."

"You're not doing a great job," she sighs, her forehead resting against mine for a moment. Then she reaches over me, her perfect breasts dangerously close to my face, and grabs her phone from the bedside table. "Oh, we need clothes... Will asked if we want to get brunch.... An hour ago."

"Well...shit."

Chapter 9

ELISE

"Wilkes, thanks so much for joining me," I say, closing the door to my office behind him. It's only been a couple of days since the gala, and I have seen him in passing, but with a few back-to-back games, he's been busy, so there hasn't been much time to hang out.

"What did you need to meet about?" he asks before adding, "not that I'm not happy to see you."

"I didn't have anything in particular." I step towards him, his hands going to my waist since we are in a private spot. I know that we could get caught, and that this isn't exactly an approved situation but it's exciting to have this secret with him. "I know that you'll be going home before your pre-game routine, and I wanted to see you real quick." I slowly bring my arms up and lace my fingers into the hair at the nape of his neck.

"Are you coming to the game?" He places a hand on my neck, his thumb brushing my jaw lightly.

"Yes, I'm sitting with Sarah." My eyes flutter shut for a moment as his other hand slides to my back, resting just at my hip.

"Are you wearing my jersey tonight?" His lips are so close to mine it would take only a small movement to kiss him.

"No," I smile instead.

"No? Well, now I think this meeting is over, Ms. Connors,'' he laughs before bringing me in again. This time when our lips meet it's gentle. He is tender at first, it's almost appropriate for public, but that changes, and the next thing I know he has me sitting on my desk. I'm pretty sure if I wasn't wearing a pencil skirt he would be between my legs.

"I think we're going to have to schedule a few more of these meetings- they seem to be helping me," he jokes, his lips brushing mine as he speaks.

"Done," I sigh. I sit back, letting my arms rest on his upper arms, feeling the taut muscles under the shirt he is wearing. "I would clear my calendar if I were you. So many meetings."

"Done." He smiles, and I can't help but smile back, thinking of all the stolen moments that are to come.

"I have to head home soon, so I'll have time to head back before the game. I've decided not to look like I'm working tonight."

"You're going full fan mode?" He asks as his fingers brush along the curve of my hip and lower back. The chance that people might catch on, or see a quick kiss placed on my cheek, seems to thrill him, and if I'm honest, I kind of love it too.

"Not this time." I want to look like a classy lady. Thankfully, we're not sitting near the wives and girlfriends. I don't want him to think that I assume we are in a relationship. I don't want to spook him or myself. I mean, I haven't been in a relationship since college, and well... everyone knows when he last dated someone.

"Take a rideshare to get here," he requests, "I want to drive you home."

"Ok," I nod. "I have to get going."

"Me too." He steps back, letting me hop off the desk. I miss the warmth that had been there, so close that I forgot my usual cold hands.

"I'll see you later," I say, looking into his eyes. I could look at his face all day, like how is it ok to be that handsome? How can someone like him ever want to be with me? Who knows how long he's going to want to be with me? I just hope that I don't get my heart broken in the process.

"I'm counting on it," he kisses me again before making his way to the closed door. He gives me a quick wink before opening it and walking out. Shit, sneaking around with him while I work might be the best idea I have ever had. I take a deep breath before grabbing my purse and head home.

Once home, I change into my most comfortable jeans and a simple gray t-shirt with the team logo on it, and I quickly walk into my home office with just moments to spare before my session. The screen lights up, and the video chat starts. "You look really happy," Dr. J states with a smile. "What's going on?"

CHAPTER 9

"I kind of met someone, and we are trying things, I suppose." I beam at the woman on my screen. "Right now, he makes me happy. I just want to enjoy it, day by day."

"So, you're not thinking long-term?"

"Well, I mean, who knows, really? I would rather enjoy each moment as it comes right now. And maybe someday it will be more."

As usual, the hour with my favorite therapist goes quickly. She's been with me for years now and has seen just how much has changed for me. It feels good most of the time now to just release everything that has been building up between sessions. It's a huge difference from when I started, when I was barely able to get through them. Now I feel like there isn't enough time ever.

I grab my sweater, which happens to be the team's colors, and my purse before heading outside to meet my rideshare to head to the arena for the game. Sarah will be meeting me there so we can sit together in my favorite seats, ice level in the corner, where you get a higher chance of seeing a fight.

* * *

"Hey, Wilkes, can I borrow you just for a quick moment before things get too crazy? In private?" I say after he sets his things down at his locker. I watch the look of confusion flash across his face as he makes his way towards where I wait.

"You're not wearing my jersey?" He asks in a hushed but shocked tone as we walk away from the rest of the team that is here already.

"No. I'm not. I told you that I wouldn't." I reply, teasing him a bit.

"That's kind of lame." He seems almost hurt until I lead him into an empty equipment closet, pulling him in close by his shirt.

"Sorry, maybe next time."

"Ok. Did you need something?" He asks with a smile, his large hands finding what is becoming their usual place on my back. He leans down a bit, so our faces are closer together.

"Oh, just wanted to say you look hot as hell in this suit," I whisper, letting my lips brush against his ear lightly. He groans in what I can assume is frustration before giving me a firm kiss.

"I like these meetings a lot," he states against my mouth, lips brushing against mine. "I almost don't want to play tonight."

"But I'm here to watch you," I state, scratching up and down his back beneath the suit jacket he is wearing.

"Ok, ok, you need to stop touching me then. Otherwise, I will not be able to make it on the ice." He sighs as he steps back. "I'll see you after the game."

"Kick some ass," I say with a wink, walking past him to meet up with Sarah. I make my way through the halls waving at the players that are paying attention, and I give a good luck hug to Will, my found brother.

"There you are!" Sarah says when I finally reach her in the stands.

"Sorry, I made a small detour on the way here. My work is never done," I say with a smile.

"I forgive you," she says, taking a sip of her drink. "I'm just happy to be child-free for the night."

"How long is Tom's mom in town?"

"The rest of the week. I love that woman. She is forcing us to

CHAPTER 9

go out and says she wants to spend as much time with the kids as possible. And I am not going to fight her on it at all."

"Sounds like she wants another grand-baby," I comment with a smirk.

"Oh, dear lord, no! This factory is closed. Condemned even!" I can't hold in the laughter as we cheer on the team. "I plan on drinking enough tonight that Tom has to carry my ass into the house, I think."

"That sounds like an excellent plan! Here's to condemned baby factories and drinking enough that we have hockey players carry us home!"

"Here, here!"

Watching the game with Sarah is way more fun than watching from behind the scenes. I haven't been to a game like this in a long time, and I have missed the feeling of being in the crowd,. Right now, I'm just a fan with a huge crush on a player. The only difference between being a normal fan and who I am is that I don't have to pretend that I'm in a rom-com and the handsome hockey player would sweep me off my feet. He already swept me off my feet and is taking me home tonight. I scan the glass and see several signs with Liam's name on them, even some asking for a date or just a kiss. Little do they know those kisses are all mine.

* * *

LIAM

"Liam," she giggles from her perch over my shoulder. I couldn't resist celebrating the win by grabbing her by the waist when we got far enough away from the arena. "Put me down, someone will see." Her hands slide around my torso like she doesn't want that.

"I was the last player to leave."

"Coaches! Which honestly would be way worse." She wiggles, and I am forced to set her on her feet. "Just wait until we get to the car," she adds with a wink as she almost skips to the car. We get into the car, and she turns to face me.

"So, I saw Sarah…she was bombed. Did you drink as much as her? Should I expect another drunken confession?"

"Nope. I'm just feeling good," she elongates the good, throwing up a double ok on either side of her smiling face. "How are you feeling?"

"Good, really good." I always feel like I could both stay up all night and crash as soon as I hit the mattress after a game like tonight.

"That high after a win," she sighs. "That always got me."

"Exactly." I like that she gets it, everything that I experience on the ice, and after a game- win or lose. I glance towards her as I drive us to her place. She is completely relaxed in her seat, running a hand across her chest slowly. I'm not sure if it's the many drinks she had during the game or something else, but I can't watch her hands trailing slowly across her body and get us home safely, I shake my head and focus on the road.

"You know, aside from the win. I enjoyed the fight. That's why those are my favorite seats." She shifts in her seat, turning towards me a bit.

"That fight that happened because of my goal?"

"Yes, why was that so hot!" She casually places a hand on my bicep, as if it was second nature to do so, and a warm current

CHAPTER 9

runs through me.

"I don't know. Why don't you tell me why?"

She shrugs and, smiling, says, "It just is."

I don't have time to ask more because before I know it, we are in her driveway. She makes her way to the porch as I pull out my duffle bag from the back seat. She waits for me at her front door, a wide smile on her face, and for the first time in a while, I feel like I'm not drowning in grief or regret.

Chapter 10

ELISE

The amount of covert flirting, 'meetings', and stolen glances over the past couple of weeks was just the tip of the iceberg of our new relationship. Liam was over almost every night he was in town, and we had semi-secret video chat sessions when he wasn't. Not that it was a big change for me, but I went to as many of the games as possible. It's sort of thrilling being sneaky at work only to come home for the day and find him waiting for me to get there. The chance that people might catch on or see a quick kiss placed on my cheek before he ducks out of my office honestly gives me butterflies. It's exhilarating, really.

CHAPTER 10

I never thought I would be this happy again but spending time with him is easy. Like our lives fit, with all our broken bits lining up seamlessly. He doesn't know about all of mine, though, and I'm starting to feel bad about keeping it from him like I'm hiding something. To be fair, we have been busy with other things. I'm hoping that I can get it out of the way, rip the band-aid off, soon.

Will and Liam are coming over for a laid back Thanksgiving today, neither of them having the time to go home for the day since there is an early game tomorrow. Sarah, who has become a good friend, and someone to talk to that isn't a man, is coming with her family later for dessert. While I value the friendship with her, Will gives me a feeling of family that I didn't realize I was missing.

I'm finishing up meal prep, listening to my current audiobook while I mashed potatoes, when I head the door open. Liam walks in with an overnight bag in his hand. "You better take that upstairs before Will gets here."

"I feel like he probably knows…"

"Feel like or know? I just don't want things to get weird, or get ruined," I frown. He steps close, wraps his arm around my waist, and places a kiss on my temple. The sweet greeting that I have gotten used to from him.

"I'll take it upstairs, then put me to work," he smiles before taking the stairs to my room. I sigh contently as I pull out the serving platter and carving knife he could use to carve the turkey and go back to my task of getting the sides completed. "You are the only person I know that listens to books instead of music while they do other things around the house." I hear from the bottom of the stairs.

"What? I have to know what happens to Ingrid and Cason!" I start to defend myself, realizing that I was pointing the knife I was using in his direction. "Ope. It's a really good book." I add going back to my chopping.

"I'm not judging you. It's cute." He held his hands up in mock surrender.

"Carve the turkey, please," I ask, letting things fall into comfortable silence. It's almost as if we are a family, waiting for our brother to come and celebrate the holiday. It had been three years since I had had a proper Thanksgiving dinner, any holiday really. Thinking about it brings tears to my eyes. I take a deep breath and feel his hand on my back.

"Hey, what's wrong?" His voice is soft, tender, really.

"It's just been too long. I forgot what it's like to have people around for a holiday... I haven't had that in three years. Not since..." I shake my head to clear the fog, and Liam takes his thumb brushing away a stray tear that rolled down my cheek. Now seems as good a time as ever to let him know a little bit more about me. "You know how I mentioned that I could have been in the Olympics with you when we were skating that day?" He nods and waits. "I didn't go because that's when my dad got sick. Cancer. It was too quick, barely a year. It's equally terrible watching someone you love wither away slowly, unable to help as it is for them to be torn away unexpectedly."

"Why didn't you say something?"

"Why didn't I say something when we first talked? When you hated me? When you were terrible if anyone tried talking to you about anything? Hmm, let's see... I'm not sure an 'oh by the way, I'm an orphan' would have been a great thing to say when you were an ass to me."

"That's probably true," he frowns. Then with a resolute nod, he adds, "You're coming with me to my family's place for Christmas." I open my mouth to counter, but he adds, "No arguments. It's happening."

"Carve the turkey," I whisper, before turning away from him with a small smile resting on my lips.

Will arrives a short time later, just in time for food. We joke and eat way too much, a standard for the holiday. It was nice having people to spend the day with again, but was a reminder of what I could lose if things don't work out between Liam and me.

A couple of hours later, Tom, Sarah, and their two kids came, and our turkey comatose is snapped by the giggles of the toddler attempting to sneak up on Liam, who graciously pretended not to notice. Before she can finish the sneak attack, though, Liam turns quickly sweeping her up from the ground and tosses her in the air, as if she were as light as a feather, causing her to giggle more than before.

"I can't believe you were going to scare me, Rosie-Posey," he says before throwing her again.

"Her brother has been into battles lately... they're both sneaking around constantly," Sarah explains, as I take the pie she brought from her full hands. She adds just to me, "It's terrifying being scared by a child- something out of a horror movie."

"Sounds like you could use a drink," I comment, leaving the guys to play with the kids. Sarah and I go into the kitchen where I pull out a bottle of wine before anything else.

"You're an angel." She takes the glass from me and takes a long drink. "I love Tom's family but they're a bit much all of them together and they didn't have enough wine for me to get through it. There are so many of them!"

"Well, I have plenty," I smile, eyes drifting to where the guys are playing with Jake and Rosalyn. I smile, thinking about how great an uncle Will would have been, and Liam....

"So," she says, refilling her glass already. "I have a guy I want you to meet."

"Oh, I don't know..."

"Come on, you only talk to hockey players. And this guy is a doctor, a legit doctor."

"Is there a different kind of doctor? A doctorate is a doctorate." I glance towards Liam, and even though he's trying to hide it, I see a slight scowl on his face. "I'm not looking right now."

"You're no fun. Just talk to him. What do you have to lose?" I stare into my wine glass, trying to avoid telling her that I'm not interested in a doctor, and that I'm pretty sure I am in love with Liam already. I can't though. Not if we are keeping things between us for now.

"Well, I just—" I'm cut off by Liam and the deep kiss that he plants on my lips. In front of everyone.

"She's taken," he says gruffly. I open my mouth to interject, but nothing comes. I'm shocked that after weeks of keeping things quiet, he disregarded it all to keep me from accepting a number for a man I had no intention of contacting. I grabbed the bottle of wine and took a big chug, feeling every set of eyes on me.

"Who wants pie?" I ask, trying to change the subject.

"Nope, you don't get to change the subject," Sarah says, giving me what can only be described as a shocked mom look. The one you get when they think you've been lying or hiding something from them. "When did this happen?"

"Umm, the night of the fundraising gala."

"That's like a month! You've been hiding it for a month?"

"I wouldn't say hiding it," I reply sheepishly. Liam tries to step away but I grab his arm. "You don't get to run away. You did this."

CHAPTER 10

"I'm sorry, I don't want you being set up with doctors!"

"I don't either. You should know that," I swat at him, "I didn't want to cause a big scene, I mean we technically work together..."

"We didn't want to cause a scene," he states, looking down at me. "Guess I ruined that, huh?"

"You think," Will interjects. "Not that I didn't already know this was going to happen. I was just waiting for you to do it already." He takes a giant piece of pie and walks back into the living room, where Tom is sitting on the floor playing with his kids.

* * *

LIAM

"Liam Andrew Wilkes," Elise groans after shutting the door behind Will. "What the hell was that?" Her hands are firmly on her hips. She's clearly mad at me, but looks hot.

"I'm assuming you mean the kiss?" I smile.

"Oh, you can wipe that smile off your face right the fuck now." She is definitely angry with me, no question about that. I probably could have handled things better. "We talked about this."

"I wasn't thinking...."

"Clearly." She makes her way up the stairs to the bedroom. I'm following close behind to make sure she isn't so mad at me that she wants me to leave, of course.

"I only thought that I couldn't stand the thought of you going out with anyone else." I grab her hand and turn her to face me. "I hate that I can't say anything when someone comments on how gorgeous you are, that I can't kiss you for good luck before a game or after a win until we are alone or in a damned closet! I want all those things."

"I want them too, but it's not as easy as that." She sighs, running a hand through her hair. "Liam if I didn't work for the team... if I didn't have to work with you..."

"We never would have met." She looks me in the eye then, resting her hip on the bathroom counter, her face blank as if she is in deep thought, trying to figure out the next steps.

"Well yeah, but it complicates things. I need to make sure this is done correctly."

"I know," I reply, stepping close to her and taking her hand in mine. "I'm sorry..."

"You're a Neanderthal," she smiles. "Sarah's face though..."

"I was distracted by your face..." I admit.

"Well, you missed the pure shock."

"You looked shocked too."

"I mean, I was... that was not a kiss I would ever expect with an audience," she smiles as she lets out a deep breath. "Well, can we be just a bit more tactful when it comes to work?"

"I will try to not want to shove my tongue down your throat constantly," I answer as seriously as possible. "Amongst other things, that is." I grab her hips, pulling her close to me, her hands resting on my chest.

"Liam." Her voice is soft as she slides her hands to wrap her arms around my back, her head coming to rest on my chest. She fits here so well, with her soft curves pressed flush against me. "Are you sure about Christmas? Won't it be weird?"

CHAPTER 10

"Of course, I'm sure."

"It's just that... I don't know. I'm used to being alone, so it wouldn't be a big deal if you changed your mind" She looks me directly in the eye, as if searching for any bit of hesitation. "I wouldn't be mad if it was too weird having a girl at your family home for Christmas."

"Do you not want to?" I ask, brushing a strand of hair out of her face.

"I do, but I just feel like it's a big deal for something we aren't public about...."

"We're a bit more public after today, though."

"True... I'd love to spend time with you and your family. But if you change your mind at all you have to tell me."

I hold her face between my hands and kiss her gently. "I want you there, I want you in my life."

She climbs into the bed, holding the comforter open for me and we get comfortable. Her back is to my chest, and I wrap my arms around her. As we lay there I think of taking her home, and I realize that the words ring truer than I thought. I do want her in my life. Am I ready for that?

Lights flash, red, blue, red, blue. I'm running, trying to find her, trying to get to her in time. My feet pound against the linoleum floor. They are all I can hear, along with the sirens and shouting of doctors. The halls stretch, and no matter how fast I run, I can't get any closer. I can't get to her. I can't do anything to help her, to save her. I need to be with her. My heart is racing, and the hall starts to disappear. Everything is turning black, and I know I can't save her. I can't save Elise.

I sit straight up. Elise is lying close with her back to me. Her feet are touching my legs as if she just needs a point of contact;

reassurance that I am there even in her sleep. I sit staring at her for a while, trying to catch my breath and to get my brain to realize that it was just a dream, not reliving that same nightmare again. The dream had changed; instead of chasing after Kaylee, instead of not being able to save her, it's Elise. I can't lose Elise. I can't go through that again. So I remind myself again that she is lying next to me. I can see her. I hear her breathing. I can touch her. She is here. She is safe.

Chapter 11

LIAM

"Last chance, are you sure?" she asks as l load her bag into the back of my car. It's the same question she's been asking me for the past several weeks, since Thanksgiving. Honestly, she is incredibly cute when she's nervous.

"Elise, you are packed, and my mom can't wait to meet you in person. You don't want to disappoint my mom, do you?

"Well, no, I would feel awful canceling now. I just... I don't want to impose on your family. And I know that they are expecting me, so I won't cancel," she explains, holding her hands nervously in front of her. "Liam, I'm sorry. I know I'm being weird, I'm sorry."

"It's fine, really." I pull her into my arms, kissing her forehead. "It makes perfect sense to be nervous. But I can tell you that they will without a doubt love you more than they love me." She laughs, shaking against me. "You think I'm joking?"

"Liam, they're your family. There is no way they will love me more than you. Not when you are a very famous, very talented hockey star."

"You say that like they care about what I do for a living. Besides, you were very close to hockey stardom. You made that very clear when we first were on the ice together."

"Ok, ok, you've convinced me. Liam, I really can't wait to meet them, it's just been a while is all and before that, it was just my dad. So, it's all kind of new for me in a sense. It's been too long." She looks away from me and sighs heavily. I wrap my arms around her, holding her close against my chest

"You say that like I'm going to leave you there with them all alone. You should know by now that I can't go very long without you nearby," I admit as I run my hand up and down her back soothing not just her but myself as well. It was completely true, she has become someone who I need, and want nearby. Someone who makes me feel better when it's not a good day. Part of me is terrified of being with her, but more terrified of not being with her. She is almost too good for me. I can admit that with very little doubt.

"You know, I honestly can't go very long without you either." She looks up at me and smiles. "Sorry, we should go. I've kept us long enough with my random insecurities."

"Don't worry about it," I reassure her with a kiss on her forehead. She turns to climb into the car, and I can't resist giving her a quick tap. She gasps, turning towards me again.

CHAPTER 11

"Liam! You can't do that when we're going to be in a car for several hours!" She grabs my shirt, pulls me close, and I smile, wanting her to kiss me, wanting to delay the trip just a little bit. Just as her lips get close enough, she pulls away with a mischievous smirk. "Let's go, Wilkes."

* * *

ELISE

The drive is longer than I expected but traveling with him is easy. I'm not sure he's enjoying my singing, but he seems to be surviving just fine. For part of the trip I read and he keeps his hand on my thigh. It's so simple, and the warmth of his palm is so comforting. I'd be lying if I said I wasn't a ball of nerves the whole way, but just his presence keeps it mostly at bay. As we near his childhood home, his mood shifts, as if he is just as nervous as I am. It's not until we park in the driveway, and he turns off the engine that he seems to relax.

"All right," he says, releasing a breath. "Are you ready?"

"As ready as I'll ever be. Though I think I'm more nervous now than I have ever been."

"I'll be right here with you." He takes a hold of my hand giving it a light squeeze.

"I sure hope so," I lean towards him, pressing my lips to his lightly. He steps out of the car and grabs both our bags before leading me to the front door. The door swings open so fast, I flinch in surprise. Standing there is an average height woman with a mass of dark curls on her head and eyes just like Liam's.

"My baby," she says, wrapping him in a tight embrace. "You look good, sweetheart." She turns towards me, and I offer her a timid smile, attempting to hide my nerves. "You must be Elise. I have heard so much about you." Instantly, I am pulled into a hug, and for a moment, I stiffen but only for a moment as the comfort of a mother's hug hits me. It's something that I haven't had most of my life now. I take a deep breath to steal away the heat of tears that wants to escape.

"It's so nice to finally meet you, Mrs. Wilkes," I say as she steps back.

"You as well, dear, but call me Vivian. Now get in here, both of you. It's far too cold out." She walks into the house, and Liam pauses for me to follow her. I'm hit with a warm and cozy feeling, the smell of the pine tree in the living room, and... is that fresh baked cookies, too. "Honey, they're here! Stop eating the cookies and come say hi to your son."

"I only had one." A tall man who looks like Liam walks into the room. It's as if I am looking at him in the future, except his father's eyes are dark, and his hair is stick straight standing up in all directions, without the help of product.

"Hi, Dad" Liam smiles, he has set our bags down and comes to stand next to me, his arm wrapping around my waist. I notice Vivian's eyes track the movement and her mouth twitches into a sad smile for a moment. I know instantly she is thinking of Kaylee. I'm not sure how to feel about it, but I know that this has to be hard for them too. They should be celebrating Christmas with a new baby, not some random orphan.

"You're not being very polite, Liam. Did I not teach you to introduce your friends, so they don't have to stand there awkwardly?" His father comments, and I chuckle at the jab.

"You know, I've been trying to get him to work on his manners too, but it just isn't sticking," I say, extending my hand out to him, and he gives it a gentle shake. "Elise. Thank you so much for welcoming me into your home."

"Owen," he states simply. "We're happy to have you here." He wraps a comforting arm around his wife, giving her a squeeze. "Liam, you know where to take the bags. Lilith will be here soon. She just had to pick up a few last-minute things."

"Classic Lils, if she didn't wait until the eleventh hour to do things, I don't know if I would know her anymore. I'll put our things in the room." He gives me a quick kiss on the cheek before making his way upstairs, leaving me with his parents.

"Well, this is awkward... want a cookie?" Owen asks me, breaking the tense feeling that I have not knowing if they want me here or if I'm just a reminder of everything that they lost. That Liam lost.

"Come, take your coat off, relax a bit, dear," Vivian says with the same smile she gave us on the porch. "I hope you're ok with a roast for dinner tonight. Liam didn't mention any allergies or dietary restrictions."

"That sounds amazing, actually." Liam rejoins us, taking a seat at the kitchen island. It's both weird and amazing to see him here. Like he's not a famous athlete, but just as a member of this family. He pulls me closer with a gentle tug and runs his hand along my back, soothing away my nerves.

This trip has just started, and I'm already overwhelmed by it all. There are so many things running through my head that I can't focus on being present. We all know what would have been if things didn't make a turn the way they did; it's obvious. I almost feel like I am imposing on them.

"Elise, are you ok?" Vivian asks.

"Yeah, sorry." I shake the foggy feeling from my brain and

smile. "Long day is all. I'm more tired than I thought, I suppose."

"Why don't you go rest for a bit before dinner? Liam, show her to your room," Vivian almost orders him. I smile at her before Liam takes my hand and leads me through the house and up to his old room.

It's a standard teenage boy's room, nothing too special aside from all his hockey trophies from years of playing the sport. It's like a time capsule, like they haven't changed anything in here since he was drafted. I smile thinking of him as a small child in hockey gear.

"Are you ok?" he asks, concern etched in his face.

"Yeah, just a bit tired. And a little overwhelmed if I'm honest," I admit. He wraps his arms around me, my head resting on his chest as he starts massaging the nape of my neck to ease a bit of the tension I am feeling.

"Tired I can fix," he whispers into my hair. I feel our weight shift and him lifting me slightly, so we are laying on his bed. I curl up against him and sigh as he brushes his fingers through my hair. "Overwhelmed though... I understand why you're feeling that, but I'm not sure how to fix it for you aside from telling you not to worry."

"It's not so much worry as it's knowing... I don't want to dig things up for you, Liam."

"What? That Kaylee and I would be celebrating our baby's first Christmas here? Elise, if that's what's wrong..."

"I'm sorry, I just feel like I'm imposing on something that should have been so special for you and your family."

"You are special to me."

"That's sweet..." I can't look him in the eye, knowing I will have a rough time keeping my emotions in check.

CHAPTER 11

"Elise, I can't say that I know a whole lot. But I do know that my family is happy if I am happy. And right now, you are what makes me happy. You've been the only thing that has made me happy in a while. I think my parents aren't sure what to make of it. I was in a dark place after the season ended last year. I know I wasn't behaving the best the last part of the season, but I gave up once I didn't have a team relying on me."

"Liam, you don't have to explain anything..."

"My family saw that firsthand... I don't know if they were prepared to see me as a mess again. I think my mom is waiting to see if it will last. My dad just wants cookies," he chuckles at his joke trying to ease the tension.

"You have every right to still be a mess. Life is messy. I'm still a mess." I lean into his chest, resting my head against his chest, still not sure what to think about being here. I haven't been sure since he invited me to come with him. I almost didn't.

"I know. You're the only one that isn't scared of my mess though. So, I'm sorry it's a bit weird, but don't worry about what would have been this year for us. This, right now, is what I have instead. It's different, but it's pretty great too."

"Ok," I whisper, I let my body relax next to him.

"You came into my life and threw it for a loop in the best way possible." His hands roam slowly over my body, the heat that builds in my belly curled up with him, being this close to Liam makes my pulse quicken regardless of the situation. The air has shifted between us, he seems to pick up on it too, his hand slides to bring my thigh over his hip. I run my fingers through his hair as he brings his mouth to my neck, kissing down and then along my collarbone.

I fight back a moan, trying to keep quiet in his family home. His hands push my shirt up and over my head and he pushes me onto the bed. His lips return to the base of my neck, and his hand trails down my torso to the waist of my pants. I squirm beneath him, my body craving his touch, I know that it's only been a few hours since we've been like this, but we can't seem to stay away from each other.

"Mmmm, I love the little sounds you make when I touch you like this," His lips graze my ear as a hand pushes my pants down over my hips. I feel the soft touch of his lips in the hollow of my throat as he whispers, "But, every sound you make, I want them to be into my ear." I whimper at his touch and feel him smile as I struggle to take off his shirt and he pulls it off for me. He smiles as I struggle to take his shirt off and pulls it off for me, my hands go to the zipper of his jeans instead.

"Liam." I reach for him, as he slowly undresses in front of me. After what seems like ages, he is settling between my legs, his hard member resting against my wet entrance. When he pushes in, I gasp against his chest to stifle the sound. Even after being with him several times, I'm not quite ready for how full I feel with him. I wiggle beneath him, and he starts moving inside me, slow and torturous. I move my hips up to meet his trying to get him to speed his thrusts, but his hand slides down my body to my waist, firmly grasping me there, holding me to keep the tempo he knows drives me crazy, setting every nerve ending a blaze.

I give up and relax into him, focusing on every delicious stroke. His mouth trails rough kisses down my neck to find my breasts until he brings a stiff hard nipple into his mouth. I grab his head, my fingers latching onto his hair as I fight the moans that beg to escape. His mouth moves to my other breast, and I arch against him, the pressure building in my belly. The liquid heat pools deep inside, warming more and more with each stroke he makes

CHAPTER 11

burying him deeper and deeper in my dripping flower.

Liam slides his hand between us as he lifts his face to mine, fingers connecting with the bud of nerves. "Come for me." I feel my release, my body tensing, contracting beneath him. I bury my head in his shoulder, biting down gently to try to keep quiet. "Mmmm yes, I'm going to come." I feel him join me, his body stiffens as mine continues to pulsate around him.

He rolls us to our sides, staying connected as our bodies calm down, heartbeats slowing to a normal speed. After a couple minutes I adjust making myself comfortable in his arms, and I let him hold me here and I drift off to sleep.

* * *

When I wake up, Liam isn't there, so I dress and make my way towards the living room, hearing his voice carrying up the stairs. He's talking with his dad about the rest of the season. Both are very excited about a potential playoff run. Honestly, I am excited too and would love to join the discussion, but instead, I kiss the top of his head as I walk by and continue into the kitchen where Vivian is starting to get sides done for dinner.

"Would you like some help?" I ask.

"Oh, you really don't have to. You're our guest, dear," his mom replies with a smile.

"I'd like to, actually. Cooking isn't really fun when it's just for yourself. If that's ok, that is...," I trail off at the look she is giving me. Her face is soft as she contemplates my words until a small smile spreads across her face.

"I'd love the help," she says, taking my hand in hers for just a moment. I take a deep breath, and it's like an entire conversation is happening between us at that moment. As if she is letting me know that she is still grieving what was lost too but is happy that Liam is doing better. Also like she knows that I understand much more than most. "Ok, let's get you an apron, so we don't ruin your clothes," she says after a few seconds.

Soon after, we have several things started, desserts for Christmas dinner, more cookies, and dinner has started I see a tall thin woman come into the house. She has the same dark curls as Liam and his mom and his dad's fairer skin tone and hazel eyes. This must be his sister; the thought makes me incredibly nervous all over again.

"Lils," Liam nearly shouts as he stands to hug her.

"Hello, big brother," she laughs. She makes eye contact with me over his shoulder and smiles, adding, "I thought Mom said you were bringing a friend. I'm not going to lie, I was hoping for someone a bit more masculine but ..."

"Lil, this is Elise." Liam is by my side, wrapping an arm around my waist.

"Sorry, I'm not a buff hockey player," I smile. She eyes me, and I worry for a moment that she will be the one to make me feel terrible about crashing their family time.

"I forgive you, this time."

"Lilith Evelyn, be nice," their mom says, walking up to her daughter, and giving her a bone-crushing hug. I don't hear what they're saying after that, but Liam kisses my forehead as if he is trying to calm my nerves once again.

"She's a bit much, but she's all bark," he says as he takes a seat at the kitchen island. He keeps me close for a while, giving me small touches to keep me from getting overly nervous as the whole family talks over each other, one talking louder than the other; it's like ten TVs on all at once. It's incredibly hard to keep up with them. As soon as I catch part of the conversation and try to contribute, they're onto the next thing, so I sit there perched on Liam's lap, lost. This isn't something that I thought I would have. Honestly, I thought it was just something that I saw on TV or in movies. I didn't know it was a real thing; the bustling conversation of family.

Chapter 12

LIAM

After breakfast, I send Elise upstairs to get ready for the day, telling her simply that I have a surprise for her this morning. A tradition that has been happening every Christmas Eve morning since before I was born in our small town. All the kids in the area go out to the park where a full rink is set up, whether it's cold enough to freeze or not. When I was a kid, my dad would take me there for most of the day, and we would take turns shooting at the goal on one side while Lilith would skate around with her friends on the other side of the rink. Today though, dad is

CHAPTER 12

staying home to read his paper and drink coffee in peace, and Lils, well, she went back to bed.

"Are you ready?" I ask, stepping into my old room. She's dressed in thick leggings and a sweater that almost hides her curves.

"Yep," she pulls on her thick sock and stands in front of me. "Are you going to tell me what we're doing now?"

"Nope." I grab her hand, leading her downstairs. I grab our skates and slide into a pair of boots at the door.

"How do you have my skates?"

"I grabbed them before we left. Now put on your coat and boots."

"Liam." She laughs, the clear tone sending warmth through my body, as she wraps her arms around my waist. "We're skating?"

"Yes, we have an outdoor rink in the park across the street. There will probably be a bunch of neighborhood kids there, but I thought it would be fun. My mom has released you from kitchen duty for the evening."

"This sounds amazing." She does a little happy dance in my arms, her smile getting wider.

"I was hoping you would think so." I tighten my grip around her waist and carry her out the front door.

"Have fun!" I hear my mom call as I close the door behind us.

We make our way to the park, I can hear the kids before the rink comes into view, but when it does, I am thrilled. Memories flood me of all the years playing here the morning before Christmas. Like previous years, there are small kids trying to skate with the help of their parents, and older kids skating around them. Elise and I stop at a bench and put on our skates, leaving our boots tucked underneath it. When we start skating around the rink, I hear tiny whispers of 'That's Liam Wilkes' or 'Do you know who that is?' and I find myself smiling.

"You're literally about to make their day," she skates close to me, taking my hand as she turns to skate backwards for a moment.

"The perks of your parents staying in the family home," I brought over a pile of hockey sticks from the past couple of games and two new ones for Elise and me to use on the ice. I always make sure to have them on Christmas trips here so that any kid who wants one can have one. "Shall we see if we can join the game?"

"Obviously." She smiles as we skate to the edge of the rink, adding in a whisper, "I didn't come to fuck around Liam; better bring your A-game." She skates off with a wink, grabbing a puck from the edge of the ice as she goes.

A few hours later, when our limbs are tired and a bit frozen, we head back to the house, knowing that we have plans for the rest of the day. There will be a simple lunch with an assortment of snacks and drinks before we have a regular sit-down dinner. Tomorrow my mom will have a giant meal planned for midday.

"That was so much fun," Elise exclaims as we walk into the house and strip off our extra layers. She hangs our coats as I place our boots and skates beneath the entry bench. The smell of my mom's cooking wafts through the house. Memories flood in of all the years we've celebrated together, and the traditions my family has built since my childhood.

"I'm glad you enjoyed it. It's my favorite part of coming home for Christmas, aside from my mom's cooking, that is." Her cheeks are rosy from the cold, and she is beaming as she takes her hair down, letting it fall in loose curls over her shoulder.

We find my dad where we left him this morning, with a full plate and a classic Christmas movie on the TV. In the kitchen, Lills is sitting at the island frosting cookies as my mom takes out another batch from the oven. She always bakes a ton, and I end up bringing a giant container home.

"Did you have fun?" Mom asks, kissing my cheek in only a way a mother can. I look at Elise as she grabs a cookie and starts decorating them beside my sister.

"It was probably the best morning I've had in ages," Elise sighs, smiling at us. My chest fills with pride for my hometown and happiness that I could share it with her.

"We used to fight mom on leaving the ice. She'd have to practically drag us home. Kicking and screaming," Lils comments, an almost sad smile on her face.

"Put that cookie down, Elise, and eat something. You two were out there for too long not to eat something." Mom takes the knife out of her hand and replaces it with a plate. "Eat."

"I'm constantly reminding her to eat too."

"I'm busy making sure you and all the other hooligans on the team look good, it's hard work...."

"You should make sure that you eat, dear."

"Now I have two Wilkes and Will hounding me!" She laughs as she places a sandwich and some fruits and veggies on the plate. She settled back on the seat next to Lils and eats as we all talked, reminiscing about every childhood moment possible.

* * *

We spent the rest of the day like any other family would, I suppose, dinner, movies, joking around, etc. Elise found her place in the conversation after a while. Melting into the banter and tradition is easier than I expected. We sit in the living room half-watching another random Christmas movie, and I can tell she is starting to feel more comfortable; which may be in part because of my dad's traditional eggnog. I remember when I was first allowed to have some, I woke up the next morning on the couch, still in my clothes from the night before with drool crusted to my face.

Elise is well on her way to that point, thanks to my dad and sister, who rarely let her glass get below the halfway mark. They are joking and sharing embarrassing stories with her, but I don't mind because she seems happy. I catch my mom's eye from across the room, and she smiles at me in a way that only mothers can when they are happy for you. She looked like this when I was drafted and again at my first professional game. Now, I'm a bit taken aback by my mom's approval, or her happiness with having Elise here with me. She knows more than even my dad how difficult last year was for me and how far I have come since meeting Elise.

"Are you feeling, ok?" I ask Elise quietly, wrapping an arm around her, and pulling her closer to my side.

"Just sleepy," she answers. The lights of the Christmas tree twinkling over her soft features, makes me want to pull her onto my lap .

"Why don't you go get ready for bed? I'll be up in a little bit," I offer. She nods before saying good night to my family.

"I like her," Lilith states when she is out of view.and an odd sense of pride bubbles up in my chest at the realization that my family accepts her despite the loss of what could have been.

CHAPTER 12

"Well," my mother announces, pulling me from the spiral of my thoughts. "It's almost time for bed all around... Santa won't visit if everyone is awake."

"Mom, we're old enough to know that Santa isn't real—"

"WHAT!?!" Dad shouts, feigning surprise.

"See, now you've ruined Christmas."

"Ok, goodnight. I wouldn't want to be down here when Saint Nick arrives," I joke, before heading upstairs myself.

I make my way to my room, walking past Elise brushing her teeth, her face is already bare of the minimal makeup she wore today, and her hair is piled on top of her head. I change quickly into family-appropriate pajamas and climb into my bed, waiting for her. I'm almost asleep when she comes into the room and crawls into bed with me, a bit less graceful than her usual self. She ends up half laying on me, chest to chest.

"How much did you drink?" I laugh.

"Your dad pours them heavy! I mean, I'm a whiskey girl, but like, WHOA...." I grab hold of her hips, keeping her in place. She places a hand on my chest and pushes herself up enough to look into my eyes. "Hi," she smiles.

"Hi." Elise's gaze flicks to my lips and back before leaning in slightly, just close enough that I only need to tilt my chin to press my lips to hers. She sighs, resting her head on my shoulder.

"This has been great," she comments as I run my fingers along her back. "Thanks for forcing me to come with you."

"It was my pleasure to 'force you' into coming here. I like sharing them with you." She smiles brightly, and I place a kiss on her forehead. I haven't felt this at peace in a while and I know it's because Elise is here with me. "So tomorrow, my mom does this thing with Santa, even though we are adults...just wanted to warn you."

"Sounds magical," she sighs, her body relaxing against my chest. It's not long before she is sleeping soundly curled into my body.

* * *

ELISE

I was not prepared for what the morning would bring. I wake up tangled in Liam's limbs just as the sun is starting to peek over the hills outside his window. Carefully, I slide out of his arms and make my way to the bathroom. I brush through my messy bedhead and as I brush my teeth, I hear the shaking of bells. I head back to the bedroom when Liam opens the door, yawning and stretching.

"Merry Christmas," he whispers, wrapping his arms around me and planting a gentle kiss on my lips.

"Merry Christmas. What exactly is going on down there?" I ask, nodding my head towards the staircase. The bells are still ringing and Liam glances over his shoulder toward the sound.

"I'm guessing that mom decided to bring back a couple of our childhood traditions this year." When he looks back at me, a huge smile is spread across his face. "I believe the noise you're hearing is Santa leaving the house." He releases his hold on my waist and slips into the bathroom, humming a Christmas carol as he closes the door.

The parent-made holiday magic is so much more than pretending that Santa came to a house full of adults. Mountains of pancakes are piled on the kitchen island with, thankfully, a carafe of coffee waiting; the eggnog that Owen made was way more than I had expected. As I turn to the living room, I notice presents piled beneath the tree and a stocking for each of us hanging at the mantle, even one for me. They had gotten a stocking for me, my name embroidered on it and everything.

I knew they would most likely have the usual things they did for their family, but to have them do so much for me was completely unexpected. I smiled, taking in all the added details that weren't there last night. There was a warmth to it that I haven't had in the past few years, and I am so grateful to be a part of it.

Grateful, but also sad beyond anything that I thought possible. I forgot what it was like to have a family around for the holidays. There is always a piece missing especially, after my dad died. It's like this subtle, yet overwhelming feeling that they should be here. Not just for birthdays and holidays, but future things like weddings and grand babies. It never goes away; it just is.

Chapter 13

LIAM

Elise is asleep in the front seat on our way home from spending the holiday with my family. I smile thinking about how great of a trip it ended up being. She was so sweet with the gifts she gave my family, and honestly, some were more than I would have expected from someone I just started a relationship with. She gave my dad a 21-year-old scotch! His face when he saw the bottle was priceless, almost as if he would trade me for her in a second. He hugged her so quickly that she gasped, not expecting the reaction at all. However, I'm starting to learn that Elise

CHAPTER 13

is more thoughtful than the average person, she knows how precious each day is, and she takes care of those around her, even if it's just with a thoughtful gift.

These past couple of days could have been completely different if she hadn't been there. I know this, and my family knows too. It would have been a lot less cheerful and a lot more somber no matter how hard my mom would have tried. Because before she walked into my life like a force to be reckoned with, I was a mess. I suppose that I still am a mess, but it's better now, I think. Better because of her.

She stretches in the passenger seat before taking my free hand as she sits up. "Where are we?" she asks, taking a look around.

"About an hour out still, not much longer."

"Are you going to your place tonight? You have a game tomorrow. I don't want you to not have a good night's rest." She doesn't look like she wants me to say yes. Truth is that I should go to my place and not hers, but I don't want to. I want to sleep next to her; my nightmares are typically better with her close by.

"I could use some sleep…but I don't want to go home."

"Ok, because I have a gift for you," she says with a wicked grin.

"We said no gifts," I state, confused.

"I know, but… I think you'll enjoy it. And you'll probably sleep pretty well afterward, too. I know I would anyway." Her hand runs up my arm to the back of my neck, toying with the hair on the back of my neck.

"You're a tease, Elise Connors."

"I would tell you to drive faster, but it's winter." I pick up speed slightly just to shave a little time off the rest of our drive. "We should grab something to eat. There isn't much at home, and I doubt that you have much beyond condiments at your place."

"You would be right. Order something from the steakhouse we like, and we can pick it up on the way there."

"Ok, you want your normal?" she asks. This is when I realize how much she has become a major part of my life. I thought I knew- but the little thing of knowing what I order from a specific place. Why is it that tiny thing that makes me feel like this is so much more than before?

"Yeah, that's perfect" I take her hand in mine and bring her hand to my lips, kissing her knuckles lightly before releasing her so she can call them.

We eat in comfortable silence but are a bit tired from the drive. As nice as it was to spend time with my family and for them to see that I am doing better thanks to her. She's the whole reason I am doing as well as I am. It's not hard to see now, looking back on it.

"Ok, present time... I just have to get it ready so give me a couple of minutes before you come up" She stands from the island counter and gives me an unhurried kiss.

"I'll clean up here," I reply, brushing her hair from her face. She smiles at me, and my heart feels like it will burst because I am truly happy for the first time in almost a year.

I take my time after watching her climb the stairs, throwing out the containers that the food came in, and washing the glasses we used for our drinks. Until I can't wait any longer, I grab our things and carry them up to the master bedroom, pushing open the door. I turn to set our bags down against the closet door and look for her.

CHAPTER 13

"Hi," she says softly, standing just outside of the bathroom door. I don't know if I would have ever expected this. She's in a deep red lingerie set that hugs her body perfectly, the lace trim skimming the top of her long legs.

"Fuck." I let out a large whoosh of air, making her giggle.

"So, you like your gift?" I close the distance between us, kissing her firmly. She pulls my shirt over my head before running her hands over my skin. It feels electrified, like every nerve ending is responding to her touch. I need to make her feel this too.

"Best present ever. But I didn't get you anything."

"This is for both of us," she replies as my hands land on her hips.

"Hmmm, I like it a lot...but," I lift her, and her legs wrap around my waist. "I can give you something else." Smiling, she kisses me again, her fingers sliding into my hair at the nape of my neck as her other arm wraps around my shoulder, holding tight to me. I walk towards the bed.

"Liam," she whispers when my mouth finds that spot on her neck that sends chills through her body. I set her down so she is lying on the bed and begin kissing down her body, letting my hands roam as they please. I take my time savoring each kiss working from her neck to her collarbone before stopping to greet her lace-covered breast. I take one into my mouth, the lace of the fabric rough beneath my tongue, it doesn't stop me, though. The soft moan that escapes her lips is all the motivation I need to keep going, and I switch to her other breast. My hands make their way to her long legs, still loosely wrapped around me, as if she is unwilling to let me go. Truth be told, I am the one unwilling to let her go.

"I think these are in the way," I whisper in her ear as I slide my finger around the waist of the matching red underwear, pulling them off slowly. I catch her ankle and start kissing up her leg, hearing her whine of protest. Laughing against her skin, I keep traveling up until I stop and place her legs so they are resting on my shoulders. "Mmmm dessert."

She chokes out a laugh before I slide a finger into her, cutting the laugh short, replaced by a gasp as my finger pumps slowly in and out of her. "Elise," I say, drawing her attention back towards me. "What do you want, baby?"

"Liam, more," she groans. I love when she gets lost like this. When she's so turned on she can't think or put together complete sentences. I keep working her with my finger, adding another when she is ready before I lean in and lick up her dripping center. Her legs tighten around me, and I smile as I find her clit, earning a sudden jerk of her hips. I tighten my hold on her hips with one arm, so she stays in place.

"You like that," I ask, taking a moment to ask before I dive back in, alternating between licking and sucking her clit as I find the perfect rhythm I know works for her. I have learned how to make her come, and I truly love how her body responds to mine. How I can make her come undone with just my mouth alone, but she enjoys it so much more this way. When her hands go to the arm holding her still and my hair, I know she is where she needs to be. I let out a groan of satisfaction to match hers.

"Liam, I... oh my...please." I don't stop to say anything, I just keep going. I want to please her. I want her screaming my name. I want her to be mine, only mine. Forever. I could love her. I could, and for the first time in forever, that doesn't terrify me. Her legs tighten, muscles tensing as she moans louder. She is close, so I focus on her clit as I hook my fingers to run along the wall, trying to find her spot. I know when I do because she nearly comes off the bed, arching her back. "LIAM." I keep licking her and pumping her core as she rides her orgasm, enjoying every second of it. When she is relaxed against me, I lift my head and slide my fingers from her, seeing her sated smile.

"Mmm, my favorite." I smile before sucking her juices from my fingers.

"Merry fucking Christmas…damn," she says still breathing heavily.

"Merry Christmas. I see why this had to wait until we were home." I really could love this woman.

* * *

It's game day, and as much as I didn't want to tear myself away from Elise, away from the warmth and comfort of her wrapped around me in bed, I have work to do. I walk into the locker room and take my place next to Will and Tom, who are quietly going through their pre-game routines. I start to go through mine as well, letting my mind wander.

Last night was one of the first truly restful nights I have had in a while, and not just because of the many orgasms both Elise and I had, but because I didn't have nightmares of losing Kaylee or Elise. The switch to losing Elise scares me more than I thought it ever would. Seeing her with my family, how she fits into our dynamics so easily, I can't help myself hoping that there could be more. It terrifies me.

"Wow, Cap, who are you thinking about?" I hear a new trade comment from across the room. "Just a few months ago, when I played against you, you were a total raging douche. So whatever ass you're getting must be good."

"No one really," I say just to brush him off, hoping it will deter him from asking more.

"Whoever she is, can I have a go when you're done with her?" He laughs, and I'm on my feet in seconds, making my way across the locker room to stand before him. I am tempted to punch him square in the jaw when I see Elise talking in the hall outside the locker room with the coach. I remember her mentioning that she needed to touch base with him about an event, a meet and greet with the season ticket holders for the New Years' game. I let out a growl of frustration before turning to the rest of the team that now have their eyes locked on me.

"If I hear any of you talk about anyone like that again, I will see that you never play for this team again." I hear murmurs of confusion and agreement, but I only see her look of confusion. I go back to my pre-game routine, deciding to take out the frustration on the ice.

* * *

ELISE

I'm not sure what just happened. I know that I was talking with Coach Karr, and then as he walked back to his office, I saw and heard Liam. I don't know what he was talking about, but I have this uneasy feeling that it involves me. There is this urge to walk to him and wrap my arms around his torso, holding him there. But I can't. I chose to keep this quiet. I chose to not be a couple in the public eye for now. So I have to fight my instinct to go to him, to help him in any way I can.

CHAPTER 13

Instead, I make my way into the arena, to my seat with Sarah, and hope that he can use whatever he is feeling in tonight's game. I worry about him nonetheless, because I love him. There is no point in denying it to myself any longer.

Chapter 14

ELISE

Liam stayed at his place last night. It was weird to not share a bed with him, especially after spending so much time with him lately. We have been together a lot these past couple of months. Even when we weren't secretly dating, we spent a lot of time together. It's hard to believe that it's nearing the end of the regular season. After the game last night, he stopped by to have something to eat with me, but I could tell he was exhausted, not just physically, but something was weighing on his mind too. So when he suggested sleeping at his place, I nodded in agreement and reluctantly let him go. I am glad that he decided to come

CHAPTER 14

over after his workout today.

When I hear the front door open, I can't help but smile from my spot on the couch.

"Hi, beautiful," he says, his voice sending shivers through me. I stand and walk to meet him, wrapping my arms around his waist. I rest my head on his chest, feeling him press his lips to the top of my head.

"Are you excited for the game tomorrow?" I ask, breathing in his scent.

"I'm a little on edge." His tone is serious, but in a focused way that I hear when he is determined to not let his team down.

"Understandable," I look up at him, unfolding myself from my favorite place. "You guys have this, though. You all out skill those asshats in Midtown."

"We will see." He smiles as I wrap my arms around his waist, "What do you want to do tonight?" His hands run up and down my back, sending shivers along my spine. I love it when he does this; it makes me melt.

"You decide. You're the man with the big game tomorrow."

"I can think of a few things."

"Oh... I don't want to tire you out too much, Liam." His hands sink lower to cup my ass. "Let's order take out, we can eat and then have a little fun."

"Oh, I'm planning a lot of fun... and it's going to be a long night," he whispers in my ear. Suddenly he's lifting me off my feet, and I instinctively wrap my legs around his waist. "We'll order takeout to make sure you have enough energy to keep up."

"You talk a big game," I tease. He carries me into the kitchen, setting me on the counter, so I'm perched on the edge of the counter.

"Order something," he almost commands, handing me his

phone.

"What do you want?"

"You."

"Shut up" I laugh, resting a hand on the nape of his neck.

"I love that laugh," he says, kissing my neck slowly, "Order dinner."

"It's a little difficult with you…" I let out a deep breath, "You need to stop."

"No." I can feel him smile against my neck. "Pick something that will be ok if it's cold when we get to it." His hand slides up my back under my shirt, and I fight through the take-out order. Distracted by the barrage of kisses trailed down my neck and over my chest, and his wandering hands. I slam his phone on the counter and run my fingers through his hair.

"Liam."

"How long did they say?" He hasn't stopped touching me, the light constant presence driving me crazy with each passing second.

"Twenty minutes."

"Hmmm. I might be able to work with that," he smirks. I can't handle that smirk. He takes a step back, leaving me on the counter.

"What are you doing?" I grab his belt and pull him back to me. "You can't do all that and step away."

"You're going to have to be patient tonight, love," he whispers in my ear, his voice that deep husky tone that drives me crazy. "I know it's not your best quality." I take a fist full of his shirt and pull so that he's pressed against me again. His mouth is on mine, strong but slow. He's torturing me and enjoying it.

"Liam," I sigh when he breaks away, trailing down my neck again. The man knows that I love when he does this. I arch my

CHAPTER 14

back at the tingles that erupt through my body. I could get used to this, every day, forever. "You're mean."

"You love it." He emphasizes his point by grabbing my hips pulling me so that I'm pressed against him.

"Holy crap, will you just tear off my clothes already?" I grind my body against his, hoping I can get him to speed things up a bit, when the doorbell rings. "How has it been twenty minutes already?"

"Stay right where you are." I let out a frustrated sigh and watch him walk to my front door. I can't remember wanting him this much, the slow and torturous foreplay is a new trick, and it's working. I want him so bad, I need to make him hurry things along.

When he walks back in, eating an egg roll from the bag, I feel a little defeated. I want to pick up where we left off, but my stomach chooses this moment to grumble. "Eat," he orders, holding the egg roll out to me. I lean forward and take a bite. "Good girl," he comments with a wink.

"What's my prize?" I tease.

"I can think of something," he laughs standing back between my legs, and places the food on the counter. "But you need to have more than a bite. I know you probably didn't eat much today."

"I ate a large breakfast. Dinner can wait," I replied, wrapping my legs around his waist, holding him close. "I'm hungry for something else."

His hands slide up my thighs to the small of my back, and I arch into him. Placing a hand gently on his face, I'm struck by how hard I have fallen for this man. I want him always. With his forehead resting against mine our mouths are a breath away, an electric current humming between us. He slides a hand up my back, weaving his fingers into my hair, and his lips crush mine. I match his pace, savoring each and every taste. His tongue enters my mouth, and I can't fight the moan that comes from deep in my chest.

He pulls back, staring at me with piercing blue eyes darkened with desire. "I want to do so many things to you," he whispers before bringing his lips back to my neck, once again finding the spot there that turns me into a puddle. I grab onto his hair, lacing my fingers with his dark curls, my other hand gripping the counter for stability.

"Do what you want," I whimper when I gather my thoughts enough to speak. He looks me in the eyes at this and smirks as if to ask if I'm sure before taking my shirt off over my head. I barely register that it's completely gone before his mouth is on my chest, kissing along the lace of my bra. I'm lost in the sensation, every nerve on high alert, when I feel the cool air hitting my bare skin as he unclasps the scrap of fabric over my now taut nipples. He wastes no time before taking one in his mouth, sucking and nibbling like it's his last meal. I buck against him feeling how hard he has gotten, seeking any friction to ease the pressure building between my legs.

"Mmm, you like that baby girl?" he asks, switching to my other breast. He knows my body so well, what I need to be truly satisfied. My fingers curl and scratch at his scalp in ecstasy; I can't take it much longer. He grinds into me, adding pressure to my core while he continues to worship my breasts with his mouth and hand.

"Liam," I moan, knowing that I am so close to finding my release.

"Not yet," he whispers in my ear, stilling his hips but keeping them flush against me.

CHAPTER 14

"You're so mean," I groan in frustration. I take the break in contact to remove his shirt, letting my hands run over his chest. I press against him, chest to chest, and look up into his eyes. "Liam, I need you." As soon as the words leave my mouth, he lifts me from the counter, and we're moving to the stairs. Pausing for a moment with my back pressed to the wall, his lips crash into mine again with hunger.

The trip upstairs is clumsy, but soon enough, he has me lying on the bed, and is removing my shorts in a swift movement. I sit up and unbutton his jeans, his large considerable length springing out from beneath the material. I can't help myself. I lean in and lick him from base to tip. "Fuck, babe." I smile before taking him in my mouth, wrapping a hand around his shaft as I work him. His hand is in my hair instantly.

I smile, looking at him with the tip of his cock brushing my lips. He moans, his eyes never moving from my mouth. I love the power that I feel with him relying on me for his pleasure. Having him in my mouth is exhilarating. I take him back in as much as possible and moan with him this time, savoring his taste.

"Elise, if you keep doing this... you have to stop," he says, pulling me off of him. I start to protest, but he kicks out of his pants and is over me in an instant. Our mouths clash in a heady need, almost frantic. I can feel him rubbing against my slick core. "Damn, you're so wet."

"Liam, I need you... I need you in me now. Please." I don't have to ask twice because as soon as the words leave my mouth, he slides the whole of his length in me, filling me to the brim. I gasp at the pressure and the pleasure of being filled by him. He moves slowly in and out of me as if he is savoring the moment, truly enjoying the moans that he is milking from me. I wrap my legs around him again; somehow, he is deeper, hitting every sensitive nerve possible. "Faster," I breathe.

Liam quickens his pace, our bodies moving as one, knowing just what each other wholly. I feel the pressure in my belly growing, a deep aching for release. His mouth is at my breasts again, taking a nipple between his teeth, and my world is unraveled. My body shakes as my walls clench around him. He keeps the pace, never faltering as I ride out the wave of my orgasm. When my breath comes back, I push him onto his back, and I'm riding him.

"Holy shit, Elise." he groans. His voice is deep and husky with want and on edge. His hands are on my ass, and I can feel his control slipping. I quicken my pace now as my pleasure builds too.

"Come, please, Liam. Fill me up," I moan. His fingers dig into my flesh, and we find our release together. I'm lying beside him, our legs tangled together as we catch our breath. "Shit, that was..."

"Amazing," he offers, smiling at me as he wraps an arm around my waist.

* * *

We spend the morning curled together until he has to get ready for the game. Last night was the best night of my life, not just because of the incredible sex, but because I know I love him more than I have ever loved anyone. The game was close, but the team pulled it out. We agreed that he would come over after

CHAPTER 14

all the post-game interviews. I decide to greet him in nothing but his jersey, making up for not wearing it at that first game after we decided to give this a try. Hoping that he is in the same mood as last night.

"Hey, handsome," I say from the kitchen when I hear him walk in. I know we just spent the night together last night, but I'm so excited to be with him again. Just like I am every time I get to spend time with him. I walk into the living room, to see him standing there with his face so full of pain. "What's wrong?" concern lacing my voice.

"I can't do this." His tone is the same as it is during press conferences after a loss. This isn't what I expected after a win. His face is more serious and tone more distant than it's really ever been with me.

"Liam, what's wrong?" I ask more firmly than before.

"This..." he steps back, putting space between us.

"What? What's wrong?" I step closer to him, trying to get a read on his face, to understand why the sudden change.

"This isn't going to work. I can't... I can't see myself loving anyone like I did Kaylee, and I can't even imagine kids without her..." He won't look at me, in fact he's looking everywhere other than in my eyes.

"What? Liam, but you... Oh my God. You're serious?" My body goes cold like I'm going to be sick, and I freeze for a moment letting his words turn over in my mind again.

"I am. I thought that if I tried... I might... with you but..."

"Liam, what the hell? You, you promised this wouldn't happen" tears start to form, and I try to hold them back sucking a deep ragged breath. "You told me that you were serious about this. That I didn't have to worry... How the hell did I fall for that? I fucking loved you. I was falling in love with you." I clutch my stomach and start pacing trying to wrap my head around what is happening. Just last night we were in this blissful state, wrapped up in one another. Now, he's ending things, making me wonder if I just imagined all the good moments that we shared.

"Elise..." he steps towards me, reaching out as if to comfort me, his brows knitted together in concern. I jerk away from his touch.

"No. Don't fucking touch me. Just get out." The tears are freely flowing now, and I can't get a full breath. "GET OUT WILKES."

"I'm sorry. I wanted to tell you before things got serious."

"Before things got serious? Too fucking late. Get. Out." He turns to leave, and I don't register him walking away or the door closing behind him. I crumple to the floor, sobbing. I love him. We had talked about the future, and he took me to spend time with his family. What about Will? He's like a brother to me... but he was Kaylee's actual brother. Losing him on top of Liam and his whole family will truly destroy me. I break down as sobs rack my body, praying that this is a terrible dream, that the life I had let myself dream of again was just fine.

Who am I kidding? I just lost everyone in one fell swoop.

Chapter 15

5 months later...

   I wasn't expecting to see her so soon after getting back into town. But I suppose that's to be expected working for the same team. She's talking with some of the guys I have seen here, higher-up execs, I think, and her back is to me, but I know it's her. It's hard to erase the image of her glorious backside from my memory. It haunts me regularly. They're smiling at her, eating up every word she is saying. She has a personality that is hard to hate. She gives them a small wave and is turning towards me before I can process what's happening. My eyes land on her middle, and I stand there stunned, seeing the large bump of her stomach. A thousand thoughts fly through my head all at once. She's pregnant. Very visibly pregnant. And unless she was cheating, that kid is mine. I can't believe she wouldn't tell me this, regardless of us being together or not.

She sees me and takes a deep breath before walking the few feet towards me. I see red, when she is directly in front of me. She quickly says in a hushed tone, "Not here." Then turns towards her office away from earshot of anyone.

"What the fuck Elise?" I am seething by the time she closes the door behind us. "You're pregnant? And you weren't going to tell me?"

"What? I'm pregnant? I had no clue. This isn't a burrito," her voice is dripping with sarcasm. She walks calmly to her desk, and it makes me furious. It's as if she doesn't even realize what she's done.

"Why the hell didn't you say anything? I come back from the summer, and the first thing I see is you, VERY pregnant. It's not a new development with how big you are already."

"Oh, you're mad at me? You're mad at me for not telling you about a child you literally said you would never want." She sits at her desk, calmer than I can manage.

"That is not what I said," my voice failing me for a moment.

"Pretty damn close."

* * *

ELISE

I can't believe he's mad that I didn't say anything. I can feel my blood pressure rising, but I try to remain as calm as possible. I

CHAPTER 15

take a deep breath and attempt to calm my heart rate. "You said that you would never be able to love anyone like you did Kaylee and that you would never want children if they weren't with her. You broke me and took away what family I had made since coming here. So, I'm so sorry for not wanting to burden you with the idea that I was having your kid. But I was not going to let you make me feel bad for keeping what family I could have." My voice cracks as I try and fail to contain the emotions bubbling within me. I would blame the hormones, but I'm not sure I can at this point. "Not telling you was awful, but having you guilt me into getting rid of them... that wasn't happening."

Everything that happened after he broke me, shattered my heart, and left me to pick up the pieces as if I didn't lose everything flashes through my mind as if I'm reliving it all at once.

I can't believe that it's over. Things were going well, and then suddenly, it was done. I stayed in bed for a week straight, sick with grief from not just losing him but his family that welcomed me with open arms. I did as much work as I could from home, trying to avoid seeing him and completely losing it.

After about four days of crying and puking my guts out every time I ate, I called Sarah. She had been texting me daily to check in, knowing how much I had fallen for Liam.

"Sarah," I half-whispered through the tears when she answered the phone.

"Oh Elise, you're not ok, are you?"

"No, I'm not. And I think I need to see a doctor." I swallowed the wave of nausea that threatened me.

"What's wrong? Maybe you just have a bug."

"I'm nauseous, exhausted, and I'm late...."

"Oh," she gasps. "Ok, did you take a test?"

"I don't have one...."

"Ok, I'm going to bring one. You're going to pee on this stick, and then we go from there. Do you have an OBGYN yet? I know you've only been here less than a year, so if not..." I could hear her getting her things together. "TOM, WATCH THE KIDS. I'M LEAVING." I laughed at her shouting through the house to her husband, if only to avoid crying again.

"I don't yet."

"Ok, mine is really good at keeping things private, we will call them if it's positive," she answered firmly, her car starting in the background. I had started sobbing, terrified of what might happen when the relentless thoughts started popping into my head again.

"What if he wants me to get rid of it?"

"Whoa, we will cross that bridge when we get to it," she replies. "I'll be there in a few. Just breathe."

It was positive. I'm pregnant by a man who doesn't want to be with me or have kids. I went to the doctor to confirm everything, but I knew in my bones that I am. I knew as soon as I decided to talk to Sarah that morning. On the freeway a wave of nausea hit me. I pulled over and immediately lost all the breakfast I had managed to hold down earlier.

"Ma'am, are you ok?"

"Yeah," *I managed before continuing to throw up.* "Just pregnant." *I got control of my lurching stomach and saw a state trooper standing by the back of my car, watching the traffic passing by. He turned and looked me directly in the eyes. He'd be handsome if I wasn't in love with Liam and heartbroken about it.*

"Are you ok to drive?"

"Yeah, thank you."

CHAPTER 15

"Drive safe," he replied with a tip of his hat.

When I finally got home that day, after pregnancy tests, a doctor's appointment, and puking in front of an officer I had a semi-emergent session with my therapist. Thankfully she was available, the weight of the day crashed down on me and I needed someone there to talk to that knew me before Liam, even if It was someone that was paid to know me.

"So nothing was going on with your coworker?" Dr. J asked after I spilled everything in our session.

"Shut it, Doc, I don't need your sass," I half laugh, half sob.

"What I meant was that clearly, something was going on there," she clarified, compassion written across her face.

"Yeah, I fell in love...."

"I deserved to know, Elise! My mother deserves to know." His statements snap me back to our conversation.

"She does know." I try to remain as calm as I can, I want to yell at him. I want to make him feel awful for leaving us. Instead I keep my voice down and speak as clearly as I can. "She called shortly after I found out to apologize for you being a complete ass. I had to hurl, and she guessed," I comment, not willing to let him say that I kept this from his mother, in fact I know that she has a picture of the ultrasound on her fridge. "I'm kind of surprised she didn't say anything to you. And I tried telling you. You didn't answer your phone."

"You told my mom." The shock in his voice is more than I was prepared for. As if he truly thought I would keep this from her. like he thought I wouldn't let his parents be the grandparents they're meant to be.

"I was terrified and didn't have anyone to talk to aside from Sarah and that seemed weird because Tom. So when she called everything poured out."

"My mom knew and didn't tell me...," he whispered.

"I'm surprised by that."

"You didn't tell me. There are plenty of ways to get in touch with me." He runs his hands through his hair in frustration, a tell of his that I had once found endearing.

"You don't get to make me feel bad, Liam." I'm losing my resolve, my tone changing from calm and factual to irritated and upset. "You have very little say here- we aren't in a relationship anymore. If you don't want to be in our lives, that is fine by me. I am prepared to take care of them without you. If you choose to be there, then we will figure it out. But you do not get to talk to me like that. You don't get to make me feel bad about the choices I made when you had made it clear you wanted nothing to do with us." The sting of unshed tears burns my eyes, but I refuse to cry over him again.

"You keep saying them," he says, his face contorted in confusion.

"Yeah them, twins. Hence why I look like a house already at five months." I can't keep this up much longer, he made his decision months ago, and the only thing that will change is his level of involvement in their lives.

"What... do you know what...." His eyes search my face, and I can almost see the man I fell in love with. Almost.

"Boy and Girl." He sinks into the chair across from me. "I don't want anything from you."

"They're mine?"

"Of course they're yours! Do you seriously not know me? I know that I didn't know shit about you after months of screwing around- since that wasn't a relationship to you..." I trail off not wanting to say what I really want to say. What I shouted in the

CHAPTER 15

dark bedroom where we spent so much time together.

"I'm sorry you had five months to process this. I have had five minutes." He's quiet, obviously thinking about everything that I've now told him.

"Yes. They're yours. They're healthy too, not that you asked." I cross my arms over my chest in irritation.

"We'll get married."

"Ha! No way in hell I would marry you at this point. Had you asked 5 months ago I would have eloped with you in an instant... but not now." I understand that this is a lot to process, but he needs to know that we are still broken up, just like he wanted. I can't forgive him just like that and start over as if no time has passed.

"Why...?" he asks, stepping towards me.

"I don't trust you, Liam" I reply, trying to keep the distance between us.

"They need a family," he says firmly, like getting married will fix everything.

"I will not marry a man that doesn't love me." I look him dead in the eye, unwavering.

"I loved you, no matter what that meant to you. Whether you ever felt the same way or not, Elise. I loved you... I still do really, and I care about you regardless of how I hurt you."

"You can't just say that... you can't say that and have everything go back to how it was before. You can't take it back."

"I know," he whispers, "I know I hurt you."

"You did. So much." I place a hand on my stomach feeling the small movements of them both. Liam moves towards me, about to say something but he stops himself. The look of concentration that I have seen so many times on his face as if he is trying to collect his thoughts.

"Hey!" I hear from the door after a short knock. I see Will standing there with a take-out bag in one hand and what I'm hoping is a chocolate milkshake in the other. "Oh, hey... sorry I'm interrupting. I brought you some food."

"Thanks, Uncle Will," I reply with a smile still caressing my swollen abdomen.

"HE KNEW!" Liam yells and points angrily towards his friend.

"Yes, I knew. You would have too if you would have answered her calls," Will comments, matching his anger.

"You could have said something," he seethes as Will places the food on my desk. "We've talked and you didn't say a damn thing!"

"You should have talked to her! I told you that. I told you to call her back. You didn't!" Will points accusatory at Liam, punctuating each word.

"You should have told me what was going on!"

"Like it was my place? She tried to talk to you numerous times. I had to talk her into even trying to talk to you after the first two months. You failed her, and you failed the babies. Not me."

"Spencer..." He goes towards his friend and teammate as if he is about to punch him. I step between them, placing a hand on his chest, his heart racing beneath my palm.

"Liam! You need to stop."

"What the hell? How did you confide in him? They're mine!'

"LIAM!" He stops finally, the anger visible on his face. "I am no longer yours. I'm no one's but my own." His eyes focus on mine, and I see the anger shift to loss and sadness. "You need to take a walk and cool off. I do not need my blood pressure getting higher than it already is."

"We're not done here."

"Yes, we are. For now." I turn towards my friend and give him

CHAPTER 15

a reassuring nod adding, "Will, thank you for the food."

"Elise." Liam's voice shakes as if he doesn't know what to do.

"We can talk about this later. I need to eat, and you need to cool off. Please." I look him in the eyes, feeling a wave of emotion rising in me. Tears threatening to fall once again from my eyes. "We will talk later. I promise."

"Tonight?"

"Ok." He walks out of my office, and I let out the breath I didn't realize I had been holding onto. I knew this was coming. I couldn't hide from it forever. I didn't want to hide at first. I wanted him there with me, with us, but he wasn't. He chose to walk away from me and then not return my calls and texts. I probably came across as a clingy ex, so I stopped trying until Will Spencer showed up on my doorstep after the team was kicked out of the playoffs. I had kept my distance from the team, watching games at home and working as far from the team as possible, whenever I could.

But now, all that space I gave myself to heal from the heartbreak seems pointless. Liam knows finally, but I feel like I've been thrown back into that hurt all over again. I take a sip of the drink Will dropped off and run a hand over my belly, knowing that it will be better for them to have their dad, but I'm not sure if it will be better for me.

Chapter 16

ELISE

Liam knows. This wasn't how I wanted him to find out but he knows now. And it's a weight off my shoulders. It's not like I hadn't thought he would be here today; it was a possibility when I came into work today. However, I was hoping it wasn't in the hall in front of several other people. The day went by slower than I had hoped, but when it was finally time to head home, I was ready to face him again. Or as ready as I could be.

When I pull into my driveway, I see him sitting on the porch waiting for me, just like he had done many times before. I take a moment to take a deep calming breath before gathering

CHAPTER 16

my things and climbing out of my car. To my surprise, he meets me at the bottom of the stairs and takes my bag from my hands, letting me walk up the stairs easier than normal. I may only be five months along but carrying twins makes this more difficult than it would be for someone carrying only one child, and honestly, I am exhausted.

"Thank you," I almost whisper. I would be lying if I said I didn't miss him. I do so much. I miss having him around, but I can't let that sway me. He broke my heart and didn't bother trying to reach out after I tried several times to contact him, and after others told him that I needed to talk to him too. I walk with a new purpose to the kitchen, to create some distance between us, grabbing water from the fridge. But when I turn around and see him at the counter, I remember the night before he left. Let's be honest, he has left traces of himself everywhere in this place.

"Ok, you're here. I don't know what else there is to talk about right now. I'm pregnant, they're due at the end of October, but that could be very different. I don't expect anything from you, especially since you said that you could never love anyone like you did Kaylee, or that you don't see yourself having kids with anyone else."

"Elise…"

"No, I won't keep them from your family, but I don't expect anything from you. I've been doing this on my own so far, and I can and will continue to—"

"Let me speak, damn it!" He's never shouted like this. This is different. This has hurt more than I ever expected from him. "I'm sorry. I'm sorry I didn't return your calls. In hindsight, I should have. I know that I can't change that. But I want to… I need to be a dad to them. Even if we aren't together."

"Ok…" I sigh, placing my hands on the island counter. "I have an appointment coming up."

"I'll be there," he says instantly. "Anything you let me be a part of I will be there."

"This doesn't change things between us."

"I understand... I just... Elise, I loved you then, I still do. I'm sorry I ended things. I shouldn't have but I did...."

"That doesn't matter, Liam. It's done and over." I can't hear any excuse he gives me right now; nothing can change the fact that he left.

"It does matter, though. I hurt you."

"You did, that's true, but the only thing that matters now are the babies, and that's all I want between us. I can't..." I draw in a deep breath to try and calm my nerves and fight back the rising emotions. "I can't handle more than that."

"I understand."

"So, I have an appointment next Thursday. I can send you the information. Most of my appointments are worked around the practice schedule anyway, so it should work out for you."

"Just let me know, and I will be there."

I nod, not sure what else to say to him. There isn't much left to discuss. He broke my heart, didn't answer any calls or texts when I told him that we had something to discuss, and then when he finally came back to town, he flipped. All of this could have been avoided if he had just talked to me. I grab the bottle of tums off the counter and chew on a few as we sit there, not looking at each other.

"Are you ok?" He asks quietly. I look up at him, unsure of what to do.

"Physically? I feel weird as hell, like my body isn't my own anymore. You know how awful I am at taking care of myself. I have to think of them now more than myself. It's weird being

CHAPTER 16

slowed down so drastically because of it."

"Is that why Will brought you food?"

"Yeah, he came to see me after a couple of days— wanted to make sure that I was ok. He randomly came by after that too. Then one day, we were talking, and I had insane morning sickness."

"That makes sense... you always sucked at taking care of yourself."

"I can take care of myself just fine, thank you!" This makes me madder than I normally would be. How dare he come here after so long and insult my ability to take care of myself.

"I didn't mean it like that," he says quickly, standing in front of me. "I meant remembering to eat. Elise, I know you're capable, I do. I just know that you lose track of time when you're in the zone and forget to eat. You can't do that when you're pregnant."

"I don't need you to come here and lecture me."

"I know, I'm sorry." He lets out a big sigh running his hands through his hair. "I haven't had a lot of time to process all this, and I'd be lying if I said I wasn't terrified." His voice is softer than I would have ever expected from him.

"I'm terrified too. Regardless of how long I've had to process this."

"I understand..."

"I need to eat something, and I'm exhausted. I will send you a calendar invite to the appointments."

"There's so much to talk about still."

"I know, but I don't have the emotional energy right now to consider how you're feeling... I'm sorry I can't talk anymore today."

His shoulders visibly drop as he exhales, "Ok."

"Lunch? Thursday?" I offer, feeling a pang of guilt for pushing him out of my home. I need time to process the sudden change in things. I had just gotten used to the thought of having a baby, then twins. Adding in him and his emotions is a lot, especially when my hormones are raging.

"That would be great," he smiles, but it doesn't reach his eyes. He stands and walks to the front door, turning slightly to look my way before closing the door behind him. My breath catches, and I feel a sudden heartache that I thought I was over, a slice of how it felt months ago when he left me here.

I grab one of the meals that I had prepped in my fridge. I had decided two months ago that I would have to order meals from a local nutritionist that some players work with so that I can be sure to have healthy things on hand. It's what is best for my babies. I throw it in the oven and set a timer before heading upstairs to change into lounge wear. My office attire has changed a bit since I started showing, and it's more comfortable than previous outfits but even now I can't wait to get into something far more comfortable.

* * *

LIAM

I'm still in shock, even after talking to her about it and knowing she tried to tell me. In hindsight, I should have answered her calls or at least her text requesting to talk to me. It wasn't like she was bugging me about it; she simply said that she needed to talk to me. I ignored her nonetheless and now I'm regretting it.

CHAPTER 16

I spent the summer mostly alone, aside from a couple of weeks with my family on vacation, but that's about it. I wanted to be with her, but I couldn't. I wouldn't lose someone else that I loved. Yes, I can admit that I love her, but the last woman I felt this way about was ripped from my life and left me more broken than I had ever thought possible. I can't go through that again. I wouldn't survive.

No one, not even my mom, knows how close I had come when Kaylee and our baby died. It was a dark few months for me, and the only thing that brought me out of that was Will coming to the cabin and forcing me to get my shit together just in time for the new season. And then meeting her— she was what brought me out of it fully and why I can't fathom losing everything again.

So instead of wallowing, I pull out my phone and dial, getting an answer after a single ring. "Hello, Liam?"

"Mike, hey. Do you have a moment to talk?"

Chapter 17

It's the first family event for the preseason when the team all gets together, wives and kids come in, and enjoy a family fun day at the practice arena. A bit of fun before things get too busy and serious for the players. Today is the first time I am seeing a lot of the players since shortly after Liam and I broke up and after the season ended back in March- when they didn't make the playoffs, barely. Many of them had no idea I was pregnant; I barely knew I was pregnant then either, to be fair.

I take a deep breath hoping to calm some nerves that bubbled up as I watched a few of the families walking across the parking lot. Dads carrying kids and bags, and their wives holding the hands of others. It's a sight I wish can happen someday. Even with the rocky start to things, I want this for my kids. I want them to have a dad who spends as much time with them as possible and loves them. I hope that Liam can do that for them even if I don't think that I will ever have a chance at that love myself now.

"Elise, hey, are you ok?" I hear from the hall behind me. I turn to see Sarah, with a questioning look on her face, almost as if she knows Liam was here.

"Not really," I replied, letting out a breath, deciding to just get it over with. She's going to find out everything anyway. "He knows, Sarah."

"Who knows... Oh shit, he's here? Liam knows...How did that go?" Her shock changes to concern in a quick moment. We discussed what would happen when he came back to town for the season, but it didn't prepare me for the actual moment he did.

"Fan-fucking-tastic," sarcasm seeps from my voice, "luckily, we were in my office. But then Will was Will and brought me food because he knew I didn't want what I brought with me, and Liam freaked out again!"

"Yeah, it sounds like bad timing there. But hey, he knows now. One less thing to stress about!" Her positivity was both what I needed and something that I wasn't prepared for. I was prepared for Liam to be mad at me. I was prepared to be sad seeing him around the arena again. I was prepared to feel like a blimp. I was not prepared to have people be supportive and understanding.

"Sarah," I sigh, placing my hands on my swollen abdomen. "How the hell do I do this?"

"Oh, Elise. It's not ever easy, but Liam will be a good dad. I know it. And you will have Will and Tom and me. And oh my goodness, Liam's family will never put the babies down." She was right. His mom called me at least once a week already, and the babies weren't even here yet. I know that she will be as involved as I let her. And considering that I have no family of my own, I would never tell her no if she asks to see them or send gifts. I couldn't keep her away from them.

"I never really thought about this happening. I never had the time to think about being a mother...." I was too busy with high school and college sports and then taking care of my dying father to think about my future. I wasn't the girl growing up that needed to play house or dreamt of a giant princess-style wedding. Motherhood hadn't been on my radar, but here I was, pregnant.

"Hon, do you love him? Honestly. Take the baby factor out of it." Her question hit me hard. He had been someone that I never thought would even look at me as more than someone that he had to work with. I never expected him to want to spend time with me outside of this building. I sure never expected the flirting and more that happened so quickly.

"If I didn't have to think about them now, I would have ran into his arms as soon as possible. But it's not that simple... I love him, Sarah, but I love them more." Tears well in my eyes at the thought. I would choose them over my love for Liam, I have already, really. As much as I love him and want to be with him, to build a family with him, possibly even grow old with him, I can't. I have to choose my children over him. Maybe one day, he will be ok enough to discuss why he left so abruptly, but until then, I know that my heart will be guarded like Fort Knox. "You should head down. I'm sure everyone will be skating already. The kids are probably waiting for you."

"You're coming with me. This isn't just for players but the

CHAPTER 17

whole organization."

"Sarah, most of the players don't know that I'm expecting. And even more, have no idea who the father is."

"Do you think that Liam will announce to everyone that they're his?" She laughs, thinking it was an absurd thought, but I think he might do something to give it away. Or people would think Will was the father since he has been so attentive. "Do you think that?"

"Yeah, I'm nervous that he will be weird or Will... what if people think that Will is the dad. He's been so supportive, like the brother that I never had. Then Liam will cause a scene if he sees that. I'd rather avoid it all. I don't want to cause a scene at what is supposed to be a fun time for everyone. It's better if I just stay here and work."

"Nope, you can't hide away forever They're going to figure it out eventually."

"How the heck do I avoid all the potential drama?"

"There could be no drama at all. You're just creating it in your head right now. You and Liam had a serious conversation already, right?" I nod. "So if he causes anything, you can pull him aside and let him know this is why having him around is scary for you. That is what is keeping you from enjoying the experience. And that it's not good for the babies to have all the drama; you can't get your BP up too high. He should know that."

"True."

"Besides, you love skating."

"I do, and I've been avoiding it because I didn't want to run into him..."

"Stop avoiding things that you enjoy because he might be there."

"Ok fine," I cave. Sarah has a point. I have been avoiding

things because I didn't want to cause drama or make things awkward for him. "Let me grab my skates from my office, and I'll be down.

"Nope, I'm going with you, this way, you don't have to walk in alone."

"Thank you."

Sarah and I chat as we gather my bag and head down to the practice rink, where we have set up games and have food catered in for everyone to enjoy. It's great seeing all the familiar faces again, but I would be lying if I said I wasn't a ball of nerves when I saw Liam across the ice talking with Mike, one of the team doctors we have on retainer. He catches my eye and gives a faint smile before taking a card from him and gesturing for me to stay where I am.

"Looks like someone wants to see you after all," Sarah gives me a hug and strolls over to where Tom is tying the laces of their kids' skates.

My eyes track Liam as he makes his way to me. I am still nervous to see him, even after the conversations we have had in the past week. He is, or was, the person that I started seeing a future with. He was who I thought would always be there, and I have never felt the kind of loss I felt as when he left. He was still there. It was his choice to leave. He chose to leave me, unlike my parents.

I have to stop thinking of it this way, I know there is more to it than him just leaving, but I can't. Until he talks to me and explains why he just left me like that I can't let him back in. I can't let him get that close again.

"Hi." His tone is softer than I expected, and it catches me off guard, not used to hearing him talk like this. "How are you feeling?"

CHAPTER 17

"I'm feeling ok, just large."

"Good, that's good. Not the large part, but I mean, you're pregnant, so that's kind of normal, I think. You're not large though you look great. You aren't huge, but you look pregnant. You're beautiful...."

"You can stop already." I smile at his bumbling despite myself.

"I'm glad you're here."

"Sarah talked me into it."

"I will have to remember to thank her." He looks as if he wants to pull me into his arms, and a part of me wants him to. I miss being close to him and the protective warmth of his arms around me, but I would break down if he touched me right now. "Elise, I..."

"Please don't apologize right now. I need way more than an apology, and if you can't give me that, then please wait until you can. I just want to enjoy today without thinking more about where we could have been...."

"Ok."

"Ok." I take a seat on the bench, placing my bag beside me, and I brace myself for the struggle that will be putting on the skates that I haven't worn since Christmas at his parents' house.

"Are you planning on skating?" He points to the pair of skates that sit on the bench next to me.

"If I can lace these up, yes. I've been wearing slip-on shoes for weeks now, so I'm not sure I can."

"I'll help." Liam kneels before me and gently slides off the ankle boots I had on with my leggings and an oversized sweater. One by one, he places the skates on my feet and methodically laces them up, asking softly if they felt all right and weren't too tight on my already swelling feet. I couldn't form words as he helped me stand after he put his skates on. It was like the last time we skated together while visiting his family for the holidays. Except for this time, we were around people that knew too much of what happened in his past, and most knew nothing about our relationship.

Liam takes my hand and leads me to the ice as if he is afraid to let me go. As if he's worried I would run away. I'll admit skating is different when pregnant. My center of gravity is off-balance, and I'm glad to have him there as I get used to being on the ice like this. We take a few laps around in comfortable silence like neither of us wants to burst the bubble and acknowledge the faces that watched us.

"Do you want to drive separately to the appointment tomorrow? I can pick you up, if you want to go together instead."

"Uh, that's fine yeah. I'll meet you there." I'm not sure what to say after that. I wanted him there for every appointment. I had wanted him there to hold my hair back as I puked the whole first trimester. There were so many times that I had wanted him there. But he wasn't.

"I'll be here," he said, sliding a hand from the small of my back. The warmth of his hand left too soon, and I needed space. I made my way to the opening and stepped off the ice; he followed. I knew he would. "Are you ok?"

"Yeah," I answered, trying to make sure that I sounded like I was and that I wasn't hurting and missing him. I turn towards him and smile, "Just thirsty." I walk to the bench and attempt to take my skates off, struggling already to unlace them. Liam doesn't hesitate to take them off for me. The longer that I am near him again, the more I want this to all be over, the more I want it to be like before.

"There." He slips my boots back on my feet and holds out a hand to help me up. Taking it, I avoid eye contact, instantly regretting looking around when I see people watching us, wives and girlfriends, and back-office staff. "Elise, do you want to go somewhere else?"

"Yes." This was too much, there are too many people around. It's too much to be under their scrutiny and to wonder what he was thinking. I make my way away from the crowd, grabbing a bottle of water from the table as I pass.

I can feel him behind me, keeping a distance but walking close by as if waiting for me to let him be close again. We needed an actual talk, to at least feel like friends again would be nice to have. I miss being around him too much to keep pushing him away. Our kids need us to have a decent relationship. I want us to have a relationship, I want things to be ok again, but I also have to keep my walls up a bit. I can't let my feelings get in the way of my kids having their father.

"I need food, real food. Can we do that instead of just finding a place to talk?" I ask him, meeting his eyes fully.

"Of course we can, Frank's?"

"Mmmm, yes." A small smile spread across his face, and even though we can't be together anymore it makes me happy to see after all he's been through.

Chapter 18

ELISE

I couldn't admit that I'd been here at least once a week since my cravings kicked in. Between the burgers and fried pickles, I probably knew the staff here better than Liam ever could. And I wasn't looking forward to whatever conversations we would end up having, but I was looking forward to those fried pickles. I made sure to take my time pretending to peruse the menus still, trying to avoid awkwardness as long as possible.

Liam opened and closed his mouth several times before the waitress came to take our orders, cutting him off. He didn't try right away after that, so we sat there looking around the

CHAPTER 18

restaurant we both were too familiar with to notice anything new. Honestly, I didn't know what else we could talk about without us either yelling at each other or me crying. Because of hormones. I will always blame the baby growing hormones no matter how this goes.

"Looks like you're stuck with me for lunch twice within a week." His tone is forced. He's trying to joke but failing. He's more nervous than I think I have ever seen him.

"I wouldn't say stuck. There's still time to get mine to go." I can't help but smirk, knowing that I would never leave him here, just like nothing.

"Please don't."

"Liam," I sigh, trying my best not to give him hope that things can just go back.

"I know, Elise... I just hope you'll forgive me someday."

"Liam, it's not going to be that easy, I want you to be in their lives, but I can't let you back into mine that easy." The waitress returns to the table with our meals, and we eat in a heavy silence.

Leaving the restaurant a short time later, I feel like I can't get a full breath. The air is too heavy with things unsaid. He had a chance to be upset, to get things off his chest, but I haven't. And if I say it now, it won't be pretty. I'm still working through all my anger with him with Dr. J.

"Elise, please..." He reaches for me, grabbing hold of my upper arm and pulling me closer to him. I fight looking at him. I want him to hold me and tell me that everything is going to be ok, but it's not ok. It won't be ok.

A wave of anger washes over me, and I hit his chest, punctuating each statement with a thud as I speak, "You broke me, Liam. You're the one that left. You're the one that walked away, we had the hottest sex of my life, and the next day you come in and break up with me out of the blue. You shattered my heart and the life that I had started picturing."

"I know." His voice is more tender than possible, making me feel awful for voicing what I was feeling. What I have been feeling for months now. It's just that with him here in front of me, it's the first real-time I've been able to tell him how I feel.

"I'm not saying this to make you feel bad. I just can't let you close again. I can't."

"Elise, I know. I'm sorry. I can't change what I did."

"I want us to get along, but this can't be like it was before." I can't stop the tears rolling down my face, damn baby-making hormones. "Tomorrow, you can be there for them."

"I screwed everything up."

"Yeah, the question is why Liam... and you don't have to answer for me. You do have to answer for yourself."

"I am sorry, truly. I wish I could change what happened."

"Don't tell me that." I take a deep breath, trying to hold in the waterfall of tears that will fall if I let them. I wipe my face and take a step back, distancing myself from him a bit more, "I have to go. I have work to do. I sent you the address to the doctor's office. I'll see you there at three pm."

"OK," he sighs in defeat, actual defeat. I can tell I hurt him, but I can't let that stop me from leaving. I need to walk away and keep him at a distance if I am going to survive this; if I am going to make sure our children survive this. I get into my car and pull out of the parking lot. He is still standing there watching as I drive away from him.

I don't have time to wallow in what just happened, because my phone rings. "Sarah?"

"Elise, where did you go? Is Liam with you?"

"We got something to eat, it was awkward and emotional, and

CHAPTER 18

I drove away leaving him in the parking lot because if I stayed a moment longer, I would cave and let him back into my life as if he didn't break my heart. He has so much that he needs to work through, even if he doesn't know it yet. I can't take care of myself and these babies if I am worried about him too. I can't, I want to, but I can't."

"Oh, hon."

"It's ok."

"Where are you headed now?"

"Home, I need a nap and to mentally decompress."

"Go, we can talk later."

"Thanks, Sarah. I'll call you later on."

* * *

LIAM

"I've been having these dreams since after my then-fiancée was killed in an accident." I can't believe I'm telling someone about this. It feels weird, especially since the only person I've ever told about this was Elise.

"Tell me about the dream."

"I can't get there in time, I didn't get there then, and I can't get there in time in the dream either." I can see it all right now. I've dreamt it enough that it's seared into my brain.

Lights flash, red, blue, red, blue. I'm running trying to find her, trying to get to her in time. My feet pound against the linoleum floor. They are all I can hear along with the sirens and shouting of doctors. The halls stretch, and no matter how fast I run I can't get any closer.

I can't get to her, I can't do anything to help her, to save her. I need to be with her. My heart is racing, and the hall starts to disappear, everything is turning black, and I know I can't save her. I can't save them.

"So, for a year and a half, give or take, you've had this same dream over and over?"

"Almost every night, but it has shifted slightly."

* * *

The next morning, I can't seem to get out of bed. I'm not sure if my body is exhausted from the daily practices or that I spilled my guts to an almost stranger. Nonetheless, I feel exhausted. I choose to skip today's optional workout, I know I shouldn't, being captain and all, but I need to prepare myself for this afternoon so I can be that close to Elise and not hold her close enough to chase away my demons. I can't though, she doesn't want that, and it's my fault.

I take one of the prepared meals from my fridge, something that I do during the preseason mostly to get into game shape, and throw this one into the microwave to heat, checking my phone as it heats up. I can't help but smile when I see her face on my phone's background. I screwed it up big time with her; I know I did. I check how far the doctor's office is from here and mentally set my schedule for the day, noting when I should leave. The timer on my breakfast goes off, and I take a seat at the kitchen island to eat, continuing to look at her face on my phone.

I can only think about one way to show her that I will be there

CHAPTER 18

for them, and it's weird as hell for me to do. I don't talk about my mental health; it's not something men are ever told is ok to do. I have to, though, I have to for my family. I spend the day relaxing after taking a run through the park near my house, a park that I could see the kids playing in a couple of years. I've showered and dressed to head out to the appointment, leaving enough time to grab Elise a double chocolate milkshake for after the appointment.

I sit in my car for a few minutes before I see her pull in, parking a couple of spaces away from me. Standing at the end of my car, I wait for her to reach me before falling in step beside her.

"Hi Elise, how are you feeling?" The receptionist asks her as we cross the lobby.

"I'm good, Trish, thank you. How are you today?"

"I'm good, thank you, hon. They'll be up to get you soon." I'm taken aback by the familiarity that she has with the office staff.

"What?" she asks, having read the confusion on my face. "When you're carrying multiples there are a lot more appointments. You get to know the staff really well."

"That makes sense. How often have you been coming then?"

"Now it's every two weeks."

"Elise, we're ready for you." We stand and walk towards the waiting nurse, "Oh, Dad was able to make it this time. That's great."

Elise places a hand on my arm for a moment as I catch my bearings, and we make our way to the exam room. The nurse runs through the standard vitals before handing Elise a blanket to draw over her legs for measurements. I sit quietly in the corner, watching everything, remembering the few appointments that Kaylee had that I was able to make because we were in the middle of the season. Elise's belly is much bigger than Kay's ever got already, and I know it's because we're having twins, but it's hard not to think of the differences at this stage. Kaylee was 5 five months along around Thanksgiving, not showing this much. The doctor said she was carrying on the smaller side then.

"Alright, Dr. Frank will be in soon, and then we will get that scan done."

"Thanks, Jenn." I hear her say, as the nurse walks out of the room. "You ok over there?"

"Yeah," I smile at her.

"Sarah set me up with her doctor. They all sign NDA's, so you don't have to worry about the press getting information from anyone here."

"I wasn't worried about that."

"You're worried about something, though. I know you well enough to know that."

"It's just different," I admit.

"Gotcha." She holds a hand out to me. "Help me sit up, please. This is uncomfortable." I stand and help her up slowly so she can adjust how she's sitting. "Thanks."

"Of course." I rest my hand on her stomach for a moment and feel a small movement under my hand.

"They've started monitoring the babies' sizes a bit early, just because multiples are rarely full-term and other complications that could happen. Could, not will."

"Could happen...."

"Don't freak out. It won't happen." She says quickly as we hear a knock on the door, and the doctor comes in.

The rest of the exam is quick, and before I know it, we are walking out of the building. I'm still focused on what we saw on the screen during the ultrasound. The two hearts beating, tiny

CHAPTER 18

hands and feet, and little faces. I saw the last ultrasound pictures. Elise sent them to me after I found out she was pregnant but seeing them moving and hearing both heartbeats is different. I can't fight an overwhelming feeling that washes over me, an urge to protect and provide for all three of them. Though I know that Elise wouldn't let me do more than necessary.

"I'm starving," she says as we walk down the hall towards the exit.

"I grabbed you a milkshake... it's probably melted. I didn't think that through."

"How about we get a fresh one and fries? Fries sound divine." She smiles, letting me off the hook for the melted gesture.

"You want to go to Frank's again?" I ask, unsure how often someone can eat there. It's good but not that good.

"Yes, I do." She looks at me directly in the eye as if challenging me. "You have no idea how I would love something else, but your children refuse to let me eat somewhere else without hurling, still. Maybe I'll be lucky in the third trimester, and I'll be able to stomach something else."

"Frank's it's."

Chapter 19

He's been attentive and kind. So kind. He's been to every appointment he can make it to and even started sending meals to my office, but letting him in again would destroy me. So I can't, I can't be more to him than the mother of his children. I can't let him in and have it lead to being less than the best mother I can be. It's just so difficult to keep him at arm's length when I still love him and want nothing more than to have him here for us.

Today is another appointment that he isn't able to make since they have one of their last preseason games in a few hours and needs to get ready. I had to convince him he didn't need to be there, that it was just another appointment of the same thing,

CHAPTER 19

which it was. He made me promise to tell him if anything was going on that he needed to know.

"Your blood pressure is slightly elevated. Are you feeling ok?"

"Yeah, I feel fine. It's been a little stressful with the regular season about to start, but it typically eases up then."

"We just need to keep an eye on it. Get a cuff and check it a few times a day. Keep a log for me. Hopefully, it's just a today thing, but if it's consistent, we need to do a few tests."

"Uh, yeah, will do...."

"If you have other symptoms, you need to give us a call."

"Should I be worried? You're making this sound like it could be bad."

"It could be nothing, but if your BP doesn't level out, you could develop preeclampsia. Which could get bad. We're going to do our best to avoid that. We want two healthy babies, after all."

Leaving the appointment, I am stressed, more than I had hoped to be, but I made my way back to the office to tie up a few loose ends for the regular-season opener and make sure the team that we put together over the past year has everything in order for the next few months- through the end of my pregnancy and my planned maternity leave. While I will have the capabilities to work from home, it won't be easy to coordinate some of the events from home, hence the extra hands.

* * *

Now that the regular season has started, I've been able to see most of the home games, only missing two so far out of sheer exhaustion. Tonight is our first big rivalry game, so I stayed at the office rather than driving back and forth today, not wanting to miss it. After changing into my game-time clothes, I settle a few last-minute things before I plan on meeting Sarah in the box to watch the game and to eat the poutine that I have been craving every day since we were back playing games.

"Elise," I hear from the doorway.

"Hey Will! Shouldn't you be getting ready?" I see my pseudo-big brother standing at the door.

"Just wanted to see how you're doing today. We haven't talked in a couple of days."

"Regular season is busy. you know that," I reply, smiling at him. "I like this suit, by the way; the plaid is classic." I walk towards him with my bag over my shoulder, and we walk towards the locker room where I will meet Sarah.

"Thanks," he smiles, "Kaylee said that it was too loud, but I like it."

"Well, not to talk shit about your sister, but she was wrong."

"You're doing ok, though?" he asks, taking a look in my direction as we walk. I can tell that he's a bit upset about the strain on his friendship. "Liam isn't talking to me right now...."

"Still? What a dick. I'm going to kick his ass." I half joke, I will give him a stern talking to at least.

"Maybe after the game, ok?" Will replies with a wink.

"Sure thing, I'll wait." Will always makes me laugh; Kaylee was lucky to have him. I'm lucky to have him. If I had to choose anyone to be my brother, it would be him. "I'm feeling ok, same as before, really. I have to take my blood pressure every day, and it's annoying, but I'm feeling ok. Minus the general swollen feeling of pregnancy."

"It still stands; if you need anything, Elise..."

"I know, Will." I can't help the tears welling in my eyes. "Now

CHAPTER 19

stop it. You can't be all sweet or you'll make me cry for no reason."

"Sorry."

"Ok, quit stalling. You have a game to prepare for." I give him a hug, wanting so bad for things to be different. I wish that things between Liam and I hadn't changed things with them. "I'll see you after the game, loser."

"You wound me." he feigns hurt, placing a hand over his chest.

Will heads into the locker room, and I make my way to where Sarah waits for me to walk with her to the box we have reserved. I haven't seen Liam since yesterday, but we texted, it was him mostly checking on me, but it was sweet. He is making an effort, one that I appreciate. Sarah and I chat about everything and grab some food before settling into our seats. The game starts, and the energy in the arena is amazing; I can imagine how it would feel to be on the ice with them. When I played, there was a buzz that can't be replicated anywhere else. I just wish that I could have felt it on a large scale like this. The anthems are sung, and the Captains shake hands before the first face-off, and the game is underway.

It's the beginning of the second period when I start to feel a stabbing feeling in my temple. I could ignore it at first, but that quickly changes to something that I can't brush off any longer.

"Elise, are you doing ok?" Sarah places her hand on my knee, turning fully in the box seat to face me.

"My head is throbbing," I admit, a veil of worry settling in over me.

"Do you have your blood pressure cuff?" She's already digging through my bag before I even start to answer. I simply nod as I try to breathe through the sharp, stabbing pain. Sarah pulls out the cuff, and I feel it squeezing my arm before it beeps a warning that the numbers are higher than they should be.

"Ok, that is way too high. We need to call your doctor." Before I process what's happening, she takes my phone and starts dialing for me. I don't protest as we get a nurse on the emergency line, and I'm immediately directed to the ER.

"Sarah, we have to let Liam know. He will freak out if something happens...," I stop walking for a moment, turning towards her, knowing that I look and sound scared of what could happen.

"Hey. Nothing's going to happen. We just need to go to make sure everything is ok. I'll let him know." She practically forces me into a wheelchair and all but runs through the arena to the team parking lot.

"You can slow down, damn Sarah," I half-joke as we walk towards the car, surprised that she didn't push me all the way to the car. "What about my car?"

"Don't worry about your car. We can figure that out later. How are you feeling?"

"Head still hurts, not feeling great," I reply, getting into her small SUV. I'm trying not to freak out, but I'm terrified. There is so much that can go wrong right now, so much that I can't anticipate or control. Still, I'm terrified for the babies, myself, and Liam.

"I sent Tom, Will, and Liam a text about where we're going. Between the three of them, Liam will know." She puts her phone in the cup holder and drives out of the parking lot towards the hospital.

* * *

CHAPTER 19

LIAM

I don't typically check my phone during a game, but since Elise has had some high blood pressure lately, I want to make sure if she needs me, I'm there for her. And today, I'm glad I have my phone on. I noticed the screen light up as I walked into the locker room between the second and third.

From Sarah: I"m taking Elise to Memorial, her doctor is on call there.

That's all that was there. I scroll hoping for more. There was no explanation, nothing to let me know what was going on beyond that they were going to the hospital, and it was like a lead balloon settled in my stomach. I look around and lock eyes with Will, who is also holding his phone in his hands. He nods, turning toward where the coach is talking. I change quickly from my uniform to the only thing aside from my suit. I leave my locker in a complete mess, but I have to get there. I can't let the same thing happen again.

I can't lose everything again.

Chapter 20

LIAM

I probably ran a few lights getting to the hospital, but I don't care. 'She's fine.' I keep telling myself. I repeat it over and over again, trying to calm myself. Trying to breathe through the fear that has dug its nails into me all over again. I park the car and run into the hospital, not stopping until I get to the nurses' station to ask where she was. Taking every turn at high speed to the maternity ward. It's fine if she's there, right? That means she's ok.

I was out of breath when I saw Sarah walking down the hall, her phone to her ear. "Liam!" She shouts when she sees me.

CHAPTER 20

"Is she ok? Is Elise ok?"

"Yeah, she's ok. The doctor is there with her now. I was just leaving you a voicemail. She's ok. That's as much as I know right now, but like I said, the doctor is in there now. So I'm sure you'll know more soon."

"I'm freaking out, Sarah." I sit in the empty chair across the hall from the room Elise is in. I rest my head in my hands, taking a moment to settle the fear pumping through me. My legs shake as I take a big breath.

"Hey, everything is going to be ok. She is here, they have her all hooked up, and they're monitoring the babies," Sarah reassures me as she rubs my back in a way that only moms can. "Now. Why don't you take a few breaths, calm down a bit, and then you can go in there." I sit there, fighting off flashbacks of losing Kaylee. Fighting off the nightmare of losing her, of losing Elise. I know that she is ok. She is in a normal room in the maternity wing. Not the ER, or in surgery, or anything else beyond a regular room. She is safe. They are all safe. "Liam, you need to stop beating yourself up for Kaylee. Elise is strong and healthy, and everyone will be ok."

I nod and sit up in the chair, having to wipe my face before composing myself. "I can't lose her too, Sarah," I admit.

"You're not going to. Unless you keep being a moron. You've been a huge dick to several people."

"I'm trying." I give her a smile, straightening up in the chair.

"Ok, well, get in there. I'll talk with Will and Tom after the game to see about getting her car home. Which means you'll have to give her a ride home."

I don't pay attention after that; I just walk towards the door, trying not to lose my cool again, but then I see her in the hospital bed. My heart crashes when I see her ok for myself, and suddenly

I'm glad Sarah made me calm down before coming in here.

"You weren't supposed to leave the game," she says, watching as I walk to her side. I take her hand, holding it in mine for a bit before giving it a squeeze.

"You weren't supposed to be here either, and yet...," I look at Dr. Frank, and wait for him to fill us in on what's happening.

"I was just telling Elise that right now her numbers are a bit high. We're going to give some IV meds and keep the fetal monitor on. Probably will mean an overnight stay, at least. We'll reevaluate if things change. Until then, get comfortable."

"Thank you, doctor," Elise answers for us. Watching the doctor leave the room, I run my hands through my hair realizing that everything was ok, for the most part.

"You're ok," I sigh, sitting at the foot of her bed.

"Liam, I'm ok. They're being cautious, which is good. I feel better now," she grabs my hand. "I'm sorry this was probably scarier for you than things would usually be,"

"I don't think I took a breath the entire way here. Elise, I was terrified."

"I didn't want you to worry, but you needed to know what was happening. Everything went so fast, and you were playing. I didn't want you to worry... I didn't want things to feel like they were with Kaylee...." She speaks so fast that I can't really understand everything she's saying.

"It's not... I didn't. I have to tell you something."

"Ok?"

"You know, forever ago, when I told you about the nightmare I had about her." She nods. "That dream changed a while ago. You have been the person I've been scared to lose for months now. It changed to being you instead. You don't have to say anything, but I was terrified all over again to lose everything.

Even if we are just friends at this point... if that."

Elise's eyes water, and she clears her throat before turning on the room's TV. "Well then, we should probably see how well they're doing without you." I smile and settle into the chair next to her so I can watch the rest of the third with her.

Nurses come in and out periodically, placing an IV of fluids and giving her the medications that her doctor ordered. Sarah comes in and says goodbye, after grabbing the random blanket and pillow she keeps in the car for her kids for me. I decided to stay overnight, knowing that if I went home, I wouldn't sleep at all. Here I would get some sleep even if it was on the very uncomfortable pull-out that they have for the dads.

Elise and I don't talk very much. She rests as much as she can, and begs the nurses to let me get her something to eat, having left her poutine in the box before they rushed here from the game. I called my mom, letting her know what was happening, and she immediately said she would leave in the morning and go to my place, saying she wanted to be here in case Elise or I needed anything.

All I could think was, Elise is safe, our babies are safe.

* * *

ELISE

Liam stays the whole night with me. I know that it can't be comfortable for him, with his feet hanging over the edge, and his neck at a weird angle. I know he is going to be sore in the morning, but it's nice to not be here alone for the night. The nurses fawn over his comfort. One just flat-out flirted with him until I stared her down as she took my vitals. Yes, I made sure she knew that he was mine, even though he wasn't, giving her a dirty look when she finally made eye contact with me.

I get very little sleep, the bed is not comfortable and they come in and check on me so often it feels like I am never going to sleep. Morning comes too fast, and since Liam is awake too, it's difficult to rest, wondering what would change after today. We're expecting the doctor to come in and give an update on what our next step should be. I have no clue what to expect, and I refuse to google anything, knowing that I would just feel worse than I already do.

When Dr. Frank finally comes in after another round of tests, I am beyond ready to get home and shower the feeling of the rough gown and sheets.

"Alright, so good news is your numbers are looking better."

"Good news, right?" Liam asks from the chair beside me.

"Well, here's the thing, I'm strongly suggesting bed rest for the remainder of your pregnancy, Elise."

"Bed rest? Really, doc?" I can't possibly stay on bed rest for that long. I have so much that needs to be done. I had planned for when they were here but not this early.

"Yes, if you want to get to term and not be in the hospital on bed rest, you need to be at home. Those are the options."

"They're shit options." I cross my arms over my chest like a child throwing a tantrum.

"But home would be better, Elise." Liam finally weighs in.

"Obviously," I say begrudgingly. "Fine, bed rest at home. But like, how much rest are we talking about? I'm not very good at doing nothing."

We discuss the appointment schedule we will follow going

CHAPTER 20

forward and what bed rest truly means for me. It's going to be tough, but I'm sure I can make it work. I have to make it work. There is no other option if I don't want to spend the next two months in the hospital. I start making plans for getting my laptop and other things I need from the office to work remotely and look into getting a few things delivered so that I can maintain my sanity.

"You can drive me home, right? I also need to figure out how to get my car."

"Don't worry about your car, Will and Tom made sure it got to your place. And I will make sure that you get to your place."

"Thanks," I smile, pulling on my clothes from the game, which I'm thankful I had only had on for a couple of hours.

"Elise, I think I should stay with you. I'll stay in your guest room." I start to protest but stop when I see his face, "I can't go home. I can't be at home worrying about if you are ok, waiting for a call that you need something, or worse, something happened to you. I will stay in the guest room. I will make sure everything is taken care of. You can't push me away. Please don't. I need to be there."

"Ok." The idea of his being there is comforting, honestly. I had been trying to push aside the fear that everything wouldn't be fine next time. Yeah, he'll have to go to practices and games, but for the most part, he will be close in case I need him. I won't ask for help, but since he is offering.

"I'll take you home, then I should head to practice. I need to explain a few things to coach, make sure they aren't pissed that I left."

"Sorry," I frown, perched on the edge of the hospital bed, waiting for the discharge papers. "You can blame me. It's my fault after all."

"Elise," he kneels in front of me, resting his hands on my thighs. "I would leave the championship game, tied, with seconds left in the third if you needed me to."

I'm saved from having to respond by the nurse coming in with a folder she hands to Liam and a wheelchair she makes me sit in. Liam kisses my forehead before making his way out of the room to pull his car around for me, taking my bag with him.

"You two are just so sweet." The middle-aged nurse comments with a sweet smile on her face. I smile and let her push me through the hospital to Liam. It's weird having people assume that we are together again, but I can't say that it wouldn't be a dream to go back to being together. It would be. If it hadn't hurt so bad when he left, then maybe.

We get to my place, and he helps me get in and settled before he heads to the arena. I have a drink and snacks within reach because he wouldn't leave until I did. I pull out my phone and called Jenna, my second in command, to fill her in and see if she can run my things down to Liam so he could bring them home for me to work. I let her know that I would help her behind the scenes, but I was relying on her to take the lead. I was nervous to let go of everything, but I knew that all the training I put into getting her ready would pay off. She was ready to take a bigger role in the team.

I call Sarah to let her know what's happening, too, filling her in on Liam forcing himself into my home, but instead of being annoyed by it, I was glad to have him close. She was already making plans to watch the games with me at home rather than watch with the random WAG's. Liam's mom sent me a text letting me know that she was here too if I needed anything, and while it made me miss having a parent of my own, I was happy to have her there for us all too. And just like that, I had nothing

CHAPTER 20

to do and too much time on my hands. It was just the first day. I'm not entirely sure how I'm going to survive these next few weeks.

* * *

I have to do something to pass the time, so I shop. I spend way more than I should have, but two babies mean twice as many things to buy... or at least look at. I have to compare different cribs, bassinets, a rocking chair, bottles, etc. It gets overwhelming real fast, though. I think about clothes shopping, and that doesn't happen either because I'm now the size of a single-family home- quickly expanding into a duplex, and there's no way I would be able to get a size that would work right now.

This is why I am blasting late 90s early 2000s pop ballads by my favorite women while I clean the guest room for Liam to stay, singing along with them at the top of my lungs. How can I resist singing 'All coming back to me'? I can't. I'm not a monster. This is how I don't notice Liam getting here and walking into the bathroom I am currently cleaning.

"What are you doing?" He yells over the music. I see an angry look on his face.

"Cleaning..." I hold my hands out in a 'what does it look like' gesture. Thinking that it should be very obvious with the cleaning supplies and rubber gloves.

"Elise! You're supposed to be resting. This is not resting!"

"Ok. Calm down. Damn."

"NO, I won't."

"I need to do something! Do you not get that? I need to do something, or I will lose my damn mind!"

"REST! That's what you need to be doing." He runs his hand over his face, something he does only when he is extremely frustrated and exhausted. "Dammit. I just need you to not."

"So you're going to clean my house? What about cooking? Or laundry? Anything else you think I shouldn't be doing?"

"Elise..."

"Liam."

"I need you to rest and not fight me on it. I can't worry about you when I'm not here. I can't handle it."

"What do you mean you can't handle it?"

"If something happens... to you."

"Fine." I pull off my cleaning gloves and place them on the partially cleaned countertop and walk past him and head back to the living room. I see that he brought a large duffle and a few suits over as I go, and a part of me feels good to have him here again, even if it's temporary. A larger part of me is pissed he is acting like I can't take care of myself.

Thirty minutes later he comes back down to grab his things and I can barely look at him. I know he is right, but I can't handle the look on his face that he would break again if something happened to me. That's too much pressure.

"I was going to order some dinner. Do you want anything in particular?"

"Chicken parm."

"OK."

"Thanks." I keep things short, not really ready to argue with him again, especially over something ridiculous like food.

"I'm sorry I yelled at you."

CHAPTER 20

"It's fine." I shake my head, trying to dismiss the subject altogether.

"It's not. I'm sorry. I shouldn't have yelled at you. I was still keyed up from being chewed out by Coach."

"What? He yelled at you for leaving?"

"Mostly because I didn't talk to him. Will told him I was leaving. Then they had to adjust the whole line, and yeah."

"I will have some choice words for that man! What the hell! What if there was an emergency with his family?" I want to call him up right now and give him a piece of my mind. How heartless can that man be?

"Calm down, killer." He smiles, taking a seat in the chair close to me. "He understood when I explained what happened. Though I'm not sure he would be able to handle your feistiness. I barely can."

"We're going to have to say something. Officially that is. Luckily it won't be big news really, since it's early in the season, and like every other sport is going on right now. The World Series will outweigh anything else for a little bit. Maybe a blip on the NHL network." I go into full PR mode, trying to get ahead of the story, our story that people might twist into something that it isn't. "We just have to decide what to say.Together."

"How soon?"

"Preferably in the next few weeks. In case they decide to arrive early," I reply, rubbing my stomach as I referred to our twins. They start moving around like they always do when Liam is talking in his calm and collected voice. "Come here," I say, grabbing his hand and placing it on where our children grow. "Keep talking. They like it."

Liam does just that, kneeling in front of me, both hands on my stomach, talking to me and the babies. I can almost pretend there was never a time when we weren't together, where we weren't on the right track. For just a little while, I'm going to pretend.

Chapter 21

LIAM

My mom got in about a week ago, and between her and Sarah, I wasn't as terrified that something would happen when I was at games or practices. I don't like the idea of away games, but they can't adjust the schedule so I can be close by. I missed being around Elise, I know that this isn't the same as it would have been before, but it's nice being close to her again. I'm not going to take this for granted. I'm going to enjoy being close to her while I can.

As I pull into the driveway after morning practice I see her attempting to bring in several grocery bags. She's been getting groceries delivered to the house for as long as I've known her, but this seems like way more than usual. I park and quickly jog to the porch. She straightens and smiles at me like she knows she was caught. A smile I've been getting a lot whenever I catch her doing things that she shouldn't.

"I, umm, didn't know when you would be back... didn't want to leave cheese in the hot sun..." she explains, trying to justify her lifting the heavy grocery bags. She looks like a teenager that was caught sneaking out of the house. "But now you're here. I would like nachos."

"Nachos?" I can't fight the laugh that her expression brings out of me. "What kind of nachos? Are the ingredients in here?" I grab the grocery bags, carry everything into the house, and set them on the kitchen counter.

"Mmmm, yes," she smiles, and I'm staring. My mouth hangs open thinking about the night I had her writhing on this counter, begging me to make her... I clear my throat and go back to unpacking the groceries, separating the obvious nacho ingredients. "Chicken fajita nachos," her voice is shy and quiet, and I can't help but hope that she is thinking about that night, too, "like we had before. I can make them, though. If you want some, we have plenty of stuff."

"Sounds good." She's babbling; it's not too often I catch her off guard like this. She's rarely shy, but this gives me hope. Hope that she might be willing to let me into her life and not just our children's. She turns quickly and grabs a baking sheet from the cabinet, starting to put together the nachos.

"I'll be back down in a bit then." It takes all I can not to kiss her on the top of her head and just go up to my room. It's getting harder the more I am around her not to revert to how it was before, but I know she doesn't want that. I won't do anything

CHAPTER 21

she doesn't want me to, no matter how much it hurts me.

* * *

ELISE

I get the nachos in the oven and soon I will be elbow deep in cheesy goodness. I know it's not the healthiest of things to be eating but the babies and I don't want anything else. I also desperately wanted Liam to kiss me earlier, but thankfully he left the room and my damn hormones calmed down after I wasn't smelling him anymore. That man always smelled so good, it hasn't changed, and I doubt that it ever will. Having him here is rough, I want him close but it's too much too soon at the same time. It's like I'm warring with myself every single day.

Liam hasn't come back down yet and food will be ready soon, so I head upstairs to let him know. The guest room door is wide open, but I can hear him in what will be the nursery. "Hey Liam," I announce, seeing him on the floor putting together one of the cribs I ordered last week.

"Yeah?" He's surrounded by bits and pieces of the crib, nuts and screws piled to his left. I slightly pray that none go missing.

"Lunch is almost ready," I say quietly, trying not to get emotional about seeing him doing something that is just so dad-like it's ridiculous.

"Did you make a lot?"

"Yeah..."

"Like Will level a lot?"

"I don't know about that," I smile, thinking about how much

Will can pack away. I haven't seen him as much since the season started, and because things have still been a bit rocky between them. "Why?"

"He's coming over to help with this since we don't have a game today."

"Oh. Well, when will he be here?"

"In a few minutes."

"Ok, I'll go make some more because otherwise, we won't be eating." I smile at him, leaving him to the currently disassembled cradle. Seeing him there really shouldn't have caused such a big reaction in me, but it sent a rush of emotions through me as memories of my dad working on things in the basement of our house flooded my brain; watching him put together the wooden dollhouse that I begged him for and the built-in bookshelves in my high school bedroom so I could recharge on off days. So seeing Liam building this for our kids, it's both everything I wanted out of life and so completely wrong. Wrong because we aren't together, we aren't a traditional family. Part of me desperately wants to be a family.

It's hours later when Will leaves, and if having Liam here felt good, having them both here is near perfect. Hopefully, once the babies are here, we can all spend time together, and they can grow up around their dad and uncle. Liam heads up to his room early as I finish up an episode of my comfort show. I can't help but want this to be different, and I know it's partially thinking about our children, but if we were together, it would be exactly what I hoped for but never really thought I would have... I guess I won't have that anyways. Close, but not really.

I head upstairs, deciding to take a bath to relax the best I can, not thinking about what could have been. Walking past his room

CHAPTER 21

though, I can't help overhearing his conversation.

"It's been rough," I hear him say as I stop to listen. "I was so scared that night. It was as if the nightmare had come to life and the relief that everything was ok was too much. So offering to live here was instinctual, but now. Now I have to keep reminding myself that we aren't together...."

"And why is that?"

"It's because I was an idiot and ended things because I was terrified that I was going to lose her. I mean, who does that? I was scared of losing her, so I ended things. How much of an idiot am I?"

"I wouldn't say, idiot. But you were reactive."

"Well, now, I regret it. I regret all the pain I put her through and all the things she had to deal with alone when I ignored her trying to get a hold of me...."

I back down the hall slowly. I shouldn't be listening to this. This is a private conversation between Liam and who I'm assuming is his therapist. He got a therapist. I'm having a hard time wrapping my head around that fact, but I am so happy that he is doing this. For himself. And for our children. If we never work things out, if I never get to have him romantically again, at least they will have a father that is whole again. I could live with that. I could handle not having him if they have that.

Instead of my planned bath, I grab the baby name book I picked up but never looked at. Curling up on my bed, I search to narrow down the list, trying to see what names would sound best with Wilkes. I'm not sure if he is expecting them to have his last name, but I wanted them to always have that piece of him at least long before he came back into my life.

ON ICE

* * *

LIAM

Things are getting easier. I can be around her without needing to touch her, well, I still want to. I just don't have to fight myself from reaching out to brush the hair from her face or grabbing her hand every time. Being this close to her, it's difficult not to fall back into the routines we had before I was a massive idiot.

Getting home today, all I want to do is take a shower and just relax on the couch with her. Maybe we could watch a movie together. Maybe I can pretend that things are back the way that they were for a bit. As if she knew I would want that, she's already curled up on her couch, flipping through, trying to find a movie to stream. From this perspective, it would be so easy to think we were back then. She has her hair up in a messy bun, without a stitch of makeup on, under a pile of blankets that, from here, blocks her swollen belly. I know it's there, protecting our growing babies. She is gorgeous.

"Care if I join you?" I ask, making my way through the room to stand beside her.

"Sure." She smiles her real true smile. The one that always makes me feel amazing. The smile that I'm working on myself to see daily.

"Give me a couple of minutes to get back down? Maybe we can order something for dinner too."

"Yes, please. I'll place the order if you want."

"Perfect, you know what I like." I smile as I turn towards the stairs and jog up to my room. Today is going to be a good day. Today might just be the day things shift towards the better for

CHAPTER 21

us.

I'm pretty sure she's figured out that I've been talking to a therapist by now, but I really should talk to her about it. I'm not sure if that is a part of today being a good day or not, but it needs to happen, and I need to do it soon if I want to make things right between us again. She actually wants to spend time with me now, I'm not sure when that changed exactly, it's been gradually moving in that direction, I'm just glad that it happened.

Back in the living room and find her in almost the same spot on the couch, sipping from her bottle of water. I grab a drink for myself and then take a seat on the opposite end rather than the chair further away from her. We settle on watching one of the 'Top 10' movies on one of the random streaming sites and watch the beginning before our food arrives.

I wasn't paying attention to what she chose, but as the story unfolds, I see that it's a romantic comedy, and every time the love interest screws something up, I'm reminded of myself and the even bigger mistake that I made. I'm not sure what she is thinking but she startles me a little when she sits up, placing her hand on her stomach. I can see it moving around, one or both of them moving around like crazy.

"I'm not ready for this. Being a mom scares the shit out of me," she says, her voice more terrified than the joking tone I was expecting.

"Being a dad scares the shit out of me too." I turn my whole body to face her.

"I didn't have a normal family. It wasn't the standard two parents, white picket fence, tire swing in the yard sort of life. But I desperately wanted my kids to have that someday but...."

"But what? Who says that can't happen?" I find myself scooting closer to her on the couch, closing some of the distance between us.

"We did this all wrong, Liam," she says softly, as if holding back tears.

"What do you mean, Elise?"

"We went too fast, too far. We let the sexual attraction keep us from really getting to know each other. You weren't ready for a relationship, and it hadn't even been a year since your fiancé died. I don't know why I thought that you would be ready for a relationship." Her voice is louder now, and her arms are flailing about. "And then it's like a year and a half later, and you're going to have two kids with someone random."

"You're not random, Elise," I kneel in front of her, taking her face in my hands. "Why would you think that you're random? Yeah, there was a lot of sexual chemistry, but I didn't have sex with you because I was drawn to you physically. I was drawn to you because of your personality, and you made me feel like myself again most of the time. For more than I have felt in ages anyway. Yeah, this is all backward and fast, but that doesn't mean it was all wrong. I don't regret having children with you; it's probably the best thing that I've ever done, really."

"Liam..."

"I messed everything up, and I regret that every single day. You made me better. You were, no are, the best thing that has ever happened in my life."

"This is a huge mess. I'm a mess." She looks down at her hands folded over her stomach as if she truly believes I ended things because of something she did. I'm not sure if I'm ready to tell her that it was all me, that she did nothing. I take my hands from her face and rest them gently on her thighs, still wanting to have that physical contact.

"If you're a mess, so am I," I joke, and a smile curls on her lips. "Good news is we are in this together. You're stuck with me. Eighteen years minimum."

"Minimum," she smiles, a stray tear rolling down her face.

"You know what, you need ice cream. I know you've been hiding a pint from me in the back of the freezer. The flavor that we both love. So, you were either hiding it from yourself, or you were afraid that I was going to eat it."

"A little of both," she admits, with a single chuckle. I go to grab it and two spoons before coming back to sit close to her so we can share. She sighs and adjusts her position, so she is cuddled into my side. I want more than eighteen years, but I will settle for this moment for now.

Chapter 22

We've made it a total of five weeks so far in our arrangement. It's been difficult but also kind of perfect at the same time. It's nice to have both Liam and Will here when they can be. It seems like they've patched things up since the ER trip. It almost feels like old times, even before my relationship with Liam. We've been able to have some semblance of normalcy, at least. They put together all the furniture I had delivered for the babies' room. Sarah and I have spent every game here, and part of me thinks that Liam may have said something to her, to make sure that I'm never alone, or rarely alone at least.

"So, brunch on Saturday still?" Sarah asks, trying to confirm plans that I wouldn't dream of canceling since I haven't really

CHAPTER 22

left the house for weeks.

"Did you ask baby daddy?" I joke from my now everyday spot on the couch.

"He suggested it," she says with a smile. "You need to get out of the house for a bit. He's taken the bed rest thing seriously, but a brunch out one morning isn't going to put you into premature labor." She curls up in the oversized chair nearby as the commercial break ends for tonight's home game.

"Where are we going?"

"Oh, you know, that place near the river. It's gorgeous this time of year." She waves her hand like I should know that. "Let's dress up too. You need to feel like a woman as often as possible before they come because there is going to be a hot minute where you will feel very un-human."

"Dress up? I have no idea what even fits me now; I'm a house, Sarah."

"You have to. What about that flowy floral dress you got for maternity pictures that isn't the vibe you were going for? It fits, perfect for a brunch."

"Yeah, I suppose that one would work."

"When are your pictures anyway?" She grabs a snack from the table and settles back into her seat as the game comes back on.

"Next weekend, before the week of away games on the west coast."

"Perfect, sooner is better at this point, while you still feel somewhat normal. I know when I got close to eight months, it was a lot harder to feel normal."

"I already can't breathe," I joke, "too many babies, not enough space. And I'm only seven months; I can't begin to imagine what it's going to be like for another month or two."

ON ICE

* * *

When Liam gets home after the game, I'm already in my room trying to get comfortable enough to sleep. The giant body-wrapping pillow has helped so much since I've gotten too big to sleep on my stomach. I see him walking into his room, hearing him moving around is comforting. It's too quiet when he isn't here now. It isn't too long before I see him in my doorway in his gym shorts and a tee.

"Hey," he says quietly, in case I was already asleep.

"Hi."

"You doing ok? I was going to go to sleep for a bit..."

"Yeah, I just can't get comfortable."

"Can I help at all?" he asks, coming closer to the bed, stopping within arm's reach of me. "Not sure how I could, but I can try."

"Umm, actually, can you lay behind me for a bit? The pillow is great in front of me, but my back feels like it's not getting any support. I don't want to be miserable at brunch with Sarah tomorrow."

"Sure." He climbs into bed with me slowly, as though he is scared to hurt me if the bed jostles too much. An arm slides under my pillow, cradling my neck, and his legs fit behind mine. "I'm not sure how to help."

"My lower back is tight; can you just rub there," I place a hand where I'm talking about. "Please." I know that I sound whiny, but I'm desperate for any kind of relief and possibly a decent night's sleep.

"Sure," I hear him clear his throat before applying just enough pressure to my back. He has always been so good at things like

CHAPTER 22

this, knowing how to relax my aches after a long day. This time though, is the first that I've asked since becoming pregnant. "Is that too much?" All I can do is shake my head 'no' and just try to relax.

I want to soak it all up, as much as possible, while I can because as great as having him here has been, this is short-term. Yes, there isn't a set end date to this, but that could change at any time. I want this to last, to go back to where we were before everything, but I can't. We can't. Every time I think about how great it would be to have him here all the time, I keep thinking about how easy it was for him to leave before. Yes, I realize he was dealing with things then, but I don't know if that will happen again or not. It could. He could leave me. He could leave us.

Liam's hand slows, and I can hear the change in his breathing. I should tell him to go to bed, but I am finally comfortable enough to sleep, and I don't want to change anything if that means I get to sleep. So I don't say anything. I just let myself drift off for a bit, knowing that I will have to wake up to pee several times anyway.

When I wake up, Liam is still there, and it's much later than I thought it would be. Somehow I slept for seven straight hours even though my bladder is about to burst. I struggle to get out of the pillow and Liam's hold on me. The arm that was massaging my back is wrapped protectively around my belly. I have a hard time getting out of the bed without waking him. He needs the sleep as much as I do. I could tell that these past few weeks have been hard on him, the constant worry that something will happen when he is gone. I decide to go ahead and shower to get ready for brunch with Sarah, since I am already up.

Liam is still asleep an hour later when I decided to blow dry my hair, but this is when his children decide to make things difficult for me by stretching so that someone's feet are pushing up into my ribs. "Damn it!" I shout, not meaning to speak so loud with him sleeping in the bedroom. I sit there trying to get them to move back down when I hear him walking towards me.

"You ok?" He yawns.

"Yeah, I just wanted to dry my hair. Things are so much harder when pregnant." I can feel my eyes water as I look up at him.

"Hold on a moment," he says before walking out of the room. I wait, taking deep breaths to stop my hormones from taking over. I can't cry because I can't dry my hair; that seems really dumb. Liam comes back carrying my desk chair and sets it in the middle of the bathroom. "Take a seat." I do as he asks and nearly do bawl though, when he starts drying my hair for me.

It's not a long process, I enjoy not having to do it myself, and the gentleness that Liam has as he helps me is almost too much. When he is done putting my blow dryer away, he reaches for the chair to take it back, and I place a hand on his squeezing it. "Thank you, Liam."

"You're welcome."

* * *

Liam drives me to brunch with Sarah. She called earlier asking if he could since there was a kid emergency this morning. I'm not sure the details of said emergency, but I am sure that I want to know. At this point, I would like to live in my oblivious state for

CHAPTER 22

as long as possible. I'm sure there will be lots of kid emergencies in my future. Liam looks nice today. He has on a pair of dark blue slacks and a white dress shirt, with light brown shoes and a belt. He mentioned some sort of press interview about how the season is going that they want to use for promos. Nothing that isn't normal, really, I'm just not used to not knowing about these things. It makes sense, though, since I'm not in the office anymore. Jenna is handling things so well; it will be great to have an extra hand to make sure everything runs smoothly now.

"Sarah texted. Said she had something that Tom left in the car I need to take to the arena. I'll walk you in," he says as he parks the car and cuts the engine.

"Oh, ok," I smile, climbing out of the car, trying to make sure I don't step on the floor-length floral sundress I have on. Thanks to Liam, I was able to have the energy to not only do my makeup but curl my hair as well. Something I haven't had the energy to do in a while.

"You look beautiful, by the way," he comments as he opens the door to the restaurant. I'm almost in too much shock at his words to notice the entire room is full of the team and their families. His mom and Sarah come forward and wrap me in hugs, making me realize that this is no normal brunch.

"What the hell?" I ask when I'm released.

"Umm, it's a baby shower, duh," Sarah states as if I should have figured it out ages ago.

"Hello, sweetheart." I walk into the open arms of Liam's mother.

"Vivian, you're here."

"I am. I'll be at Liam's place for the time being. I'm here to help where I can."

"Thank you, both of you." I can't handle everything; this is too much. There are too many people. Too many emotions are hitting me all at once. "I'm sorry, I need a minute. Bladder smooshed and all." I joke so that I have an excuse to step away from everyone for a minute to collect my thoughts. I'm almost away when I see Liam following me.

"Are you ok?" He runs a hand along my arm, comforting me as I compose myself.

"Not really. This is a lot."

"Everyone wanted to do something for you."

"I don't know why!" I'm honestly not sure why so many people are here. It's not like I have been around them for years. We barely know each other, really. Yeah, I work close enough with the players that we've all talked and might have some jokes between us, but I didn't think it was like this.

"Because you're their friends and family." I break at his words, feeling warm tears start to roll down my face.

"I don't have a family, Liam. This isn't...."

"You do. You have a family, Elise. Don't say that you don't." He grips my shoulders firmly, holding me in front of him, and I can feel his eyes burning into me, waiting for me to look at him.

"I never... I never thought that I would have this. I was expecting to never have a shower. Or to have people that would care enough to ever...I was planning to be alone in everything."

"You're not alone. You'll never be alone again. You have me and my family. Will. Sarah. We're all yours."

"It's just overwhelming." He cups my face between his hands, making sure that I look at him, and I can see tears building there, threatening to spill too.

"I'm sure it is, but you have family, and we're not going anywhere."

"Did you do this?" I wonder, not sure what answer I want to

CHAPTER 22

hear.

"I may have helped. But it was mostly Sarah and my mom."

"Thank you... So there isn't a random press thing today that I forgot?"

"No, no press thing. Just had to look good enough to stand next to you." I turn towards a mirror in the hall of the restaurant and try to make sure I don't look like I've been sobbing in the hallway. Liam takes my hand when I'm ready. He kisses the back of my hand and we walk back into the party they planned for us, for our children. I still can't believe that they did all this for me.

* * *

Vivian is over a lot, and it's been such a help for us. She was able to get the nursery set up and ready for the babies' arrival, which could happen at any time. She also makes dinner daily for us, though I can't deny that I don't miss the milkshakes and fries from Frank's. Liam is back in time for our maternity photos. I had been planning on doing them alone, but now I'm glad he will be a part of it. Vivian came over after picking a floral crown for me and is steaming the dress that I bought, I think partially to stay out of the way, and Liam is changing into the outfit I picked out for him. I may be going a little overboard for this, but this might be my only pregnancy. I want to have a fairy tale photoshoot. My dress is a deep burgundy tulle that flows with a bit of a train, and Liam will be in a navy suit. Classy, and magical.

"Are you about ready? The photographer will be waiting for us." I step into the dress, not caring that Liam and his mom are in the room. They will be seeing a whole lot of me shortly when the babies come anyway. I'm hoping that Vivian will be there in the room with us, since she is the only grandma.

"Yeah," I say, reaching and struggling with the zipper of my dress. Liam comes up behind me and brushes my hair out of the way, dragging the zipper up effortlessly. "Thanks, you might have to help get me out of this later."

Vivian is smiling at us and takes a few pictures on her phone like the moms I saw during proms doing for their children. And while I ache to have had those memories myself, I am very happy to have her here. I grab the floral crown and Liam and I head out to meet the photographer at a nearby botanical garden.

"Thanks for doing this with me," I say to break the heavy silence between us. Reliving earlier when I said he'd have to help me out of my dress, I want him to, but not in a platonic way. For the first time in months, I wanted him to do more than just hold me in my sleep, and that was amazing enough as it is. I'm missing the old us more and more.

"Of course. Though I'm not sure about the whole theme...."

"Trust me, the pictures are going to look amazing."

"I don't doubt that one bit." He smiles at me from the driver's seat. We make it to the garden sooner than I thought we would, but Anne, the photographer I had found while scrolling through social media, was waiting for us in the parking lot.

"Hi! This day could not have turned out better if we had planned the weather ourselves," she says as I walk towards her, the floral crown now placed on my head with my full curls. Liam falls into place next to me, a hand resting on my back.

"Perfect," I agree.

We go through the motions of initial photos getting comfortable with each other and Anne's process. Finding nooks in the gardens that are private enough that if there are hockey fans in the arena they won't bother us. Eventually, Liam is just standing there talking with me, and the babies kick his hands, making us both laugh, and he crouches in front of me.

"Hey there, kiddos. You stay in there just a bit longer, but I can't wait to see you both." He places a kiss on my belly before standing in front of me again.

"Liam," I look up at him, "I can't wait for you to be a dad."

"I can't wait to see you as a mom," he replies, leaning down enough to rest his forehead to mine. "You're going to be an amazing mom. I know it."

"Ok, this is incredible. You two are the cutest couple I have ever had the chance to shoot." Anne smiles from behind her camera. Neither of us corrects her, mostly because part of me really wants it to be true again. Maybe we can be. "Let's go to the fountains. They should be on now. It will be spectacular."

She walks in front of us, turning every once in a while to take our picture. Liam has my hand in his, and I'm not sure if it's for stability or just because he wants to hold my hand. I hope just because.

Chapter 23

The pictures came back and Vivian is simply gushing over them. I decide to make her an album of photos in my free time. She has been such a blessing to have around, a motherly presence that I didn't know I was missing. I had another appointment this morning, and everything seems normal enough that I can stay at home for a bit longer, barring any major changes.

Liam asked me out to dinner, just us. Maybe we can chat this time and clear the air a bit. He still hasn't told me about seeing a therapist, but I didn't want to push him until he's ready. Maybe he will be ready soon. I want to know he is doing well, at least. It seems like he is but, to know for sure, to talk to him specifically about it will ease my mind a bit about letting him close. A part

CHAPTER 23

of me worries that he isn't ready, that he isn't going to stay if I do this time. This time would be very different, exponentially so. It wouldn't just break me, but it would damage our children.

"Liam is here," Vivian said from my bedroom doorway.

"Thank you. Can you help me zip this, please, Vivian?" I ask, walking out of the closet towards her. "I should probably stop choosing dresses with zippers if I can't reach them now."

"If all you need is help with a zipper, keep wearing them. You look beautiful. I know that my son thinks so, at least."

"Thank you for everything." I smile, wrapping her in a hug as close as I can with my enormous belly.

"Oh, sweetheart. I'm so happy to be here. Now get going. I'm sure he's been sweating this dinner all day. I mean, he had to if he had to get ready at his house instead of here."

"Right? It's like a legit date. What's wrong with him?" We laugh together as we make our way down to the living room, where he waits in the charcoal gray dress pants that I love, with a black dress shirt unbuttoned at the top. I love when he wears his suit like this. If he had a suit jacket on as well, it would be perfect. He looks too handsome, like a mafia boss from a romance novel, but maybe that was his plan to look insanely good. I have a dress on that I thought for sure wasn't going to fit but luckily was just loose enough that I didn't feel like I was wrapped in sausage casing.

"Wow, Elise."

"Hi." I smile at him, suddenly forgetting all the bad between us, just by his reaction. He is completely slack-jawed in shock, more so than I thought possible.

"Alright, you two have a great night. Elise, I will see you tomorrow," his mom says, kissing my cheek and then her sons before walking out of my house. We both just stare at each other, smiling for a moment longer before Liam blinks away the fog and opens the front door for me.

We make it to one of the fanciest places in the city, downtown off the river. The view is amazing, and I can barely believe that we are here. It's not that we didn't go out on nice dinners together when we were dating, but it seems different. We are completely different people now. I want to get to know who he is now. Hopefully, he likes who I am.

We are seated in the back, our table is tucked away from everyone else, and we have a decent view of the river. There are no choices to make, a chef's menu, but Liam lets them know to forgo the wine pairings. There's no pretending to look at the menu, no musings over what sounds the best, so we just sit there for a month too long.

"How are—"

"How are you?"

"I'm fine, getting over being on a forced vacation." I smile, answering him.

"I'm sure you are, but soon we will have too much to do and not enough time. Pretty sure we should enjoy this level of chaos while we can, right?" I smile softly as he takes my hand in his.

"True. Liam, how are you though, really?"

"I'm doing better," he sighs, leaning forward in his chair, his fingers tracing over mine. "I'm sorry for what happened with us, Elise. I wasn't ready for all this, but I wouldn't change it, not at all... ok, well, maybe the part where I break up with you."

"Liam, please stop apologizing. I know that you were going through a lot when we met. We're both to blame for how things happened."

CHAPTER 23

"I have to apologize. I have to explain." I nod, staying quiet but showing him I was listening to whatever he wanted to tell me. "I was terrified, still am, really. You remember the dream that I told you about, about the night we lost Kaylee and how it changed." He waits for me to nod again. "It changed to me losing you. You were the one that I was running to see before something terrible happened. So it changed from me losing that life with her to losing what we could have had together. The future that I wanted desperately."

"Liam," I sigh, feeling my eyes watering at this explanation.

"You were right that we did this all so fast, but that wasn't what scared me or pushed me away. It was my fear... my fear of losing you as I did her." He pauses, looking out the window for a moment before adding, "I started seeing a therapist after I found out you were pregnant. I didn't want my issues ruining my children's lives. I still need to work on things, of course, but things are better."

"I'm so glad you're doing better." I give his hand a squeeze, and his large fingers wrap around my hand, holding it tight. I don't want him to let go, ever.

"I should have listened to you about it ages ago now. Maybe things wouldn't have become such a mess."

"Messes can be fixed." His eyes snap to mine, a flicker of hope there for the first time in a while.

Our conversation slows to something less serious as our meals arrive, course after course, until I can barely manage to breathe in full breaths. Liam drives us home, and after he helps unzip my dress again, he says goodnight with a kiss on my forehead. Tonight was what I needed, confirmation that this was going to be ok. That even if he wasn't going to be mine anymore he would at least be theirs. He was doing everything he could to be a good dad, and that's all I could ask for even if a part of me wanted us to be together again.

*   *   *

LIAM

It's the middle of the night when I hear Elise calling for me. I sit up in my bed for a moment to make sure I'm not dreaming. She calls again and the fear in her voice sends me flying from my bed towards her room. The panic I felt in the pit of my stomach subsides only a little bit when I see that she is mostly ok.

"What is it?" I ask, as I kneel in front of where she sits at the edge of her bed.

"My head is throbbing, and my vision is blurry. We need to go to the hospital. Now."

"Ok. Let's go," I say, standing and immediately grab her some shoes and the bag she had ready to go in case there was an emergency.

"You need a shirt, Liam. I would like the nurses to focus on us and not you. Though it's nice and distracting." She's doing the thing where she jokes to deflect how she is feeling. We're in the hallway, and I take a detour grabbing the first shirt that I see, the one I was planning on wearing to practice in the morning. "Liam…" I can see the tears welling in her eyes.

"Hey, everything is going to be fine," I reassure her the best I can, pushing aside my own fear for a moment. She is more important right now; she is more important always. I pull her into my chest, kissing the top of her head, "We're going to get there, and they're going to get everything all checked out. We'll call the doctor's emergency line on the way there."

She nods against me, and we head to the hospital.

Chapter 24

"We're going to have to do an emergency cesarean," the doctor says after reviewing all the test results. We talked to his emergency line, and they were waiting for us to arrive. Check-in was quick, and they got her hooked up to machines so fast that I was both scared something was majorly wrong, and relieved that they were taking things seriously. "I know that this wasn't what we were hoping for but it's what is best for you and both babies."

"But we aren't full term yet. Are they going to be ok?" She's only eight months along. What if they're not developed enough and end up in the NICU for weeks, or longer?

"We're going to give you something to help with that, and I

CHAPTER 24

will make sure that we are ready for them. We will do all that we can to make sure they are healthy."

"I guess that's all we can do." She looks up at me, the fear evident in her eyes.

"When do we get started?" I ask, taking a deep calming breath.

"The meds have been ordered, and an OR is on standby."

"That's really soon. Liam, is your mom almost here? Does Will know? Sarah?" She is crying now, tears rolling down her face.

"Elise, they know. Mom is on her way. She's just stopping by the house to grab a few more things for us. Everything is ok…"

"I'll let you both have a minute. The nurse will be in soon, but everything will be just fine," Dr. says, squeezing her shoulder.

"See, everything will be fine."

"I'm so scared," she admits, curled into my side. "Liam, if something happens, promise me you will go with the babies. Leave me with the doctors, go with them, make sure they are ok."

"All of you will be fine. This is going to be the easiest surgery ever."

"Don't jinx it, Liam."

"Hey," I gently place a hand on her face, making her look at me. "You are going to be ok. And so will they." I wipe the tears from her face now. I have to stay strong for her right now. I'm terrified that something will happen to them. I'm terrified that I'm going to lose her again. I'm just terrified. But she needs me to be strong through this. Heaven knows that she has been incredibly strong through her entire pregnancy. She curls back into my side, clutching onto me more than ever before.

We stayed like that for a while, breaking apart so the nurse could give her the meds our doctor said would help their lungs be more prepared for delivery. Elise keeps looking at me like she is terrified and thinking of her past. All I can think of is that she has had to do things like this all by herself before. She's been alone for so long. I will not let her do this alone.

I change into the scrubs they gave me to wear into the OR and settle back next to her. Not letting her worry that she is alone. She isn't. She never will be again. I will always be here. She is mine, and I will make sure that she knows that every single day. She is the only one for me.

"We're ready for you," the nurse says, walking in with a smile, "you're going to be parents very soon."

"We're going to be parents," she says wide-eyed, looking over to me. "I mean, I knew this the whole time, but still."

"Yeah, that's the normal reaction. Alright, let's get the show on the road."

"Your mom?"

"She'll be here soon, but knows that we're headed to surgery now. She'll be here when everything is done." I brush her hair back from her forehead and under the hairnet thing that they gave her.

"You look like an extra on Grey's. It's kind of hot."

"Are you feeling ok?" I smile.

"Just needed to let you know. If hockey doesn't work out, that's an option. Give McDreamy a run for his money."

"I'll keep that in mind."

It feels like we are in a whirlwind after that. Suddenly she is on an operating table and I am sitting there at her head as they get her draped for major abdominal surgery. "Are you as scared as I am?" she asks, taking deep breaths, trying to calm her nerves.

"I think we would be crazy not to be scared." I take her hand in mine trying to comfort her, and myself.

CHAPTER 24

"Valid." We can hear and see the flurry of activity around us as they begin the surgery. There are two warmers ready to our left and a set of doctors each to take them if they need to. It feels like too many people, but if something were to happen I'm glad that there are so many people here to help.

"What do you want me to do? How can I help you?" I ask her, trying to avoid peeking over the blue drape that blocks where they have cut into her flesh. It makes me queasy just thinking about it, and I can't be the guy that passes out. She needs me to stay strong today.

"We haven't decided on names yet..." She stops talking when she hears the doctor say that he's about to deliver baby A, our girl.

"I thought that you wanted to see them, to know for sure." We both wait a beat as if holding our breaths in anticipation.

"True."

"Are you ok?" I ask seeing her close her eyes tightly.

"Yeah, just feeling pressure." Just like that, our daughter is out, and team A flies into action, taking care of her and making sure she is ok. I turn my head following them with my eyes, until Elise squeezes my hand slightly. "Liam..." On to Baby B.

"You're doing great. We need to give them a moment to get them checked out." They take our boy over next to his sister and it's like my heart stops waiting for them to say or do something so we know everything is ok.

"You're doing great, Elise. We just have to close you up," I hear the doctor say as I shift my eyes from Elise to our children.

"Liam, why aren't they crying yet? They're supposed to cry right?" I'm wondering the same thing, but trying so hard to keep my emotions in check.. "Go with them Liam, they are almost done with me, please check on them. Please."

I kiss her forehead and stand, quickly making my way to the babies. They're so small. I let out a breath when I see our daughter, wiggling around her arms and legs as they get vitals, and our son is still getting his airways suctioned, but both sets of nurses nod and smile as they work. "They look so good, Elise. They obviously take after me in the looks department."

"Oh good," she sighs, her voice softer than I expected. I turn towards her, and notice that her color is far too pale. Panic sets in instantly, the sterile hospital smell stifling.

"Get him out of here" I hear Dr. Frank say, "There is too much blood."

"Mr. Wilkes, we need to take the babies to the nursery, why don't you come with us."

"Liam…" I hear her soft whisper of a voice fading away. My stomach is instantly cold, a pit of dread weighing heavy in me.

"What's happening?" I'm led out of the operating room. "What is happening?!" No one answers me as I lose sight of Elise. And I'm hit with an instant pit of dread in my stomach. She has to be ok, she can't… this can't happen. I can't lose her. Our children can't lose her.

Chapter 25

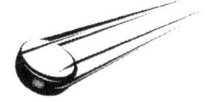

I remember laying there hearing that my children were ok, that they looked good, and then things blurred. I didn't hear anything but a ringing rushing sound surrounding me. I felt cold, and then I was just there. Like I was waiting, not sure what for though. It was a weird middle ground like I was in that not asleep but not awake that blissful state before the world crashes in on you. I want to enjoy this for as long as possible knowing that I will not be getting much sleep after this. I just wish that Liam was here cuddling with me.

But wait, he was here. He was here, then he was dragged away from me. Why was he taken away? Why am I here, alone? I don't want to be alone. I can't be alone again. Liam and I were just getting to a good place again, at least as far as being able to spend time together and not have that awkward silence. I love him, I could love him again as I did before, but he's not here.

"Elise..." I hear faintly from a distance. It pokes at the edges of my dream-like state, taking the edges of the fuzzy room and making it move in this dizzying wave. They're talking to me, continuing to pull me from my warmth. Everything gets fuzzy again, but it's clearing rather than blurring this time. "Elise."

I feel groggy, and my head is dizzy, but I see him here. Liam is here, waiting for me, sitting next to me. "Shhh." It's too loud around me right now.

"You're awake." He takes my hand holding it tighter and kisses my knuckles. "Thank God you're awake."

"Why are you so loud?" My voice is barely a whisper, raspy and thick. I'm not sure what happened, but he obviously was worried.

"Elise, you scared the crap out of me. Don't ever do that again."

"I didn't do anything." I blink seeing the lights and machines around me, the nurse checking the monitors smiles, before sending a message to someone letting them know that I'm awake.

"I know you didn't, but you almost left us."

"I didn't want to." I finally turn my head to look at him, Liam. Tears had been running down his face, his eyes still very red from crying. He looks like he was hit with the worst news ever and that caused a wave of panic to wash through me. "The babies?"

"They're good, small but good." He smiles at me like he is so happy and so relieved at the same time. He looks up then to another nurse that walks into the room. He pushes my hair back from my face gently, looking between the nurses and me.

CHAPTER 25

"What happened?" I ask, looking at the one that just came into the room.

"You gave us all a scare; that's what happened. Dr. Frank will be in soon to go over things with you, but we sure are glad you're waking up here."

"Waking up? What the hell happened?!"

"You lost some blood. We had to put you under to stop the bleeding," she explains, resting a hand on my shoulder. "Your doctor will let you know more, but for now, you're stable, and your kids are freaking adorable."

"Thanks, it's all me."

"No way, Wilkes. It's all me, you don't get more credit than me." Liam smiles and rests a hand on my cheek. Who knew bleeding out was so exhausting? I sure didn't, but Liam was here for me the entire time. And that is a lot more comforting than I ever expected it to be.

"Don't ever do that to me again," he whispers, looking me directly in the eyes.

"I don't plan on it. Pretty sure this was scary enough for our whole family for at least a decade."

"Minimum."

Liam is my person, I don't know to what extent that will be, but he's it for me. There is no one else. I don't know how I know this, but deep in the pit of my stomach, he is. I'm pretty sure that if he ends up with someone else after all this, I will never get over it. I know that it would hurt me to the core to see him with someone else, and hopefully, he feels the same way. I can't act on this now, I'm too tired, too sore. So much changed today, and we have so much to get used to now.

***

"Vivian," I smile, seeing her quietly come into my room. The doctor left me in the capable hands of the nurses, and I finally have a chance to hold my babies.

"I hope I'm not interrupting."

"Nope, not at all. Are you feeling up to meeting your grandkids? I know it's been a bit of a crazy day," I ask her, my eyes watering.

"I'd like that very much." Her eyes are just as teary as my own. I'm glad that she is here, though the plan did not go as I had hoped.

"Well... in that case, mom," Liam walks towards her with our daughter. "This is Elowen Amelia."

"And this is Finn Archer." I nod towards my handsome son resting in my arms. "The tough part now is going to be figuring out which one to hold first."

"How am I supposed to decide?"

"No clue." Liam smiles down at Elowen, and then over at me as I hand Finn to his grandmother.

"Oh, Elise," she kisses my forehead, and I'm instantly flooded with an intense feeling of love from her and me for her and the family that I have built with Liam. "You did so well."

"Minus the whole trying to die thing..."

"Yeah, minus that part. Please don't do that again," her voice is stern for a moment before she looks down at her grandson.

She stays for a while, taking her time with both Elowen and Finn before she heads back to Liam's place for the night. Sarah and Will are visiting tomorrow to give us time to rest, but we were able to FaceTime them for a bit. Liam's dad and sister

CHAPTER 25

were on a plane here, so we haven't talked to them yet given the exciting events of the day, but they'll be here tomorrow morning to visit too. It's crazy how much has changed in less than twelve hours, but to see so many people here for my children makes me so happy.

"Hey, you should get some sleep," Liam says, taking Elowen from me and placing her in the nursery crib. "You're dozing off, and you had a major surgery."

"I just want to hold them forever." I know that I'm falling asleep. But I can't get enough of them right now.

"We will hold them forever." He pulls the blanket up around me, tucking me in. "I love you, Elise. Thank you so much for making me a dad."

"I love you too," I mumble as I fall asleep.

* * *

Three days later, they're ready to send us home. Liam has two car seats set up in the back of his SUV and loaded everything we brought with us up to go home. The nurse that pushes down to the car as Liam carries both babies helps me out of the wheelchair and into the front seat, giving me a blanket to help my incision on the drive home. I'm still wrapping my head around that I had major surgery and will have a longer recovery because of the complications.

"You ready?" Liam asks, sliding into the driver's seat.

"Very ready," I reply, already tired and ready to get into my own bed after a long hot shower. "I might be most ready to take a shower in my own home."

"I don't blame you."

We make our way home, and I take my time getting out of the car, letting him unload our bags, handing our sleeping babies, car seats and all, to his parents. When he has the bags slung around his shoulder, I'm at the porch steps, starting my climb, instantly regretting a two-story house. He takes my arm, letting me use his strong sturdy frame to get up the stairs easier than alone.

"Welcome home, Elise," Owen says, taking the bags from his son.

"Hi," I smile, my eyes a watery mess, thinking about how good it feels to have family here, but missing having my dad here. I search the room sporting Lilith and Vivian holding a kid each, bouncing them lightly, to keep them calm as Liam walks into the kitchen to make the bottles. I decided there was no way I would be able to breastfeed both babies and work. Liam would be able to help more that way. "Wait, do I smell pot roast?"

"Yeah, we figured you were really sick of hospital food."

"Owen, you are an angel sent from heaven." I give him as big of a hug as I can without hurting.

I'm in trouble here, Liam's family is amazing to me. If I can't figure out a way to keep things good with Liam, I might lose all of this, and I am desperate to not lose it. If anything, I want to make sure they never leave me.

"Hey, I've been thinking, just so that things might be a little easier," I say to Liam once his family heads back to his house for the night. "It might be better if we are all in the same room... not sure if that is ok with you."

"Yeah, that makes sense." He smiles at me as he tucks a hair beside my ear, letting his hand cup my cheek lightly. "Are you

CHAPTER 25

doing ok? You've been wincing every time you've moved today."

"It's better but still uncomfortable,"

"Well, I'm glad I will be there to help since you won't be able to get up as fast as me." I nod, looking down at Finn and Elowen. "We made them. You did all the hard work."

"You're right. I did." I don't want to take my eyes off them; I love them so much already. I never knew that it was possible to love someone so quickly. I've only ever loved one person this much, and he's standing next to me. "You just had the fun part."

"It was fun," he turns towards me, and I'm almost certain that he's about to kiss me, his glance flicks towards my lips for a moment, and then up towards my eyes holding my gaze for a moment longer than usual. "You should try to rest a bit. Why don't you go lay down while they're sleeping?"

"Well, that sounds amazing, but we're going to need to put together a press release about this. That way there aren't any stories out there, though I doubt it will be a headline anywhere."

"Always working, Elise, we can figure that out after you get some rest. You had surgery, you need rest."

"You're bossy now that you're a dad."

"I'm just protective of my family." My heart melted a bit more at his words. Family, we're family, Liam, Elowen, Finn, and I. Non-traditional but still family. I smile and head towards my, no our, room to rest for a bit leaving Liam to watch over us all.

Chapter 26

About a week after coming home with Elise and our babies, I get a call that Sports Center is showing pictures in a loop of me carrying the car seats and Elise beside me being pushed to the car. I haven't told Elise, mostly because I don't want her to worry about it. We've been so sleep-deprived and in a bubble of new parent life that I wouldn't want this to be placed on her shoulders. So, after speaking with her second in command in the PR department I am headed to the arena for a short meeting about an announcement.

"Hey, Jenna." I try to hold in the yawn that the venti coffee couldn't hold off.

"Mr. Wilkes. Thanks for coming in. I didn't want to bother

CHAPTER 26

Elise with this after everything."

"I appreciate that. She needs her rest." I left her curled up in bed, the babies sleeping soundly in their bassinets, and my mother in the living room just in case she needed help and I wasn't back yet. I wasn't sure how long this would take or what the plan was to make sure this was presented properly.

"So, the story is vague. Just that you were seen leaving the hospital with an unknown woman, with the two car seats. Other than that, they don't know anything else. I just know that Elise would want to get in front of the story."

"You're right. We discussed that a bit ago and started drafting a few things we were going to release."

"I'm thinking because we don't want things to get twisted, we should do a press conference...."

"Gotcha." A full-out press conference was not what Elise and I were hoping for, but that was prior to the photos leaking. I think she would agree that this is the best option.

"Only if you feel ok doing that," Jenna adds, knowing it's my choice. They could release a simple statement, and that's it, but seeing as I have been in the headlines for almost two years, it's probably better not to let the media run with what little information they have.

"Well, I have been out for about two weeks now, we should probably give them a reason."

"How soon can you do it?"

"How soon can you?"

I walk into the room and take a seat at the table where the mics are set up with many waiting news staff and camera crews, and cleared my throat. Jenna got everything set up quickly and will be posting on the team's page once the conference is over. I let Elise know that I need to wrap up a couple of things but will be home to help out in a little over an hour. She let me know that she already posted a picture of the twins on her social media so the story rolling currently wasn't a big deal, but we should bump up the press release. She doesn't know what was happening here though, not yet, there are things that I need to say and while I want her to know them, I didn't want her to worry about it.

"Thanks for coming in on such short notice," I start, my palms sweating, knowing what I am about to tell the whole sports community. "I'm sure you're all a little curious about my absence from games lately, and possibly about the photos of me leaving the hospital with some tiny cargo. Let me start with, I will remain injured reserved for another seven weeks so that I can spend time with my children and their mother." The reporters all start shouting at once, "I'll take questions at the end, please. I would like to give a bit of an explanation before. I'm sure some questions will be answered." I see several reporters nod and ready to take notes as I speak. "As many of you are aware, I was previously in a relationship, and we had expected a child before both were killed in a car accident almost two years ago now. It wasn't easy for me to cope with, so when the season started a few months later, the club brought in a new PR manager. She and I worked closely together for several months so that I could be a better teammate to my fellow Comets." Everything up to this point was already out there. Many in the sports news community ran stories about the tragedy that struck the Comets, having both the fiancée and elder brother on the same team. Now though, I had to explain a part of my relationship with Elise, and honestly, I wasn't sure I wanted much about us out there. "Elise Connors is an amazing

CHAPTER 26

woman, and she was, or is really, a major reason that I have healed from that tragedy. She made sure that I found ways of coping with that loss and was a major part of getting past the worst of it all." I hope that she knows how true everything I'm about to say is. "The truth is that the more time I spent with her, the better I felt, and the more I fell for her. She became a big part of my everyday life. Eventually, I realized I wasn't ready mentally and ended things with her. Pretty sure that is one of the biggest mistakes I've ever made, for the most part, that is. I realized that I needed to seek the help of a licensed professional." I pause, knowing that I had to move this away from my relationship with Elise. "I started speaking to a mental health provider and working through all the issues I had pushed down. I was able to work on myself, and after several months of taking the time to learn how to cope with everything that I have been through, I am mentally more prepared to continue on with the season and fatherhood. That can be credited in part to Elise, who encouraged me from the beginning to talk to someone. I'm anxious to get back on the ice, but as I said earlier, that won't be for another seven weeks. Due to a complicated delivery, I am needed at home a bit longer than usual. Elise and I would like to introduce them in our own time, but with the obvious news out there, we wanted to let everyone know where I am. At home, not injured, but very sleep deprived."

"Mr. Wilkes will take questions now." Jenna gestures to the waiting press to come forward with any questions that they have now that I was able to give them a brief explanation of what's been happening.

"Are you saying that these are your children with Elise Connors?" a reporter asks.

"Yes."

"Are you in a relationship with her?" they ask for clarification.

"I would marry her today if she would let me."

"You said that you have been seeking help from a mental health provider. Is this something that you decided to do on your own after your loss?" asks another member of the press.

"Partially. I did decide on my own. However, it was with the encouragement of my family and Elise that I finally felt like I could. I didn't realize how that was still affecting me, not only on a personal level but on the ice as well. Mental health is something that we should all take seriously. And something that men, in particular, tend to brush under the rug because we are expected to be strong in all situations. I hope that by sharing my struggles, I can help someone else seek the help they need."

"What would you say to someone struggling to take that step then?" I hear from the other side of the room.

"It's not easy choosing to get help, and it's not easy putting in the work. It is, however, worth every bit of the effort. Choose yourself."

"Very fatherly. How are you handling your new role as a parent?" the first reporter asks with a knowing smile.

"I'm exhausted," I chuckle, "but it's worth every bit of sleep deprivation. My life feels whole again."

"That's all for today. Please expect a full press release later today," Jenna states, officially ending the impromptu conference. That was the plan we came up with earlier today, keeping it short and advising that there would be a full statement written out later for additional information.

I smile and walk out of the room, making my way out to my car to head home when I get a call. Elise's face pops up on the screen. I put the car back in park and brace myself for the several reactions that are possible after holding a press conference without talking to her about it first.

"Hey, is everything ok? Do you need anything while I am out?" I ask as I answer, knowing that she is fine and probably doesn't need anything.

"No, everything is fine. I just watched something interesting... a press conference." Her tone is even as if she is waiting to hear that I am ok. Like she is worried this was too much for me right now.

"Wasn't sure you'd be awake," I say softly.

"I wanted to see what they were saying about the pics that someone took. Liam..."

"Yeah?" I hold my breath, knowing I am a moment away from her real thoughts on what I just did.

"You did good."

"Jenna and I didn't want to bother you with this...."

"I better be careful. She'll take my job."

"No, you're too good at it."

"I set up newborn photos for this weekend before they change too much. We can use those for the official announcement for the twins. Maybe we can take a few family photos too."

"That sounds perfect. My mom will love having a photo of all four of us."

"Ok, well, drive safe, and I'll see you soon. We'll see you soon."

"See you soon."

I'm going to marry this woman, even if it takes years for her to say yes.

* * *

ELISE

Liam twisted that just enough to focus on mental health rather than our relationship. It was as if we had a chance to go over what to say beforehand. I was very impressed with how he handled things. I was also taken aback by him saying that he would marry me today if I would let him. I felt like I would for a moment before I realized just how difficult things have been for us and how much we need to work through before that's even in the room, let alone on the table.

Elowen starts stirring in the bassinet, and I grab her before she wakes Finn as well. I am starting to get a routine in place with Liam's help for them. Staggered just enough that when he is back playing, I will be able to handle things on my own when I need to. I feed Elowen, and once she is settled back in the bassinet, Finn is waiting for his turn. I am sitting on the couch with him when Liam walks in.

"Hi," I greet, and he kisses my forehead. Something that always turns me into a bowl of jelly, but I try to not let him see it.

"How are my favorite people?"

"Fed and really to be awake for a few minutes before passing out again," I answer, placing Finn over my shoulder to burp. Liam takes a spot next to me with Elowen in his arms. She looks so tiny when he holds her. It's hard to believe that they were born almost two weeks ago already.

"Do you have clothes in mind for these family photos?" He asks, not taking his eyes off of our daughter.

"I do, you know that, though," I smile at him for a moment.

"You always have a plan."

"If only people would cooperate with that plan," I comment

partially under my breath. It was true that the press basically forced us to announce everything earlier than planned, but also for how I wanted things to go prior to the pregnancy. I had been thinking about it as I fed our kids. He said he would marry me today, but had he not left me, I would have married him yesterday.

Chapter 27

It's been three months since I became a mom and since things shifted with Liam. We aren't just friends, but we aren't together either. It's kind of a weird in-between feeling, to be honest. We aren't romantically involved, but we're not just friends. Maybe it's a parent thing, co-parenting isn't exactly something that we know a whole lot about, and the lines are blurred. I know that waiting for him to leave is a trauma response for me. I know that he won't leave. He would never leave Elowen and Finn. But there will always be a part of me waiting for my life to be turned upside down. Knowing that it had happened before, losing my whole family when I was still figuring out who I was as a person will do that to a person.

CHAPTER 27

Tonight though is the annual gala, the fundraiser that was the start of things for us, and Liam asked me to go with him as his date. I couldn't say no to him. As much as I want to keep my distance, unsure of what we were doing or what to expect, I couldn't - there has always been this magnetic pull between us. So I push aside my fears and insecurities to enjoy a night where we can just be Elise and Liam.

Lilith decided to move here, staying at Liam's place since it's mostly empty. I'm not sure what pushed her to make that choice, but there was more to it than just wanting to be close to her niece and nephew. She offered to watch the twins for us tonight. I got a new dress for the event, since I was still dealing with a postpartum belly, and spend the better part of an hour trying to get my hair and makeup just right. Not that I was trying to impress anyone in particular, but if he noticed that would be enough.

I slid into my burgundy A-line dress with off-the-shoulder straps, and just as I reached for the zipper, Liam is there zipping it for me. His hands rest on my waist for a moment longer than usual, but the relationship Liam and I have isn't typical. He looks at me through the mirror, a smile on his face. We look pretty good together, not just dressed up like this, but in regular, and lounge clothes too.

"You look stunning," he comments as I lean forward on the bathroom counter to put on my lipstick, then grab my clutch and turn to face him. He holds a hand out to me, I set mine in his, and we walk out of our room and make our way downstairs. It feels good to have him there, like before. I'm not sure if it's just having him here all the time or that knowing he has been working on himself, for himself, has made me want to do things with him again. I miss him in every sense.

"Holy Hell, Elise!" Lilith comments from the floor with the babies, snapping me from my internal thoughts. "You look too good for my brother."

"Thanks," I smile at her, "and thanks for hanging out with them. Best Auntie ever."

"It's no big deal at all. They're kind of my favorites." She goes back to paying attention to Elowen and Finn, both reaching for the hanging toys on their play mat.

"We'll see you later. Probably won't stay too late," Liam says, ushering me to the door, knowing that I will have a hard time leaving if not forced, slightly forced.

"Yea, yeah. Go have fun. You know I'm crashing here anyway, so maybe don't rush home and enjoy the night?"

We drive there in comfortable silence, for the most part. It wasn't uncomfortable, but there was something else there today. Liam looks amazing in his tux, and I just hope we can enjoy tonight. This is the first time we've been away from the twins for more than an hour or two. When we get out of the car, Liam takes my hand and leads me to the entrance, which, this year, includes an emerald carpet for all the guests and players to walk and get photos taken. There are more cameras than I thought there would be. Jenna took care of getting some local press here for tonight to bring the gala to more people rather than just the season ticket holders and investors. Liam and I pose together, his arm wrapping around my waist, holding me close to him.

Liam and I make our way through the crowd, several people ask us about parenthood and how we are doing. It's sweet knowing people are more interested in that than the game itself in a way. Knowing that there are so many people rooting for us makes me too happy. Liam deserves to be happy, I deserve to be happy. Maybe we can be happy together?

I've been hoping that we would have a moment alone to talk about things, to figure out what comes next for us. I'm not sure where we stand, but I know what I want. I just don't know what he wants. We've both continued to work on ourselves as well as figuring out what is best for Finn and Elowen. It hasn't been easy, but we have it mostly together. I just don't know what he is thinking when it comes to how we will keep things going and what happens as they get older.

Liam walks us to our table just as they start the usual spiel about the fundraiser and thanking all those who participated this year. There is a short movie about the kids enjoying the camp and spending time with the players. Liam's arm drapes around my shoulders, the warmth soaking through my skin makes my heart race a bit faster. We have been through a lot, both when we were together and before we ever met.

I'm hoping the proximity isn't why he is leaning into me. I let out a breath and enjoy it while I can, feeling like this might be the night that changes everything. He's probably planning his out. We only talked about him staying through the end of my pregnancy and then when the babies were just home. The deadline for him staying with me gets bumped out little by little as we discover new things we both need to be there for, but now, he could very well go back to his house, and we could figure things out that let him get enough sleep.

The speeches wrap up, and before dinner can even start, Liam turns towards me, taking my hand gently. "Hey, can we talk for a second?"

"Sure..." worry fills me with his words. Things have been good, too good really. What if he's about to tell me he thinks he should move out and split time with the babies? I can't be apart from them that much, and I don't want to be away from him either. He leads me out of the room, to a quiet corner, and I'm taken back to the night that started, really started, our relationship. It's almost poetry that he ends things as they began. I just hate it.

"Elise," he starts cupping my face so that I look at him.

"Yeah?" I stare into his gorgeous blue eyes, searching for what he wants to tell me. Hoping that it isn't what I think it might be.

"Do you want me to leave?"

"Leave? The party?" I ask, stalling the inevitable.

"No, your house. You're healed up now, and the babies have a routine...."

"No. I don't. Are you planning on leaving?" I answer too quickly, I know I do, but I don't want him to leave ever.

"I'm just terrified, terrified that you're going to be in love with somebody else and I'm gonna miss my chance completely," he admits. I take a hold of his hands, steadying myself and making sure that I have his full attention.

"Liam, how can you even say that? Who else would I be in love with?" Tears flood my eyes, knowing that this has been building for a while now. I can't avoid this any longer. "I have been in love with you since day one. I've just been waiting for you to figure out everything you needed to. You've had so much happen to you and very little time to deal with it. I don't want to rush you, but I don't want you to leave."

"I'm sorry it's taken so long to realize how much I need you." He leans in, our foreheads touching.

"It's ok; I'm not gonna rush you. I'm not. We both need to get better. We've been through so much, not just together but before we knew each other too. It's not just you and me anymore;

CHAPTER 27

it's our kids too. So as long as you need me to, I'll wait because I'll choose you every time. No question about it. There is no one else for me, Liam."

"Elise, I love you." He brushes his thumb across my cheek, his hand at the back of my neck. "I know I want you in my life. I want to do this together."

"Liam, I love the man you are becoming. And I have no doubt you're going to be someone our kids look up to. I love you." I want to kiss him here and passionately make up for all the lost time, but my stomach chooses this moment to growl loudly with hunger. He gives me a soft, chaste kiss instead and leads me back into the gala and to our table.

* * *

It's hours later and Liam is driving us home. I am exhausted and hyper-aware all at once. Liam admitted that he wants more and that he still loves me. And I still love him. We can be the family that I have always hoped for. It was like all my worry about our relationship was lifted off my shoulders knowing he is in love with me.

"Hopefully they are still asleep, I could use a minute to decompress before diving into dad mode," he admits, looking over at me.

"My feet are so swollen. I can't move."

"We could leave Lils here…"

"We could." I see the glint in his eye, the one that let me know he's not as tired as I thought, and to be honest neither am I after seeing, knowing, what he wanted.

"There is a whole other house."

"We could sneak away for just a bit longer, right? Everyone is probably asleep. Lils is staying in the guest room." And at this moment, I want Liam Wilkes more than I thought that I could.

"Is that a yes?"

I nod, smiling at him. We pull into his garage in less than ten minutes and Liam has me scooped up into his arms and is carrying me into the house. Before I know it, I am on his bed, and he is kneeling in front of me, unbuckling my heels and sliding them off my aching feet.

I lean forward and grab the loosened ends of his tie, pulling him up and towards me. We lock eyes for a moment before I kiss him like I have been starving for him. I am starving for him, honestly. Liam's hands cup my face, holding me as if I might run. He is hesitant to move further, I can feel it, so I make a move, slowly unbuttoning his dress shirt to slide it off.

"Are you sure?" He is being more timid than I want or was expecting. This is the man that left me naked on the kitchen counter after almost getting me off to answer the door for our take-out order. Now he is waiting for me to say yes, again.

"We can sleep when we are dead Liam and right now, we are both very much alive. I'm sure, very sure."

His mouth is on me in an instant, and he's unzipping my dress without looking. I pull the belt out of the loops of his pants as my dress falls to the floor in a pool of tulle and glitter around our feet. His hands roam my body, and there is a twinge of worry that he won't be happy with what he sees now that so much has changed, just a small fear that he won't be attracted to the added weight and curves. That doesn't come though as his hands and mouth are all over me like a man dying of thirst.

"Liam," I can't hold back the moan that escapes my lips when

CHAPTER 27

his mouth makes contact with the tender spot where my neck and shoulder meet. And I wrap my arms around him, holding him there with an arm around his shoulders and one laced through his hair. Silently begging him to never leave.

He picks me up as if I weigh nothing, and we're on the bed tangled together. I have missed him. I missed his hands on me and the way we just work together like this. His hands are all over me, roaming my body as his mouth moves from my neck to grazing along my collarbone. Liam takes my bra off, continuing to kiss down my body, stopping to pay attention to my breast in equal amounts. It's like he has all the time in the world, it always has when we've been together. Liam takes his time.

He slowly removes my panties, trailing kisses down my thigh then back up just as slowly until I feel his tongue sliding between my folds. I can't focus on anything else, and I'm lost in the sensations of him between my legs. For the first time in ages, Liam and I are together, and he is turning my brain to mush with just his mouth. He drinks me all in, nibbling and sucking on my clit, diving his tongue in me. I gasp, unable to stop my hips from moving against his face, and my thighs tighten around his head. I swear that I hear him laugh against me for a brief moment, but it doesn't phase him. He goes right back to work on my dripping sex. I feel the pressure in my belly building higher and higher with each lick and suck until I explode in release against him. He stays there, still working me as I ride the wave of my orgasm until my legs relax against his body.

Liam rises between my legs, wiping his face of my juices with a smile on his face, as if he is really proud of himself. Truly he should be, he learned everything that makes my body shudder with pleasure, and he seems to be using each of those tactics tonight. I sit up just enough to reach his waist, undoing the button and zipper of his pants, feeling his rock-hard member beneath my hand as I do. Sharing a bed as we take care of the twins has made for mornings where I can feel his hardened cock against me or see it pressing against his pants in the mornings, and I have wanted it desperately most of the time. Tonight is no different, I want him now, but unlike those midnight feedings and sleepy mornings I can have it.

"Pants off, now," I say firmly, looking him in the eye.

He doesn't wait, and he kicks off his pants and boxer briefs as fast as possible. Liam settles between my legs again, our hips lining up like a perfect puzzle. I slide my hands up his arms, wrapping one around his neck, letting my fingers lace in his hair, pulling him as close as possible. Our mouths crash together in an all-consuming desire I haven't felt since just before we broke up. I can feel him adjusting my body so we line up before he slides into me painfully slowly.

"Fuck," he drags the word out like he is trying to maintain his composure and control a bit. I am thankful for that, to know that he is just as affected by this as I am.

We both let out a deep breath, and I smile against his lips. I missed this, sex with him. He starts pumping in and out of me slowly. The slow friction rubbing against my clit has my body craving more and more with each gentle thrust. His mouth moves down to my neck, and he drags his teeth against the tender flesh there, making me gasp and moan as I buck against him. The tempo of our hips increases until he is pounding harder and harder. Each thrust leaves me gasping, and he knows that I'm getting close again. Liam throws my legs over his shoulders and quickens his pace, driving back into me over and over again. Harder and faster. Until I come undone, the pressure in my stomach is coming loose in one delicious and amazing moment.

CHAPTER 27

With a few more pumps, he finds his release, and we are laying there breathing heavily.

"Liam, that was...I love you. So much." I roll into his side, holding him close, not wanting to let him or this moment go.

"I love you. I can't wait for our lives together." He kisses my forehead and rubs my back tenderly. I needed this night. We both needed it. The chance to come together as a couple again. Playing house is one thing, but to know that we are going to try again. That we're going to try not just for our children but because we belong together.

We both don't want to move, and we don't. I can feel my eyelids growing heavier, and I hear Liam's breathing even out. So, instead of waking him up, I settle in, falling asleep in his arms.

A few hours later, I jolt awake, used to hearing babies crying for food or diaper changes. But instead, it's just Liam and me in his bed, still pressed against each other skin to skin.

"Stay in bed, I'll get this one," he says groggily.

"Liam," I laugh. "We're at your house. They aren't here."

"Oh, that's right." He sighs, and then pulls me as close as possible again. "Mom and Dad had a playdate." He kisses my shoulder, then my neck before our mouths meet in a sleepy but comforting way.

'We should probably relieve Lilith."

"You're right."

"Liam..." I look at him again, wondering just how we're going to navigate the changes to our relationship.

"Elise, this is just the beginning. I will always be here. I won't ever leave you again. It nearly broke me in ways I didn't know were possible after Kaylee. I was in love with her, but you, you are my future. You're my whole life."

"You can't do that to me ever again. Because it will break me." I'm not sure why I said it, but it's completely true. I love him too much to be ok if he left again. "You stay and we work things out, together. We have to talk to each other."

"We stay, and we talk. We're a team." Liam searches my face as if waiting for me to turn him down again, to tell him that I can't. But I want him, I will always want him. I take his hands in mine, holding them before me before looking up at him again, placing a soft kiss to his cheek.

"Ok, let's go home."

I know that from this point on, no matter where we are, as long as we work through things together we are each other's homes. Not the building that we are in, but each other. Liam and I dress and head out of the house he moved into after losing the life he had planned, to the house we have started our family in. I grab the photo of them on our way out, the one of Liam, Will, and Kaylee. I want her to be there. She was a big part of making him the man I love today, and she deserves a place of honor in our lives. As he opens the passenger door for me, Liam pulls me in for a hug; our bodies flush against each other. We stand like that for a moment, his body keeping me warm in the crisp night air. This is the start of forever, Liam and I. We're building a family, yes, a bit quick, and yes, a bit out of order, but it's ours. It's mine.

Epilogue

4 months later...

The past four months haven't been the easiest, and I don't know if many would expect it to have been, navigating our relationship, the season, and having children to look after, but we've done it. We've taken each day one at a time. Making sure to take a few minutes each day to make sure we connect. He's moved into the house that I bought, and we decided to keep his place for when his family visits. Lilith is mostly moved into his house full time now. The twins love having her around; their faces light up when they see their Aunt Lils and their Uncle Will. He's been so supportive, coming over to help as often as the hockey schedule allows. Meaning that Liam and I get some free time now and then to feel mostly normal. And Sarah, she's become my very best friend, someone I can ask every ridiculous parenting question that pops into my head with zero judgment.

I went from having no family, being completely on my own to having this huge family, it's a bit daunting sometimes, but I can't say I would change it, not one bit. The chaos, the too-full home when everyone comes over, and the quiet moments when it's just Liam and the kids here with me. Every day I am more and more grateful that this is mine. My parents would be so happy to see what I have made for myself, and I can see bits of them in Elowen and Finn. As I lay in our bed this morning, I smile, thinking about everything we've been through, and how it got me to this point. A life with so many people cheering us on.

Liam walks into our bedroom early in the morning, trying to get things done before the kids wake up. I love Elowen and Finn, but I very much enjoy the quiet mornings we get before they have us too busy to take a moment together. When he climbs back under the covers with me, I instantly curl my body to his, basking in the warmth.

"My personal space heater." I wrap my arms around his torso, squeezing tightly for a moment.

"Good morning," he kisses my forehead lightly, making me smile.

"Hi." I snuggle against him

"They're still asleep."

"Thank goodness." I run my hand along his chest absent-mindedly, loving his solid form under my hand. I feel very at home here.

"These few minutes are probably my favorite of the day. When it's just you and me. I love you and the family that we built. I love you so much. I can't imagine being away from you."

"Yeah, I love you too."

"I sure hope so because I don't want this to end. Ever. I want you to be mine, ours forever." He pulls away for a moment, and I sit up, instantly wondering what he is doing. "This was my grandma's," he holds up a gorgeous Art Deco style ring, emerald cut diamonds on a gold band. "I would like very much for you to wear it and even more for you to be my wife. I love you, and I want this to be official. Please, Elise, will you marry me?"

"Yes." I start crying as he slides the ring on my finger, my hands shaking slightly, not sure that this is real until I can feel the cool metal and the weight of the ring on my hand. "Holy shit."

"Holy shit's right. I was really worried that you were going to say no for some reason."

"No way. I'm not letting you go ever again. You're stuck with me. Forever." He takes hold of my face, kissing me deeply. "I would say that we have plenty of time to celebrate this morning, but we both know that the kids will be awake soon, and we need to get you to the arena for today's game."

"As long as you're wearing my ring, I don't care where we go or what we do."

"Whatever it's, we'll do it together."

***

We head to the arena for today's game. The kids are in their adorably tiny hockey sweaters and winter hats. Liam wanted to get there early so there is time to get his head in the game, but he also wanted to spend as much time with Finn and Elowen as possible. We decided to hang out for a little bit with him before heading to the box to watch with their Aunt Lilith.

My favorite part of games like this is our ritual good luck kisses. Liam will come out in his full gear and give all three of us kisses for good luck. Lilith snapped a couple of pictures of this a few games ago, and they now hang framed in our living room. He loves our kids so much that I can't help but swoon each time I see them. They're my whole world.

Walking down the hall to the locker room, Liam pushes the stroller where the kids are currently sleeping off their afternoon bottles. We're a family, and soon I will be his wife. HIS WIFE! I can't believe it. I knew that I wanted to be his forever and him mine, but I didn't think that marriage was going to be happening so soon. When we turn the corner to meet up with Sarah and her family, I stop short when I see Will and Lilith, very cozy tucked in a corner.

"Holy shit," I laugh, not sure how to react to this.

Will's eyes snap towards us, and Lilith backs away from him slightly. I never expected to see them together but thinking about it, they seem kind of perfect together. Will, laid back and easygoing, and Lilith is very high energy and always on the go. I smile at them and then turn to Liam, who is dumbfounded.

"You're dating my sister?" Liam's brows furrow in confusion and a bit of brotherly protectiveness.

"You dated mine," Will answered matter of fact.

"He's got a point, Wilkes." With this, he smiles down at me before placing a kiss on my lips. "And you can't kill him... you won't have a best man if you do."

"YOU DID IT?" Lilith shouts, grabbing my hand to check out the ring before hugging Will.

"Congrats, you two," Will smiles from behind her arms.

"Thank you, Will," I squeeze his hand. He's the best brother I could have asked for, and I'm glad he was the first one that I was able to tell. Sarah is going to flip, though.

"This is really happening." Liam turns towards me with a smile on his face. I saw our whole lives ahead of us. Watching the twins grow up, taking them to games, and teaching them to skate. Will, Lilith, and his parents. Holidays at his childhood home and our home together. It's all so crazy to think about. So much has changed in a short time. I wouldn't change any of it, though.

"It's really happening. We just had to place our love on ice for a little bit in the middle there."

THE END

Acknowledgments

Wow, I honestly can't believe that I wrote a book! This started as a creative outlet, turned into 'lets just finish the story', and then BAM I'm publishing it. I can't even begin to thank everyone who has helped me.

To my mom, Amy Komula. I love you. You are an inspiration to me, taking a terrible situation after dads passing and working to provide a stable home where David and I could thrive. You have always been so supportive of everything I have done and this is no different. This book is as much your accomplishment as it is mine.

All my cousins- seriously there are a lot of you. You all have been so supportive and encouraging when I decided to move forward with this project, just like you have been my entire life. I wouldn't be the person I am without you all. I love you all!

Emma Steinbrecher, who would have thought that reconnecting via tiktok would lead to this?! You encouraged me so much with this book. Your feedback especially in the beginning is what really pushed me to want to finish writing Elise and Liam's story. Without you my friend, Liam would still be Chris...ugh.

To my closest friends. Just thanks, I can't tell you how much I appreciate you being there for me.

Reanna Guthrie, thank you so much for taking my book to the next level. Your notes and suggestions helped me so much to get to this point. Without you I would still be fumbling through trying to self edit and Elise and Liam would fall flat.

Alex Taylor, the fact that you read this when there was so much more of their story I need to write is astounding. I almost feel bad for asking you to do it, but your suggestions brought so much more depth.

Katelyn Braun, thank you for all your advice. You helped me get through the first draft and to have the confidence to keep going.

There are so many people that I have met during this process that I couldn't begin to name you all but that you so much for all your support, and encouragement when writing and editing got me down and overwhelmed. Your kind words and advice helped me push through.

Made in the USA
Middletown, DE
13 August 2024